IN CASES OF
MURDER

Jan Edwards is the UK author of the award-winning Bunch Courtney Investigations, a series of crime novels set during WW2.

She has published over 50 short stories in crime, horror, fantasy and mainstream anthologies including *The Mammoth Book of Folk Horror*, *Criminal Shorts*, *The Book of Extraordinary New Sherlock Holmes Stories*, volumes 1&2, and appears in multiple volumes of the *MX Books of New Sherlock Holmes Stories*.

She is a member of the CWA.

The Bunch Courtney Investigations

Winter Downs
In Her Defence
Listed Dead
In Cases of Murder

Other Titles by Jan Edwards

Sussex Tales
Fables and Fabrications
Leinster Gardens and Other Subtleties
A Small Thing for Yolanda

https://janedwardsblog.wordpress.com/

https://www.facebook.com/Janedwardsbooks

IN CASES OF MURDER

A Bunch Courtney Investigation

Jan Edwards

The Penkhull Press

Published by The Penkhull Press
Staffordshire, UK
www.penkhullpress.co.uk

~ Acknowledgements ~

As always, there are many people to thank in the writing of any book. In this case, these thanks also go to the numerous sources for historical research into the history of London Transport, bomb damage, rationing, firearms, cars, and a few dozen other facts that needed to be confirmed.

Misha Herwin deserves a big hug for enduring my rabbiting on "in Bunch mode" for many dozens of chats over coffee (quite a few of them virtual during lockdown), acting as a sounding board for what would work and gently shooting down those crazy notions that certainly would not, and for beta reading the finished article not once but twice! My other half, Peter Coleborn, has been a star for his unstinting support throughout the writing process and afterwards for his many hours spent deciphering my eclectic/dyslexic punctuation and spelling.

There was a point when I wondered if *In Cases of Murder* would ever see the light of day after it followed a lengthy side-track and back again, a hiccup which was not helped by two long years of lockdown and viral madness. Requests from readers asking for the next volume has been a huge boost throughout that process, so many thanks go to them. The next adventure has finally made it over the finish line. My Bunch fans will be glad to know that book five – *A Deadly Plot* – is now finished and in the edit process, with book six – *A Party to Murder* – well under way.

~ One ~

Bunch Courtney settled into a mesmeric left-right rhythm with the brushes, not thinking about anything beyond burnishing her Fell Pony's coat to a sleek black sheen. Hitler's army, poised just across the Channel might dominate every minute of everybody's lives, but refereeing disputes among Perringham Estate's Land Girls was a far more immediate concern. At least today's issue had been resolved. Her horses had always been her refuge and she hoped a brief hour in Perry's company now would work its usual magic on her temper.

"Miss Rose?"

The voice calling across from the house broke Bunch's concentration. *Hell's bells, what now?* She ducked behind the door in the vague hope the housekeeper would go away.

"Miss Rose? Are you down here?" Mrs Knapp crossed from the kitchen garden and Bunch could hear the housekeeper's leather-soled shoes tapping in the cobbled yard. "Hello Bella." Knapp leaned down to pat the liver and white springer spaniel dancing around her feet. "Where's Miss Rose? Seek."

The dog gave a short yip in reply and raced to jump at the stall door, wriggling her enthusiasm from tail to topknot. "Traitor," Bunch hissed. Henry Marsham had left her the dog when he'd been called up to Scotland. A trained gundog, she had been assured. "With all the brains of a cauliflower," she muttered. "Thank you so much, Henry."

"Miss Rose?"

Knapp was close now and Bunch knew the game was up. "Yes, Knapp. What can I do for you?"

"There's a telephone call, Miss. Chief Inspector Wright."

Wright? What could he want? "Thank you. Tell the Inspector I'll call him back."

"He did say it was urgent, Miss. He called twice while you were out."

"Did he indeed." She tried a few passes of the brush across Perry's ample rump but the moment was gone. *It's not Knapp's fault, but dammit all the same.* "All right, tell him I shall be in directly." She tossed the brushes through the tack-room door and turned to scrub her knuckles against the sprinkle of white hairs between the Fell Pony's eyes. "I'd better go and see what he wants, hey Perry?" She rested her forehead against his and he snuffled at her pockets. "No apples today, you greedy old sod."

"Miss Rose." Knapp had not moved. "Chief Inspector Wright said he would hold on the line awhile. He seems rather anxious to speak with you."

"Yes, I'm coming. Burse, could you be a dear and turn Perry out into the paddock?" She waited to see the elderly chauffeur-groom wave acknowledgement from the far side of the yard before striding towards the house.

Standing next to the telephone she paused to finger-comb her dark bob and grimaced. *He can't see you, idiot.* She'd only spoken to Wright twice after their last case together; this time the long gap since their previous chat had been entirely her doing, and it made things awkward, embarrassing. She fluttered her fingers above the handset a moment before snatching it up as though it were a handful of nettles. "Hello. Bunch Courtney speaking," she said.

"Rose? Finally. You're an elusive woman. It's William. William Wright." Hearing his voice felt odd after so many months.

Bunch sighed. She was not a lover of anyone using her given name, which was irrational given that it *was* her name; she saw herself as the least flower-like of anyone she knew – tall, dark and angular, whereas her sister Dodo was blonde and petite. *It feels like an unending joke.*

The longcase clock standing just a few feet away ticked down the seconds to her reply. Her post as Police Consultant, the one she had bullied Chief Superintendent Uncle Walter into devising for her, had stopped being the fun she'd anticipated. Being shot at was not high on her list of favourite pastimes. Despite that, she had a suspicion that her current restlessness came out of a need for action beyond the slow and relentless routines of the farm, Land Girl troubles notwithstanding. *There's no reason why I should avoid looking at Wright's cases. Not if I'm just a consultant.* "Hello

William," she said. "It's been a while. How are you?"

"Busy," he said. "As always."

"Aren't we all. To what do I owe the pleasure?"

"I need to pick your brains, if I may?"

"I can't imagine what I would know that you don't, but fire away."

"We've a tricky murder case on our hands."

Her lips twitched at the various ripostes she could make before she settled on "Rather your stock in trade, I'd have said." More plock-plocks of the swinging pendulum echoed around the hallway. Her bad memories of the previous November were rapidly giving way to anticipation. Being a killer's target had badly shaken her. *But Etta Beamish is securely locked away. Perhaps it's time to get back in that saddle*, she thought. "I ask again, what exactly is it that you presume I know?" she said.

"A young woman has been murdered and was discovered in very curious circumstances."

"And—"

"With the deceased was a notebook in which were several Wyncombe telephone numbers."

"Including mine? I assume that's why you're calling me."

"Not exactly. I'd be hard pressed to find anyone in the County Set who doesn't have the number for Perringham House. Actually, it's another local number that's raised a few questions."

"Isn't PC Botting able to answer them?"

"He's traced the address for the number in question but hasn't much information beyond that. Does Haven Cottage ring any bells with you?"

"Vaguely. Who lives there?"

"It's currently unoccupied. We're trying to track down the owners, without a great deal of success."

"Unfortunately, I—"

Wright interrupted her. "But I rather hope you'd know the victim – through your many contacts. Her name is Laura Jarman. Her family owns a large property near Petworth."

Bunch was aware that Wright could not see her expression and for once was not sure she was glad of it. *One can say so much with a good scowl.* She rocked back on her heels for a moment and stared at the dusty toes of her riding boots. Wright's assumption that he could just dangle the bait of a new case and she would come running rather amused her. The fact that he was probably right amused her even more.

"Hello? Are you still there?" said Wright.

"Yes, I'm here. I was wondering why you need me since you already have her name, and you know where she lives. What may I possibly add to the pot?"

"Her family are proving to be … unhelpful. We're bumping horns with the War Office over access to them, which makes it harder than it needs to be. The Super thought that as a local with a certain social standing you might have better luck in lowering their guard."

"If their daughter's been murdered, I should have thought they'd be making a lot of noise to have the case solved by yesterday."

"Oh, they're making the right noises: demands that we find her killer are being poured into all the right ears. You know how that goes."

"Meaning what, precisely?"

"We've been able to talk with the father and taken a basic statement from him, but we don't know a thing about this family that we couldn't read in *Who's Who*."

"And you think they know more than they want to admit?"

"Possibly. Jarman, the father, had dangled the Official Secrets Act. Obviously we can't breach the OSA but the Superintendent suggested I utilise your 'God given gift of wheedling' to gain some more information. His words, not mine."

"If Uncle Walter is referring to my natural flare for diplomacy, then I quite see his point."

"Not what I meant."

"I know." She smiled to herself. She had taken Wright's lure, loaded with enough intrigue that she couldn't let it go. Putting him on edge made her feel a little less like a liberty horse twirling in pretty circles on command. "Is the timing of the death significant?"

"We're going to assume it has some relevance to the war effort."

"That sounds likely enough. All right, William, I'll take the job but not tonight. I wouldn't be able to get there until after six o'clock – and then there's coming back again and I hate Blackout driving. Plus, I think it would be an idea to have a good old chinwag with Granny. See what her society grapevine may give us."

"I wasn't expecting you would do anything today. However, I was rather hoping we could have a proper talk before you run over to see them."

"Of course. I can motor down to Brighton tomorrow morning."

"Tomorrow? I have an appointment with Doctor Letham at the mortuary. It's not the best of places for us to chat."

You call me three times in one day to lure me into your investigation, she thought. *You plainly want me to discover something in particular. So … do I play along?* She grinned. *Why not? All I have waiting for me after breakfast tomorrow is a stack of War Ag forms.* "No. It's perfect," she said.

"It is?"

The clock plocked through another long pause. "I wouldn't offer if it wasn't," Bunch finally added. "And it would be nice to say hello to Letham again. He's nice old chap. It's settled, I shall be there at ten o'clock."

"Wouldn't a little later suit you, at my office? As I said, the mortuary is not the most salubrious—" Wright began.

"Oh, tosh and rot. I run a farm, for heaven's sake. We rise with the proverbial dawn. And it won't be my first trip inside a mortuary. I take it the usual arrangements apply?" She heard him breath out. *That is not a sigh,* she thought. *It's a silent snort.* She hardly needed the money but earning for something other than for her family gave her a kick. "William? Are you still there?"

"Yes, I am and yes, the Super has authorised your consultation fee with expenses. Plus additional motor spirit rations."

"Naturally. I assume ten o'clock is acceptable?"

"Yes, I—"

"Ten it is. Goodbye William." Bunch slotted the handset back in the cradle before he could answer. His attitude stank, and she could well believe calling her had been her uncle's idea. "I certainly can't imagine that miserable sergeant of Wright's suggesting it." She stared at her booted feet. She was tempted to refuse the case if it were not for the fact that they would quite probably be secretly relieved if she did.

"Rose?" Her grandmother called from the drawing room. "Rose, is that you?"

"Yes, Granny," she called back. "I'm sorry, I've been out on Perry and quite forgot the time." She ambled into the drawing room and stopped short. Seated on a wide sofa next to Beatrice Courtney was an elderly woman. *Damn. Connie Frain, of all people,* and aloud: "Mrs Frain. How nice to see you." Bunch quietly wiped her dusty palms down the seams of her jodhpurs.

"Rose." Constance Frain inclined her head, her dark eyes sparkling at some private joke, and did not offer to shake hands. "Still set on your horses, I see."

Bunch pasted on a smile. It wasn't that she disliked her grandmother's WVS coterie, not as a body of women, but... *Constance Frain, the biggest gossip this side of the Channel. And probably the other side as well.* "Getting around the estate is much quicker on horseback. Too many jobs and too few people to do them. And now the damnable War Ag is demanding we grow flax for webbing. Would you believe it? On chalk downlands? Flax needs deep loam. Bloody fools." The glazed look in Constance's eyes at the welter of facts made her grin. "I'm parched and I still have chores to do before dinner. Do excuse my state while I grab a cuppa." She plonked herself in a chair and poured herself a beverage, carefully avoiding Beatrice's face though she could feel Granny's eyes on her. *I'll doubtless be hearing about this, chapter and verse, when Constance has gone.* She beamed at the two women, stretching out the moment with a sip from her cup, and managed not to wince at the tea's weakness.

"What did your chief inspector want?" Beatrice asked. "We've not seen him for a while."

"My invaluable skill and advice. What else? I'm popping down to see him tomorrow morning."

"Not another murder?" Constance fixed Bunch with an avaricious stare. "That's what usually brings him here, isn't it?"

Bunch regarded Constance carefully. "Yes, I suppose it is."

"Would that be the Jarman girl? I got the news from Anne Bishop. Dreadful thing to happen."

"How did Mrs Bishop hear about it?" said Bunch. *Though little goes on around these parts before lunch that isn't common knowledge by afternoon tea.*

"Laura is her niece," Constance replied. "Or perhaps I should say *was*. All very depressing."

Bunch warmed a little with embarrassment. "How awful for them all. Do pass on my condolences."

"Rose…" Beatrice began.

"I don't know the family, to speak of," Bunch continued, "and the two of you know absolutely everyone. Do fill me in on all the goss."

Constance Frain leaned forward a little more, agog at having the chance to play a part in events that were landing neatly at her feet. "Well … it all happened a week ago, though it has been kept fairly quiet. The family are rolling in it, so strings are pulled, no question," she said, with the merest hint of a sneer. "Anne told me the place has been overrun by government types. But you can't always take what Anne says as gospel. She does love to gossip. Anyway, she says the family made an absolute killing in the last war." Constance lowered her voice. "There were accusations of profiteering but there were no charges, that I know of."

"Are the Jarmans are involved with munitions?" said Bunch.

"Yes … well not guns as such. Military transport or something of the kind."

"Here in Sussex?"

"I do believe they moved down from somewhere in London," said Beatrice.

"Yes, from south of the river." Constance nodded her own confirmation.

Like a pair of old turtles, Bunch thought.

"One can hardly count Richmond as south of the river, Constance," said Beatrice. "It may be municipal but it is Surrey."

"It is," she conceded. "Doesn't make much of a difference in this case, though. The Jarmans are hardly County."

"I gather the Jarmans originally started out in Birmingham," Beatrice added. "Not called Jarmans then. They were Russian. I can't remember the old man's family name but I do remember he changed it just after the Great War broke out."

"They wanted to sound British," said Constance. "So many did."

"Including the old king," Bunch muttered.

Constance flushed and hid behind her cup for a moment. "Well yes, of course, my dear. I am sure the Jarmans were not Russian, however. I thought perhaps they were Polish. Or was it Romanian?" She trailed away, aware that both Courtneys were staring at her. "One of those, anyway. It will come to me."

"They're terribly English now," said Bunch. "And quite local."

"Yes, indeed. Laura's mother was Sussex born. One of the Inglis girls. Marrying Charles Jarman was beneath her, of course, but her family needed the money," said Constance. "They moved down to Petworth early in ... 1937, I believe."

"Oh yes. Such a shame. I knew Selina as a young Amazon of the WSPU. Only narrowly escaped prison for chaining herself to an MP's front gate," Beatrice declared. "Another reason her parents married her off so quickly. I am not surprised Selina came back here at the first opportunity. Didn't Jarman lease some of the farmland to neighbouring estates? The Parkers had most of it."

"They did," Constance replied. "How Jarman keeps the government's sticky paws off it I don't know. What could he be doing there that he can't do at his factory?"

"It's a factory?" said Bunch.

"Lord no. Selina Jarman would never put up with the noise. The factory is in London somewhere."

"What was Laura like?" Bunch asked.

"Knew her mind," said Constance.

"She was a little wild, then?"

"I gather she argued with her father rather a lot," Constance replied. "But if she had half as much spirit as Selina did at that age its hardly surprising. She didn't have a *reputation*, if you know what I mean."

"Doesn't she have two brothers," said Beatrice.

"I was coming to that," Constance snapped, obviously determined that Beatrice was not going to usurp the spotlight. "Robert is in the West Kents. And Stephen ... he's an invalid, poor chap. Polio when he was quite young. Though I hear he married recently."

"Was Laura single?"

"Oh yes. There was a chap a little while ago," said Constance. "Selina was convinced that Laura was intending to announce an engagement, but it seems he vanished off the scene just before they moved to Petworth."

"Were the two things connected?"

"I doubt it. Charles Jarman would only have moved there because it suited him."

"I see." Bunch reached for the cigarette box, took out one and tapped it against the back of her hand. The Jarman family background was a revelation and the details behind them could be relevant. *Access to this stuff,* she thought, *is exactly why William wants me on this case. Perhaps he'd be better off hiring Granny.*

~ Two ~

Bunch paused at the mortuary doors to gaze at the calmness of the cemetery beyond, wondering for a moment why on earth she was here at all. *I could have refused. God alone knows I've got enough to do on the estate.* "Yet here I jolly well am. And here I go." She plunged into the chemical-tainted interior, pausing to show her identity card to the elderly porter at the desk. "I am expected."

"Yes, Miss. Doctor Letham and Chief Inspector Wright are waiting for you."

Bunch pushed through the double doors into the antiseptic chill of the post-mortem room and smiled as Wright and Letham turned away from the body on the mortuary table to face her. "Good morning, gentlemen," she said. "Have I kept you waiting long? I do apologise."

"Morning, Miss Courtney. No, you're as punctual as always," said Letham. "You'll forgive me for not shaking hands."

He was a slender neat man with thinning hair brushed hard back from a thin face. *And must have been handsome in his youth*, she thought. *Still would be, were it not for those glasses.* Dark, much-mended tortoiseshell frames dominated Letham's face, partially hiding dark eyes that gazed back at her with a shrewdness she always found disconcerting, as if he saw not a woman but a set of muscles and bones and organs. He was never anything but courteous if, to Bunch's mind, disturbingly impish, an image only enhanced by his soft Edinburgh lilt. He executed an extravagant bow, sweeping both rubber-gloved hands out at waist level like a courtier to his queen. Bunch's smile widened and she wondered if he'd guessed how apprehensive she was feeling, and why.

"Rose," Wright said and nodded in an echo of Letham's greeting, his smile less broad but no less sincere. He glanced at the clock. "In fact, you're a little earlier than I expected." Wright was taller than Letham and looked plainly younger despite fatigue lines gathering around his grey eyes and long, almost equine face.

He must be growing on me, she thought. *In this light he reminds me a little of Leslie Howard.* She smiled and shook the hand he proffered. "Not exactly a pleasure under the circumstances but good to see you, nevertheless. Both of you. I take it that is Laura Jarman?"

"It is." Letham stood to one side. "Are you up to taking a wee peek?"

"If the Chief Inspector thinks it's a good idea?"

"Could he stop you?"

"Probably not." Bunch stepped between the men and steeled herself before pulling the sheet from the head and neck to look down at the dead woman, telling herself that the person was long gone, that these were only earthly remains. The sight of a body was never something she welcomed but something she felt she needed to endure in order to gain a sense of the person that had once been.

Laura's face was bloodless, her skin the same off-white shade of thin cream. *But she would,* Bunch decided, *have been pale even before death.* A dusting of freckles across the girl's nose and cheeks looked like spatters of tea on white parchment. Her hair was the pale brown of fallen leaves, with just a hint of red. Her eyes were closed but Bunch imagined them as blue, or even violet. Her lips that were once full retained traces of vivid scarlet lipstick but there was no evidence of face powder.

Bunch peeled the sheet back a little further and tried not to flinch at the stronger odour released from beneath the cover. *Not a fresh cadaver,* she thought. She noted several cuts to the body that were tinged dark with crusted blood, as opposed to the fresher Y-shaped post-mortem incision, roughly re-sewn. "Death appears to have been due to stabbing." She leaned a little closer to examine purple bruising around Laura's neck and left cheek, dark marks on her arms and ribs, and took note of the deep creases around the midriff. "She was subjected to some considerable violence, poor girl."

"Beaten, strangled, and stabbed. Evidently her killer wanted to ensure she would not survive," Letham replied.

She pulled the sheet up to cover the body once more before taking several steps back to glare at Wright. "I don't believe all this nonsense about the family not talking. What was your reason for wanting me to come here? You know who she is, after all."

"If you recall, I did not ask you to view the body," he replied. "But since you're here I did want you to see this. I was about to have it removed to our evidence store at the station." Wright drew her to a cupboard at the far side of the room and opened the door. A battered steamer trunk took up most of the floor space. It was leather-bound with bamboo strapping screwed down with brass studs, and the lid fastened by brass catches. The kind of luggage she had seen a thousand times on quaysides and railway platforms or wherever else the well-heeled were seen in transit.

"It's a perfectly ordinary trunk," said Bunch. "I have several of my own that are quite similar."

"The difference is, this is the one that Miss Jarman's remains were discovered inside," said Wright. "On the incoming platform at Brighton Station."

"Oh heavens." She stared at the trunk and back to the cadaver. "How long was she there?"

"The station master told Carter she could have been on the platform for most of that weekend," said Wright. "He thought she might have been left after the last train came in from Victoria on Monday of last week, but as there was a raid that night the trunk was probably moved to one side to make sure it didn't cause problems for passengers milling about in the dark, and it was forgotten about until the cleaners came across it."

"She was killed a day or two before then," Letham added. "Probably on the previous Friday or Saturday. Certainly, rigor mortis had already passed when she was placed in the trunk. She was kept somewhere dry before that."

"That long?" She wondered why Wright had taken so many days before calling her. *I know the family were being difficult, he said ... but a whole week?*

"Did you learn any more about her, Rose?" Wright said. "Anything that could explain how she'd get herself murdered?"

"I clawed a few things out of Granny, about the Jarman's background, but most of it is probably common knowledge – in certain circles, anyway." She gave Wright a quick rundown of the details she had gleaned. "I know that the Jarmans didn't appear in *Debrett's* until Laura's mother married into the line. They are what Granny defined as nouveau riche. From what I was told, I can't imagine how Laura would be involved in anything dangerous. She led a sheltered life, I gather."

Wright smoothed his hair distractedly. "The oddest thing about all this is that her family didn't report her as missing," he said. "They insist she was living in London and had no idea why she should have been found where she was."

Bunch would hesitate to accuse Wright of being disingenuous, but she could not help wondering why he had employed such an elaborate means of including her in this investigation. *The police have her name so it shouldn't have been difficult to trace her family*, she thought. *What's different then, apart from their having connections so close to Wyncombe?* "Perhaps they didn't know. If she'd joined up she'd not be living at home. She's the right age to enlist," Bunch said. "Nothing I have told you would be difficult to check. It's quite flattering to be asked, but I'm not sure why you've asked me to consult. I am not certain the family will be any keener to speak with me than they are with the police."

Wright looked her up and down from the corner of his eye. "You're not the least bit intrigued?"

"Perhaps I am, though I am more curious to know why you want my help when you already know who she is and how she died."

"I didn't think you would meekly walk away from such an intriguing puzzle."

"To be honest, I thought you'd be more pleased if I did." Their gazes locked, his startled, hers bordering on amusement. Bunch broke contact first. "I had a chat with Granny and I've told you everything I know. Now it's your turn – what is this case about?"

"Identifying the people who killed this young woman," Wright replied.

She folded her arms and stared at him. "I rather thought that went without saying." From the corner of her eye she caught Letham leaning back against his desk, gazing from one to the other, and she fought hard not to scowl. *He's enjoying the show.* "There is more to all of this than you've said, I suspect. I need to be in the loop if you want me to help."

Wright passed his hand over his hair, staring at the floor for a moment. "Two other bodies were discovered before this one.

They too were stabbed and their remains dumped in large trunks. One was on the platform and the other turned up in left luggage."

"So not a—" Bunch felt her face warming. "They were not assaulted, I take it?"

"None of the three victims were *virgo intacta*, if that is what you're asking," said Letham. "Not even the sainted Miss Jarman."

"Oh." Bunch gazed at Laura, viewing her in a different light. Bunch herself was no angel, but from what she had gleaned from Constance and Beatrice, Laura Jarman had not seemed the type to have been shielded from that sort of thing; yet at the same time she was not one of the fast set.

"The first two had led completely different lives, judging by the old bruises and injuries over their bodies. Miss Jarman didn't appear to have been the victim of any previous violent assault – before she was killed," Letham added. "Please put that out of your mind."

Bunch nodded without comment. She did not see herself as prudish but crimes of that nature filled her with horror. "I've not seen anything at all in the newspapers," she said at last.

"Not something we want to be made public. The idea of another trunk murderer in the county could cause a panic," Wright said. "They're all well aware that we had never been able to identify the 'Pretty Feet' victim, and no one was ever charged for that crime."

"Wasn't that before you came to Brighton?"

"I was at Scotland Yard back then and as the Yard was involved, we all knew about it." Wright frowned. "It's not that unheard of for bodies to be disposed of in luggage. Pretty Feet stuck in the public mind because we never found out who she was."

"Nevertheless, you don't think people need to know about the new bodies?"

"I'm not sure it will help, at least not yet. There's been a fifty percent rise in crime over the last eighteen months. Looting is rife, black-market activity is off the scale. And prostitution in the cities is epidemic. It's what comes of so many people being separated from their families." He spread his hands, indicating the corpse. "It's anybody's guess what this is all about."

She nodded. "We're all aware that things are not as they should be, but this…" She examined the top of the trunk, wondering at each crease and mark as she went over the possibilities of why this woman had met her death. "Do you think they all were killed by the same hand?" she said at last.

"I can't say at this stage, other than they have all been murdered by the same method. Only Letham here can make the final judgement."

"It was an upward thrust with a long slender blade which pierced the heart." The pathologist unfolded his arms to mimic the move. "Markedly similar to the previous victims. The marks on her neck seem to be overkill." He coughed and shrugged. "My apologies. In my profession the humour…"

"…is dark. I worked in hospitals. Would that sort of knife wound indicate a professional killing? Plenty of chaps around with military training these days." Bunch sighed. "Don't look so shocked, William. I've had military and nursing training. Anything you can add, Letham?"

"Not as yet," he replied. "And in answer to your question, yes, professional but the blade is too slender to be military issue."

Bunch nodded and looked to Wright.

He rubbed the flat of his hand across his head in an unconscious gesture as he thought out his answer. "The only common links so far are knives and railways." Wright rubbed at his hair once more and sighed. "Miss Jarman is the first of these bodies that we've been able to identify. It seems to have been a more … hasty killing than the others."

"Why do you say that?" She glanced at Letham. "Was there something peculiar about her?"

"She still has her head and her hands," he replied.

Bunch was not sure how she should react. The idea of a body being dumped in a steamer trunk was horrific enough, but having head and hands removed made her more than slightly nauseous. "The other bodies you mentioned … were they also found at railway stations?" she said.

"Yes, as I said, one on a platform, the other in left luggage. They put extra men on the overnight trains, but we have no idea whether the killer has been leaving the bodies under cover of darkness or even in broad daylight."

"A busy platform, I assume?"

"Quite." Wright frowned at Bunch's apparent flippancy. "Interestingly, one of them had a collection ticket, but... We thought our searching of luggage large enough to stow a torso would have shifted their activities."

"Or their hunting grounds."

"What?"

"Logically, if the place where they have been hunting – or leaving their victims – becomes unfeasible for whatever reason, you move on. I admit, I find it hard to imagine why they were all found in just one location. The railways could've taken them almost anywhere. If they can get these trunks into the goods wagons why not just leave them to be found at some other destination?"

"I have no idea. If we knew where they were being put aboard the trains it would help, but we don't have a clue. If they were all on the London route I'd say it was the result of some crime wave oozing out of the capital."

"Except that platform is to Hove, on the coastal line."

"Precisely. It's the excuse Scotland Yard is using to not send anyone to assist us. I was informed that since I'd worked for them in London I should be able to conduct investigations in Brighton every bit as well as they could." He managed a humourless laugh. "We're not the only force suffering from depleted ranks."

"They seem happy to view it as a local matter?"

"Except that Miss Jarman appears to have been killed and dumped in a hurry. I must be honest Rose: that is why you're being co-opted."

Huzzah, she thought. *He's getting to the point.* "And that is?"

He shrugged. "As I told you yesterday, the family is reluctant to talk to the police – other than to call your uncle every time we approach them."

"Despite their daughter having been murdered. How curious."

"Classic denial," said Letham. "If they don't admit she's dead then she is still alive."

"There is something else though, Letham. I'm not saying one of the family murdered her, but they are hiding something."

"So, am I here to infiltrate the upper ranks?" Bunch smiled and grunted. "You say she had the number for Perringham Hall in her book."

"I didn't."

"Really? You said…"

"I only said that your number seems to be known to one and all. But not in this case."

"All right then, what was it that linked her with me?"

"The Wyncombe number I mentioned was newly added on the back leaf," Wright pulled out a sheet of paper and pulled a face. "We thought you might be able to shed some light on it. The number is listed to Haven Cottage. We now know the owners are a Mr and Mrs Clement Waller. According to PC Botting's report they moved out in spring of 1939 when the war threat became real, as a few thousand others did. Since then the house had been rented out on short leases. Very short. I gather the most recent tenants left in something of a hurry after a few weeks."

"Moonlight flit?"

"Bogus references so less flit and more disappearance."

"Naturally. Did you say Laura had this telephone number in her book? I find it hard to believe the exchange has no further details. Somebody had the line installed."

"Someone who turns out not to exist."

"You want me to speak with the Jarmans to see if they know what Laura's connection was to that cottage?" Bunch paused, glancing at Wright. "I had better go alone although if they are not willing to chat with the police I can't see my turning up on your behalf is going to endear me to them. I could just have a nose around Haven Cottage."

"Since we don't have any evidence that was where she may have been killed we will need to have the owner's permission to enter the house. We are trying to obtain an order for access, of course, but the courts are backed up so that will take days."

"All the more reason why I should have a skulk around."

"You can't gain entry illegally. Haven Cottage is not your first task. I need you to talk with the Jarmans."

"I had no intention of breaking and entering, William, but yes, I shall see the Jarmans first."

~ Three ~

All over the country, road signs and house names had been removed and had Bunch not come seeking Gellideg House armed with a map she would have missed it, with its gate stanchions hidden in the hedges and the iron gates themselves already gone to Beaverbrook's "pots and pans". A swing barrier and gatehouse was set a few yards further in. The men who emerged from the gatehouse were dressed in dark serge uniforms of the kind worn by ARP wardens though their helmets were blank. Wright had warned her about them but she had an urge to giggle at their swagger as one of the men approached.

"Good morning, Miss. May we help you?" He leaned down close enough for her to feel his breath. "This is private property."

"Good morning. Rose Courtney here to see Mrs Jarman. Calling on behalf of my grandmother the dowager Lady Chiltcombe." She handed them her own card and another purloined from Beatrice.

"Do you have an appointment?"

"I called early today." *I only got the housekeeper,* she thought, *but I did call.*

"We don't have you on our list."

"No? How odd. Granny – you must have heard of her: Lady Chiltcombe?" She smiled a blandest of smiles. "Granny will be disappointed when I tell her I was turned away." She looked him in the eyes, still smiling. "I'm sure Mrs Jarman will also be disappointed." She put the MG into reverse gear and revved the engine a little.

The man hesitated for split second and then signalled for his partner to raise the barrier.

"Thank you. You're a sweetie." She changed into first gear, waggled her fingers coyly, and pulled away. *Coy* was not how she felt. Roadblocks had become an unpleasant fact of life but civilians guarding a private house was more than a little disturbing. Not even the family house in London where her father – one of

Winnie's close advisors – mostly stayed had warranted that much. But it fitted with the assessment Wright had given of Jarman, as a man full of his own importance.

She found herself motoring towards a Jacobean sandstone manor surrounded by mature trees and neat gardens. Pulling up at the frontage she got out to give the cast-iron bellpull a tug. After a minute's wait she tugged at it again. She could not hear the bell ringing but since they often rang in the butler's pantry she was not entirely surprised. After yet another minute had passed without any response Bunch eyed the vast bronze knocker at the centre of the oak-plank door. She lifted it and let it drop just once with a resounding bang, and a few moments later the door was opened by an elderly woman dressed in sombre black.

But not just in mourning, Bunch thought. *She clearly wears black from habit, although not a maid. Housekeeper perhaps? Companion? Whichever she is, I suspect she's not going to give an inch without a Jarman's say so.* "Rose Courtney." Bunch presented her card. "I'm here to see Mr and Mrs Jarman, if they are at home?"

"Mrs Jarman is indisposed. There's been a death in the family," the woman snapped.

"Yes. My grandmother Lady Chiltcombe asked me to call. She was acquainted with Mrs Jarman a little while ago." Bunch waved a hand at the bell pull. "I rang several times."

"Mrs Jarman *is* indisposed." The woman lifted her chin defiantly. "Mr Jarman has left orders that Mrs Jarman is not to be bothered and not to answer the door to anyone."

"I quite understand." Bunch looked away at the hydrangeas quivering their lurid pink pom-poms in a large tub just to the left of the door. *Wright thinks I can wave at the family like a magic wand and all doors will open. Can't have him thinking I failed.* Manners dictated she should leave her card but she was loathe to just give up Beatrice's magic pass. "I know it's a terrible imposition but I would appreciate a few words, if I may?" She took a step forward and the woman moved to block her. *A butler couldn't have done any better. Wouldn't Miss Apps have adored her for the school lacrosse team?*

The woman glanced at the card once more. "Mrs Jarman is indisposed," she repeated. "Doctor has given her something to calm her and she's sleeping."

Okay, name-dropping Granny is not making headway so onto plan B. "I must admit it's not entirely a social call. I'm also making some enquiries about the … case. I'm a consulting detective with the police." Bunch tapped the card, still gripped firmly in the older woman's fingers, with the nail of her forefinger.

"You would need to speak with Mr Jarman, in that case. He is dealing with all of that." Her pale eyes glittered and the corners of her mouth tightened, leaving Bunch in no doubt of what the woman thought of her mistress's husband. "You can try speaking with him." Her tone made it clear that she didn't give Bunch much chance of success. "You'll find him in the office."

"And where would that be?"

"Take the path between the beech trees and his offices are on the right."

Bunch felt she was being sent to the side entrance like an errant baker's boy, which was a novel experience, and she couldn't decide whether to be affronted or amused. But she had identified herself as calling on business as opposed to a simple social call, so she settled for resignation. *I wonder if she'd send a chief inspector away that easily? Quite probably, from the look on her face. I imagine Knapp would do the same.* "Thank you." She handed her Beatrice's card. "My grandmother genuinely sends her condolences, so please do give these to Mrs Jarman when she wakes. And tell her I shall call again another time."

"Yes, Miss. Thank you for calling." The woman was smiling as the door closed with a firm click.

Bunch took a few steps away and paused to glance back at the house. The curtains were all drawn back, not closed in full mourning as she would have expected, and she had spotted fresh flowers in the hallway. *That could mean nothing, of course. There's no way of knowing how close this family adhere to tradition. Not a great deal, according to Granny. Is Mrs Jarman just not talking to anyone? Wright did say they were being tricky.*

The path round to the office block was lined with clipped hedges that formed a living tunnel, which effectively obscured house and offices from each other. Bunch peered through the hedge expecting to see lawns and flower beds but realised she was being funnelled through a sparsely wooded area. She walked perhaps fifty or sixty yards before the path opened out on a range of outbuildings – and a fresh security point. Knowing she couldn't claim a social visit this time round, she reached in her bag for her police pass along with her ID card.

"Gentlemen, good morning. I am here to see Mr Jarman."

The tallest of the two men reached for her papers. "Which Mr Jarman?" he snapped.

"Well … I was hoping to speak with Mr Charles Jarman but either will do," she replied.

The other man had vanished around the corner of the nearest building whilst the first continued to read the papers. Just as she was thinking she might be refused entry the second man returned and whispered a few words to his taller colleague.

Her cards and papers were returned to her although Bunch sensed he really wanted an excuse to send her away or, better still, have her arrested. "Admin block." He pointed at the buildings. "Stick to the path. We'll be watching."

"Thank you," Bunch said and strode away. It surprised her that they made no attempt to escort her but she was aware she was under close scrutiny.

Some of the outbuildings were of the same red brick as the house, although several of the others were rendered in grey plaster. Bunch estimated that the latter had been built in the past twenty years, and constructed with more practicality in mind than aesthetics.

The building closest to her had clearly been a row of substantial farm cottages in a previous incarnation, forming three sides of a square around a small lawn and a single tree. The wings to right and left were single storey, but the middle section boasted a second level. A more modern arched doorway at its centre had been added, and was topped by a vast clockface of the kind Bunch usually associated with churches and town halls. By the side of the arch was a large sign declaring Administration. She made for the archway, let herself through a door marked Reception and found herself in a wide area set out in a Deco style; far more chic than the exterior had led Bunch to expect.

A large desk in ebony and chrome took up the centre of the room. To the left was a corridor from which came the noise of typing. To the right, a large pair of heavy office doors. A dark-haired young man was replacing the telephone receiver as Bunch entered. She noted his left hand was tucked in his pocket, which sagged a little from its weight. *Stephen Jarman,* she thought.

"Good morning," she trilled and produced a second card for him. "Rose Courtney to see Charles Jarman,"

"Good morning, Miss…" He made a show of reading her card. "Oh. The Honourable Miss Courtney." He looked her up and down without expression before examining the desk diary, turning pages with his right hand and holding them down with his left, before shaking his head as he met her gaze. "Did you make an appointment? I'm terribly sorry but I don't see your name in the diary."

You know damn well I didn't, Bunch thought. *And you know damned well who I am. Ten to one that was a warning call from the house. Standard repelling of unwanted houseguests. No wonder Wright asked me to consult.* She laid the card that he had not taken from her on the centre of the open diary. "I know it's a terribly difficult time but I really do need to see Mr Jarman urgently, and I have driven some way. I shall only take a few minutes."

"I have no doubt, but I really can't oblige. Nobody has access today without an appointment, do you see? He has a particularly important meeting with the War Department in an hour's time and he really can't speak to anyone else." He shrugged lightly, and in Bunch's opinion a touch smugly. "I'm sure you know how it is. Officialdom, what with the war … and all that jazz."

"I am here on official business," she snapped.

"We do have security and you should really have a War Office pass to get past our guards."

"I should?" Bunch looked behind her at the door and turned back to smile sweetly at him. "My family home was requisitioned by the government some time ago now. You may know it: Perringham House. I can tell you the place is absolutely stiff with armed squaddies, with barbed wire and gates, and I am told they even have a few patrol dogs of late. Nobody gets in there, not even family." She leaned both hands on the desk and gazed into his face. "That, old chap, is what you might call *being guarded.* Not a handful of civilians without so much as a pop gun between them.

You're Stephen Jarman, aren't you."

He flushed slightly and re-examined the card. "I am. How may I help you?"

Bunch took a step back and glanced at the desktop for a moment. "Currently I have been asked to look into the facts regarding the unfortunate death of poor Laura."

"You knew my sister?"

"Yes. Not well, I admit, but I've seen her at various events. My condolences. It must have been such a shock for you all. I was hoping to speak to your mother – I have messages from my grandmother for her. But a rather frosty type at the house told me she's not receiving visitors as yet."

"Mother is taking Laura's death badly. If you have any official questions about her murder you will need to speak with me … or my father." His expression had changed, self-importance giving way to a wary curiosity.

"I did ask to speak to Charles."

The young man's eyebrows met in a frown. "And I told you that he's far too busy today. He's preparing for a business meeting. If you would like to make an appointment for another day you could…"

"This meeting is so important? I'm a little surprised under the circumstances…"

"Because of Laura?" He shook his head. "We're all devastated, naturally, but we have vital war work to complete here."

"I know how that is, Stephen." Bunch tried a broad smile to soften that brittle and silent defence. "I hear you are to be congratulated. My grandmother, she's the dowager Lady Chiltcombe, don't you know, she told me you were married recently."

The frown deepened. "Yes, I was, thank you." He fidgeted with the diary and glanced at the doors behind him. "See here, Miss Courtney, I do think you'd be better off coming back. Quite likely Father really will be a while. This meeting is especially important."

"I have no doubt it is, but I drove up from Wyncombe especially and it would be such a crime to waste all that petrol. I'll wait. I am sure this meeting will not last all day. Who knows, I may even know these chaps visiting Charles. My father stalks the corridors of Whitehall, after all." Bunch crossed to the small line of chairs against the far wall and sat, her hands crossed on her lap, smiling at him. "If you could tell your father I'm waiting? It might save us all some embarrassment."

Stephen Jarman looked from her to the large double doors and back. He turned abruptly and vanished through the doors. Bunch gazed around, aware of her racing pulse and praying she hadn't pushed it too far. *Father will go berserk if I have*, she thought, *using his name in vain*. She didn't have long to worry about that. The doors opened almost immediately and Charles Jarman stalked towards her.

He reminded Bunch of a bird. *A crane, perhaps, all hunched shoulders and slender body*. He was not a tall man, and she had the impression of a powder-keg personality that exuded charisma, and the certainty that he could indeed charm, despite the puckered burn scars around his left eye that stretched around to where an ear would have been.

"The Honourable Miss Rose Courtney. I have heard all about you … and your family." He held out his hand. "To what do we owe this honour?"

"Mr Charles Jarman." Bunch knew she hadn't quite managed to hide her surprise. Wright had told her Jarman had been in and accident but being told and then seeing the reality were never the same thing. Her hesitation was momentary and she rose to greet him with hand out. "Good of you to speak with me. I only need a few minutes of your time. I would not intrude at such a time but this is important." As she shook his hand she tried not to look at the damaged face any longer than she should.

Jarman's left hand lifted to his cheek and he smiled wryly. "Not pretty is it. A tank fire," he said.

"The Great War?"

"No, no. I was in a tank in the Great War, yes, and sustained a few injuries. But this—" He gestured again at his ruined face. "I acquired this taking part in trials down near Aldershot in '36. I consider myself lucky to have got off so lightly."

"Just before you moved here?"

"Yes. My doctor said time in the country would be beneficial."

"Is that what you do here, resting while you build tanks?"

Jarman broke into a grim laugh. "Design them. Well, not whole tanks – just certain portions of them. The tracks to be precise. We build nothing but prototypes here. Research into new techniques. All under wraps with the War Department. I really can't say any more on that score, Miss Courtney. Besides, I find it hard to imagine armoured military vehicles are of special interest to you."

"Tanks are not why I'm here, of course." A door banged nearby and a pair of young men in brown overalls passed the window outside. Bunch glanced at them and smiled at their perfect timing. "Perhaps we can talk somewhere a little less public?"

He raised his chin to stare at her along his damaged nose and Bunch could sense him teetering on the edge of refusal. "I can give you fifteen minutes. No more. I really do have a meeting that could be crucial for the war effort. Stephen, coffee for our guest."

Jarman led her into an office decked out in a deep-blue carpet, a large desk, and a few leather seats flanking chrome and glass coffee tables: a waiting room, by any other name. She followed him through a second pair of black and chrome doors to the inner sanctum. More glass and chrome and deep-navy blue, which she thought jarred a little against the photographs and models of tanks and armoured lorries that decorated walls and flat surfaces. *Khaki would be more appropriate.*

Bunch gravitated towards a pair of armchairs separated by a glass coffee table and sat down without waiting for Jarman. "What a lovely view." She waved at the window, at the track heading through trees that opened onto the Downs.

"The advantage of being the boss." Jarman sat in the other chair. "Now, I should like to know what you mean by waltzing into Jarman's Engineering and demanding to know my family's personal business."

"Firstly, I must offer my condolences. And secondly to ask a few questions about Laura." Jarman nodded and she felt the mood shift. It was like a warm front plunging down to cold and stormy. Bunch realised she had no choice but to plough on in the teeth of it. "I consult for the Sussex Constabulary, though on this occasion they contacted me because Laura had my telephone number – *Well, almost* – in her notebook and without too finer point I am very curious to know why, because so far as I am aware she has never telephoned me."

"I'm not sure we can be a great deal of help on that score." He sighed heavily and stared out of the window though Bunch was reasonably sure he was not seeing the scene outside.

She waited. Wright had said the family were being difficult over the police enquiries and she wondered what or who had created such a barrier. *Some clumsy local constable treading on toes? Or the ever-lugubrious Sergeant Carter? Or even Wright himself? Does Petworth even come under Brighton's remit?* She could not afford to wait for too long for a reply yet there were occasions when letting people talk in their own time was far more productive than a direct interrogation. "Laura deserves justice," she said softly. "And your wife needs to know for her own peace of mind."

"Laura and Stephen used to be close to their mother." Jarman turned to glance at her. "But Laura, not for some little while now."

"They had a falling out?"

"Laura had become difficult of late. When my wife tried to find out why—" he rubbed at his face "—Laura got terribly angry. She's always been rather headstrong. I persuaded her to work up at the factory, away from here, and bring some peace to the house."

"Do you know why Laura was angry?"

Jarman shook his head. "I'm afraid I hadn't been paying her much attention. My work takes so much of my time so I leave domestic issues to my wife, but Selina went to pieces when Laura left, I'm afraid. Now she sees herself as responsible for Laura's death. Nonsense of course."

"Laura was murdered by a monster. Your wife is not responsible for their actions."

"I know. The girl is – was – wilful. Laura was wilful from the cradle."

Bunch thought about her own family and acknowledged the truth in that – some people were as they were despite their family's best intentions. "It is sometimes the way of things." She kept her expression neutral. The man's apparent lack of attention to his wife and daughter might be harsh, bordering on the cruel, to some, though Bunch had experience of something similar. She loved her

parents dearly and she had no doubt they loved her, but the diplomatic service always came first and Perringham second. Charles Jarman was no older than her own parents but at heart he was a Victorian industrialist who saw everything in bald terms, without nuance or sentiment. She had come across many of them in her times and she had never worked out whether they were truly as pompous as they appeared, or whether it was some kind of veneer. She felt a pang of sympathy for his wife and wondered from whom Laura had really run. *Or to whom.*

"Laura didn't deserve to be killed. And her death certainly was *not* my wife's fault."

"Coffee, Dad. Miss Courtney." Stephen Jarman entered and set a tray on the table. "Do you need anything else, Father?"

"Any sign of Mrs Bell?" Jarman snapped.

"Not as yet." Stephen Jarman smiled at Bunch. "Bell is our receptionist. She failed to appear today."

Charles Jarman tapped his hand on the edge of the table hard enough to have the cups chink in their saucers. "Today of all days, with the Brigadier due any moment. Get that wife of yours over here. We can't have the desk going unattended."

"She's out. I think she had an appointment in Petworth."

"Again? Mary is part of this family now and we have a business to run. We have deadlines to meet. She should be answering the telephones, at the very least."

"Yes, Dad." The younger Jarman nodded to Bunch before retreating.

"He doesn't have a clue," Jarman said. "Doesn't see we've a war to fight and we can't afford to carry anyone. Laura had a good head on her shoulders when she cared to use it. And now she's gone…"

"And Stephen?"

"He's had to step up after Robert enlisted. And he blames both his mother and me for Laura leaving." Jarman allowed himself a tight smile. "Which is rich coming from him."

"What has Stephen done?" Jarman laughed sharply and Bunch felt a chill run through her at his lack of empathy. *No wonder they are flying the coop first chance they get.* "Did you think Laura left here because of him?" Jarman worked his jaw as he stared past her.

Chewing bees, she thought.

"She went to work at our London factory," he said finally. "I thought it was for the best. It would give her a chance to cool down, think things over before she did something she'd regret."

"Separation may help at times." Bunch thought of her mother Theadora, now in the nursing home. She and her mother had never waged open warfare, as the Jarmans seem to do, but they'd had their share of battles. "He and Laura weren't close?"

"Stephen has had much of his mother's attention because of the polio. I told Selina not to coddle the boy but she would run around after him."

"Understandable that Stephen would need a little more care," she said. "Polio is a terrible thing. I had heard rumours that he was a cripple but he seems to be fine."

"We were fortunate. We thought we would lose him but in the end he was not as severely affected as some."

"I couldn't help noticing his arm."

"Muscle weakness, no more. His left leg was also affected. Good shoes sorted that out, but the army won't take him. All to the good, I suppose. With Robert and Laura gone I really do need him here." Jarman's face tightened. "Robert is a gifted engineer and to my mind his presence here would have been far more useful for the war effort. But he couldn't wait to join up however, and as a grown man we could not prevent him."

Bunch wondered briefly why Beatrice and Constance had omitted that particular gem. *Was it something they didn't know? That's a first.* "So, you got along well? You and Robert?"

"We rubbed along." He scowled at her. "I realise you are here to ascertain what might have happened to my daughter, but I don't see how anything else is your business. We are carrying out important and secret work here."

"I was trying to understand why Laura left."

Jarman flushed red around his collar. "Over some fiddling little thing."

"It often is." Bunch had some sympathy and felt an immediate guilt that her mother was languishing in a nursing home, in rapidly failing health. *Why am I comparing these people to mine? We're nothing alike.*

Jarman offered her a cigarette and took his time lighting both hers and his own. Finally, he let go a stream of smoke and tapped ash that had barely begun to accumulate before he replied. "Laura was a city girl and the country life bored her to tears." He grunted. "Her words, not mine. She told us that she never wanted to live here surrounded by fields and trees."

"She had made contacts not far from here, and quite recently. Did you know?"

He looked at her sharply. "Why do you assume that?"

"It appears she knew people in Wyncombe. I presume you were told that much?" Jarman gave a slight nod. "I become involved with this case because I live there." She watched his expression carefully.

"Wyncombe…" He reached for his coffee cup. "Never heard of the place before the police mentioned it to me."

Bunch had more than a strong idea that he was avoiding her eye. *Though it's difficult to tell what he's thinking with those terrible scars.* "It's a small village near—"

"Never heard of it," he said again. "Can't be much of a place. Two houses and a pub, I'll be bound."

"It is small, yes." Bunch smiled sweetly. "I have lived there all of my life."

Jarman set his cup back in the saucer, pausing to move the handle at right angles to the stripe of the pattern. "If you don't know all that's happening on *your* own doorstep—" he raised his face to look her in the eye once more "—I can't imagine why you think I should." He stood up abruptly. "Now if you don't mind, Miss Courtney, I really can't spare you any more time. I have an important meeting coming up and with my secretary missing I shall need to prepare for it myself."

"Of course. Thank you for your time, Mr Jarman. I shall call again, if I may, and have a word with your wife when she has had a little time to get over the shock."

"I would rather you didn't bother her. She's not taking this well and the doctor has her sedated. I doubt she would be able to tell you any more than I have. We haven't seen Laura here since the autumn and we have no idea what might have happened to her, or why, but it doesn't mean we don't love her."

"Of course."

Jarman escorted Bunch to the outer office where Stephen was still alone.

"I told you to fetch Mary. We have the Brigadier here at any moment and I can't have him wander into an empty office," Jarman said.

"She is still out," Stephen replied.

"Then go and get her back." Jarman opened the front door. "Goodbye Miss Courtney."

There was no alternative but to leave, which Bunch did with reluctance and relief in equal measure. Jarman was not a pleasant man but she had the idea his rudeness was also a smoke screen for other reasons. At some point, however, she would need to corner Stephen and Mary, away from his presence.

As she motored down to the end of the drive she passed a military staff car with two officers seated in the back, the younger of whom she recognised.

"As I live and breathe, Henry bloody Marsham."

~ Four ~

Bunch loved the freedom that her Roadster gave her. It was not as luxurious as the mothballed Crossley, nor was it any faster, but in an inexplicable way it was more exhilarating by far. Especially on such a warm day, with its top down and wind whipping past. *The closest thing to riding a horse without it being a horse.*

She pulled the MG through the entrance gates of the Red House and stopped, staring at the frontage for several minutes, her fingers tapping impatiently on the steering wheel. The early Victorian manor house, built of red brick as its name suggested, was two storeys high, long and low, with a pair of spotless red doors glittered with brass fittings beneath its classic portico. A half-dozen steps in a sweeping arc made for an impressive facade. There was none of the usual swathes of wisteria or ivy that you might expect clinging to the walls of such a building. Instead, there were slender columns of clipped yew marking the spaces between the pale sandstone window surrounds. At each end of the façade was a tall gate which was contained by the high garden walls.

When it became obvious that they had no facility to provide her mother with the round-the-clock care at the Dower, the family had claimed a place for Theadora at the Red House. It was close enough for the family to visit and a pleasant enough establishment that appeared less forbidding than a general hospital. It had been the retreat for a small Anglican order, opened for nurse officers from the Boer and Great wars, and a convalescence home since then. Bunch wondered that it had not been claimed by the rapacious War Office. *Maybe the Church has special influence?* she thought. *And even nowadays there still has to be places for sick civilians to waste away.*

Whatever its origins, she was never comfortable visiting such a place; she found it depressing, or more precisely she found its function depressing. Some patients did escape its confines alive, at least briefly, but Theadora's presence here had brought home the spectre of mortality – with a mighty thump.

As she sat in her car, she pondered the schisms that had dominated the Jarman clan and decided that compared to them her own family was positively brimming with bonhomie. Despite his long hours at the Ministry, Edward Courtney visited at least once every week without fail since Theadora had been moved to the Red House shortly before Easter. Bunch had found herself searching for excuses to stay away. Guilt she knew, guilt at not using the limited nursing experience she possessed to look after her mother. Although they loved each other, the bond between mother and daughter had always been eccentric. She and Theadora had their differences, yet those differences were never hard set; rather they ebbed and flowed with whatever winds prevailed at the time.

"But you're here now, dammit," she muttered and leapt out of the MG without bothering with the niceties of opening the door. She paused to straighten the line of her white blouse and black swing slacks before skipping up the steps two at a time.

The lobby was cool and crisp. Corridors, panelled to shoulder-height in gold-brown walnut, punctuated by recessed doors and semi-circular console tables, stretched away to left and right. The walls above the panelling were plain white, broken only by simple crosses, carved in the same pale walnut. The space was bathed in rippling sunlight pouring in through upper gallery windows.

Unusually there was nobody sitting at the reception's hatched window and no sound from either corridor, or from the gallery at the top of the staircase. She knew where everyone would be on golden afternoons such as this, however. Patients, or guests as the matron preferred to call them, those well enough to recognise their surroundings, would be out enjoying that sun. *Whether they wanted it or not.*

Bunch walked across the expanse of the intricately tiled floor to a pair of doors set with stained glass and gazed out at the garden. Covered walkways ran around three structural sides whilst the fourth wall was of old stone, supporting several ancient fruit trees. The quad was mainly laid to grass, quartered by flower-lined stone paths that met around a fountain pool.

Theadora, just a few paces from the French doors leading to her private room, was stretched out on a steamer chair. A glass

and a covered jug of what Bunch hoped was barley water stood on a low rattan table beside her. As Bunch stepped closer she could see, even through the lenses of her round-eyed sunglasses, that her mother's eyes were closed. An opened book lay face down on top of the light blanket that was covering her legs, despite the warmth of the sun.

It felt wrong to wake her mother when the woman rarely slept now, without powders and painkillers. Bunch paused four paces off, gazing down at her mother's face and wincing at the yellow papery bags beneath her eyes that disguised high cheekbones. Theadora was beautiful, still, but every failing internal organ was etched in her face. Bunch was aware of movement close to her and turned to smile at the elderly woman in the grey-blue robes of an Augustinian nun standing at her side.

"Miss Courtney, how lovely. You're a little early. Visiting time is not for another quarter hour, but no matter. Your mother will be thrilled to see you."

"She looks quite comfortable, Sister Bertha. Perhaps we should let her sleep. I can come back another day."

"Lady Chiltcombe would be deeply sorry in that case because she speaks of you often. For you it's only half-an-hour or so from your day but for her it is a precious half-hour of her daughter's company."

"Before we disturb her ... how is she?"

"She is much the same as on your last visit." Sister Bertha tilted her head to peer into Bunch's face. "We manage her pain as best we can and see that she wants for nothing. That is no trial because she wants for very little these days."

"How... How long?"

Sister Bertha raised her shoulders in a light shrug. "In these times, how long is there in this world for any of us?"

"Mummy looks so frail. Fragile. I should drive Dodo over to see her." She smiled at the nun's questioning glance. "My sister Daphne."

"Mrs Tinsley came yesterday with her daughter. Georgianna, is it? And her sister-in-law."

"They did?" Bunch felt her guilt return, that she hadn't known about Dodo's visit. And guilty that she barely had time to speak to her sibling over the past week. "I'm sure Mummy would have been pleased."

"It was a lively visit. That youngster has quite a set of lungs on her."

"Oh dear. Not too much disturbance, I hope?"

"Not at all." Sister Bertha nodded slowly, not looking at Bunch. "It does everyone good to hear young voices. It reminds them of what they are made. And your mother was buoyed up for the rest of the day, though of course she was very tired."

"You have heard about the christening being brought forward? Is my mother up to it, do you think?"

"A christening is such a joyful event." Sister Bertha paused to regard Theadora. "It will be taxing for her, there is no doubt about that, though it should not be a reason to delay. The benefits of such occasions far outweigh the costs. I believe your sister and father and yes, your mother, will derive a great deal of comfort from it all." That thoughtful bird-like tilt of her head again as she gazed at Bunch. "You have a good soul but a restless one. I suspect it requires a great deal more to bring it peace."

"Mother is more important." Bunch broke eye contact, a little unnerved at having the nun divine her character quite so readily. The need for things beyond her usual environment, to have an active part in the world's events, had been gathering strength for months. But she realised that there was no way of relieving that pressure without causing chaos. The estate was always going to be her main duty, even more now that her mother was on her way out of this world and her father was absent for so much of the time. No different to a million other people, she knew, but the feeling that she should be doing something extra was never more than a thought away, nagging at her mind.

Sister Bertha, Bunch realised, was still watching her but with a questioning expression spiced with a kind of pity, an emotion that snatched Bunch back to the real world. "What I wanted to ask," she said, "will this christening take far too much from Mother. What do you really think?"

"Will it shorten her allotted time on this earth? That I cannot say. It may give her strength but that is in the hands of powers far greater than mine," the sister replied. "Your mother knows the risks and… Ah, Lady Chiltcombe, you are awake. You have a visitor."

"Rose." Theadora struggled to sit up with Sister Bertha's help.

"Here let me." Bunch bent to adjust the pillows and Theadora sank back against them with a sigh.

"My darling Rosebunch, how lovely to see you."

Bunch was shocked at the rasp in her mother's voice, and by the weakness of it, yet it was *Rosebunch* that made the hint of a lump rise in her throat. It was Dodo and Emma and a select few school chums who called her Bunch, and only her father who still used that pet name in its original form. Hearing it from her mother took her back to dimly remembered times during the previous war. Strangely enough, far happier times for Theadora.

"Hello Mummy," Bunch murmured and bent to brush her lips against Theadora's cheek. "You're looking well."

"Lovely of you to say but don't tell fibs, Rose dear. It doesn't suit you."

There was a pleasure to be had in that amiable rebuke and Bunch grinned. "Then I shall do my utmost to tell the brutal truth, Mummy. You look no worse, which on a day like today amounts to the same thing. Good to see you out here enjoying the sun."

Sister Bertha was struggling back towards them with a chair taken from further along the patio and Bunch hurried to collect it from her, placing it on the other side of the little table. "You needn't have done that, Sister. I was going to fetch one."

"It's no trouble, child. I need to remind her ladyship not to overtire herself with too much talking." She smiled impishly and Bunch was in no doubt for whom the warning was intended. "And also, to ask if you would like some tea. I can send one of our postulants out with a tray."

"Thank you, Sister. That would be lovely."

"My pleasure." The elderly nun inclined her head and drifted away, covering the distance to the doors in far less time than her serenity hinted.

"The sister said you're holding your own." Bunch settled herself in the chair and leaned forward, elbows on her knees, to gaze at her mother.

"I believe the phrase is 'as well as may be expected'." Theadora laughed. "Well enough for one more weekend." She laughed again and it turned into a coughing fit and all Bunch could do was help her with a sip of barley water. As the spasm began to subside Theadora took hold of Bunch's wrist and squeezed it gently. "Your face is priceless. One thing you have inherited from me is a hate of people pussyfooting around the hard subjects. I will be there for Georgi's christening. Absolutely no arguments."

"In that case there is nothing more to be said." Bunch could not help feeling, when her mother had spent twenty years avoiding Perringham and the deaths of her sons, that this was a trait which came from Beatrice, but she let it pass and waved vaguely at the patients dotted around the courtyard, searching for a new subject to fill the imminent void. "I feel like an intruder," she muttered. "Nothing to be done but gossip and argue."

"Visiting the sick always feels rather awkward, doesn't it?" Theadora reached for the glass again and took a sip from it, her hand shaking slightly so that the rim chinked against her teeth.

Bunch fought the instinct to hold the glass for her, knowing how her mother hated being seen as an invalid, and waited until Theadora put the glass down. "I thought you were not coming before the weekend."

"I wasn't," Bunch replied, "but I was passing and it seemed a shame not to call."

"Where have you been? Somewhere exciting?"

"Petworth."

"And…"

"I was visiting a chap called Jarman."

"Charles Jarman?"

"You know him?"

"One often sees these people at the odd party. He isn't someone you forget easily with that dreadfully burned face. I knew his wife Selina a little better. Wasn't she one of your grandmother's suffrage girls? Perhaps…? I was terribly surprised when she married Jarman, though he was quite a handsome thing before his accident. Maybe she liked the older man? Many women do, you know. Once they pass forty, men usually have acquired better manners and at least a modicum of common sense."

"Granny said it was all about money."

"That would have a deal of logic to it – and Beatrice is the oracle." Theadora's laugh ended in another coughing fit, gasping to pull air into her lungs.

"Here." Bunch helped her mother to sit forward, holding the glass of barley water to Theadora's lips.

"Thank you," Theadora said and lay back with a long sigh. "Damn this disease. I feel like a three-day old kitten."

"You'll get stronger."

Theadora chuckled more quietly and with less humour. "You are a darling for trying to cheer up an old soak, but we all know I'm dying. Slowly. One organ at a time. Coughing like a demon every night … and will you just look at these hands." She held one hand out and glared at it. "Puffed up and yellow. I feel as if I genuinely have fingers made of bananas."

"Mummy—" Bunch stopped, pursing her lips, searching her mother's face for the right thing to say. Talking was not the Courtney's strong point, or at least not between the two of them, and her mother's candour and unexpected gallows humour took her by surprise. "Is there anything to be done?" she said finally. "What about surgery…?"

"That time is long past, even if half the decent hospitals in the country were not bombed to hell and half the decent surgeons swanning around in uniform treating flat feet and carnal diseases – there's no way any of them can help me now."

"Does Daddy know?"

"Everyone does, my dear. It's why Daphne's bringing the christening forward. Getting it in before I pop off."

Once again Theadora's candour took Bunch by surprise, and she felt herself flounder for an answer. There was no point in denying it, not when her mother had asked for the truth, and all she could come up with was: "She had mentioned it. Rather proves she is aware of how things are going. Oh Mummy, I am so sorry."

"Not nearly as sorry as am I."

Theadora laughed again and Bunch realised that in all her life she had never heard that sound coming so often from her mother. "I'm sorry all the same."

"I know you are, dear heart." Theadora turned her head away

and looked across the quad while an orderly set a tea tray on the table. "Enough of my doom and gloom for now. Let's talk about something a little more exciting. I take it you have been visiting the Jarmans on some macabre errand. Daphne told me you had seen your little policeman friend."

"He has a name," said Bunch. "Yes, I have, as it happens. Wright required information on Laura Jarman. She has been … murdered."

"I can't say I am surprised." Theadora waved a hand at her daughter's surprise. "Laura had turned wild, from all I hear. And her father is in industry, you know."

"Don't be such a crushing snob, Mummy. A lot of people are in 'industry', as you put it. I must say, I was quite taken aback by what I saw this morning. He has turned his estate into some kind of a research complex."

"That won't go down well with the local farmers. There they are, putting every square yard they have under the plough – and he's sitting there in his tranquil meadows playing with his toys." Theadora chortled quietly at her daughter's face. "I may be away from Perringham but I do know a few things about farming, and I read the newspapers. One couldn't miss *Dig for Victory* even if one tried." She was grinning now, the mischief lighting up her face as her voice dropped to a loud whisper. "If you look closely at these borders the sisters have planted you'll see cabbages and tomatoes in amongst the delphiniums."

"Granny has been eying up the croquet lawn for potatoes. Luckily, we've managed to divert her so far. One must have some amusements and we need somewhere to host the Oak Day fete. The village would never forgive us if we don't hold to tradition."

"You would be lynched," Theadora agreed. "Yes, indeed, we need social gatherings – and Charles Jarman alienating the locals will not help with poor Selina's social life."

"I think she's suffered far more from Charles being a prize specimen of boorishness."

"He was rude to you?"

"He managed to stay on the proper side of civility and be desperately rude at the same time. Quite an accomplishment. I can't say I was sorry to get away from him."

"A wasted journey?"

"Not entirely. And you will never guess who I saw going in there as I left. Henry Marsham. Along with some old general or other."

"Did you indeed? Henry was sweet on Laura for a while."

"Oh? Granny never said."

"He had to do something after you turned him down. Fun to know Beatrice's knowledge is not infallible ... despite all she will have us believe."

"Henry being keen on me may be stretching it. And I didn't exactly turn him down. He only took me to a few parties."

"Goodness. Practically betrothed, in your grandmother's eyes"

"Well, Granny must be slipping because she didn't know about the house that Laura had a telephone number for. Haven Cottage. Any ideas?"

"Not a clue, my darling. You would know far more about what goes on in the village than I ever could – unless it's in my newspaper." Theadora passed a hand over her face, exhausted by the exchange, Bunch suddenly realised. "Enough of all that. Pour me some tea and tell me the good news."

"Good news of what?"

"Anything that isn't about the war or you friend William and his murders."

~ Five ~

Bunch needed time to think and the company of horses, with their unquestioning acceptance, allowed her the room for private thought. The fact that her mother's liver failure was shutting down her other vital organs was not as much of a surprise as it might have been. Bunch had enough medical knowledge from her days with the FANY to know that it was not unusual, expected even, but the realisation that there was less time available for her mother than expected was a shock. Bunch needed to absorb all this information for herself before she talked with the rest of the family.

Dodo, she thought, *would have been on the telephone the moment she got home, had she known. She was always closer to Mummy and this is going to hit her far harder than any of us. George only died a year and half back, after all. Poor creature.* Her fingers went through the familiar task of fastening the pony's bridle straps. *The family will rally together of course, communicating a thousand words in a single gesture. Like we always do. Only in time, however, will we know how it will change us all.* She set thoughts of Theadora's illness to one side because that, hopefully, was not immediate but still sometime in the future. *And may not even happen. You never know, stranger things have…* There was no way that she believed that. *But mourning in advance can't possibly help.*

Instead, Bunch made an effort to review her meeting with the Jarmans. Her conversation with Charles Jarman raised far more questions than it had resolved. He was an obnoxious sort, but that was no secret based on what she had learned from both Theadora and her grandmother. *He's hiding a great deal but that was no surprise either*, she thought.

His son was more of an enigma. Something about Stephen Jarman disturbed her. Not anything he had said or anything she saw him do – her unease was based on nothing more than a particular look in his eyes. She didn't think he had it in him to kill his own sister, and as far as she had been informed of by Wright, there was absolutely nothing to link him with the two previous murders; but he also had a secret he was hiding.

Bunch mulled all these thoughts over and over in her mind as she checked the girths and led Perry to the mounting block. She had never needed the block when she was younger. Perry was little more than fourteen hands and steady as a rock. A few short years before, she was still riding him bareback when the mood took her. The injuries she'd gained in France made mounting the horse a lot harder, and she had come to the sad realisation there was a time and a place for stoicism. She stood on top of the block, gathered the reins in her left hand, and slid her right leg over the saddle.

She put thumb and forefinger in her mouth and let go with a shrieking whistle. "Bella! Come! Heel!" The spaniel scurried out of the feed room and rushed ahead to the yard gates where she stopped, looking over her shoulder, tongue flapping at one end and stump of a tail wiggling frantically at the other.

"Let's be off, shall we?" A brief squeeze of her calves against Perry's sides and he shambled a few paces forwards before breaking into a brisk walk. He was eager to ride out and it took just a few minutes to bring them out onto one of the many *wapple ways* that criss-crossed the Downs. Bella ranged through the scrubby stands of gorse and bramble and wild clematis, covering at least twice the distance as the horse and rider as the dog quartered the ground.

Hacking across the coombe always gave Bunch the room to lose herself in thought, yet she always maintained a deep appreciation of her surroundings. As she reached a tree-free high point she reined in Perry. From somewhere above the Downs came the sound of a lark and she shaded her eyes to catch a glimpse, but it had already flown too high against the brightness of the sky. Away to the southwest a solid line of dark cloud was creeping closer, far enough away to be no threat to her ride for another hour or so. Her attention was pulled back to the hillside, at a flash of colour and the chattering, wheezing call of a pair of yellow hammers flushed from the scrub by the blundering spaniel; at the hum of bees making the most of the buttercups and ox-eye daisies and scabious; at a line of ant hills marching through the turf. Her gaze fell finally on a small patch of wild orchids. She contemplated dismounting to pick a bunch for her grandmother but knew from experience that those delicate blooms would be limp and dying long before she got them home. *Dead as poor Laura.* Besides, she'd only struggle to remount Perry. She leaned forward to slap Perry's dusty black neck.

"Such a violent death and such a vile kind of disposal. Laura's killers couldn't even be bothered to leave her in left luggage. She was simply abandoned on the platform like an old umbrella." She frowned and continued to talk aloud. "On the other hand, she was bound to be discovered quite quickly there. A trunk on the platform would get in the way and somebody would investigate. It could have sat in left or lost luggage for days, maybe weeks, if the smell didn't attract attention. Wright says there were others, so is there a pattern? But the first two were mutilated – head and hands missing. Was she abandoned because of the air raid, before her killer had time to finish the job?" Bunch picked at the strands of Perry's coarse mane, running each thread through her fingers until she reached the ends. "What do you think, old fruit?"

Perry nodded his head and snorted impatiently.

"Yes, I know, you don't give a fig because you're a grumpy old horse. All right, let's walk on." She tapped her heels against his sides and urged him down the left-hand track at a slow trot. "Time to visit this house, see if we can discover who young Laura was telephoning. Walk on Perry. And Bella, come!"

~~~

A privet hedge shielded the house from the road. The hedge had obviously been let go for months and there were long fronds of rose arcing upwards and outwards over the it, with early sprigs of blossom already releasing their cloying perfume. But at the centre of the hedge someone had at least cut them back around the gateway.

Bunch dismounted and hitched Perry to one of the gate posts and peered down the short drive to Haven Cottage. The house was typical of hundreds throughout the county: white-painted ground floor with large diamond paned windows either side of the door, the upper storey tile-hung, and a low-pitched roof like a vast floppy hat with four dormer windows lifting its front edge.

Once through the gate she could see that the driveway up to a relatively new garage had been roughly widened behind the hedge with cinders and old brick. Invisible from the road, there was sufficient space for a half-dozen cars at the very least. Her first thought was to wonder if the Wallers had been back in the past eighteen months to learn what had happened to their property. Her second was to wonder why Beatrice's local WVS re-homing campaign hadn't commandeered Haven Cottage to re-house the bombed-out families from coastal towns and cities.

She strode up to the front door and knocked. After a few minutes she rattled the handle and was not surprised to find it locked. A path veered left to the side of the house and it was logical to Bunch to follow it. She had barely gone three paces when a sharp sound, like the slap of a clenched fist meeting a cupped palm, made her stop dead. She stared around her and then at Bella. The dog seemed unperturbed. She was grateful that Bella, failing hunter though she was, at least had a grasp of the basic commands of Come and Heel, and signalled Bella to her side. They crept the last few feet to peer around the corner of the house.

The noise came again, this time from above their heads. Bella growled, gazing upwards, and Bunch laid a hand on the dog's back as she searched for the source of the noise. Almost directly above them a heavy curtain flopped against the stone sill of a small window. She watched as it caught the wind once more, twitching and curling like a cow's tongue reaching for a tuft of grass, and lifting finally to flap against the tiles. *We're a pair of idiots, Bella. Getting twitchy in our old age,* Bunch thought. *Curious though that the window itself isn't moving. It must be latched open.* "Now why would someone leave a window ajar if they were going to be gone for a while?" she said to Bella. "Or open, at all?"

Initially, Bunch had only intended to look around the outside if there was no one home, but since the window was open to the elements she gave herself permission to enter. She was certain the letting agent would not be pleased that a window was left open. "It is my duty." She had not known the Wallers personally but told herself she would hate to think of the house filling up with water if it should rain. "What do you think, Bella?"

The dog wiggled at her and ran a few yards ahead, leading her round to the back of the house. Bunch tried the kitchen door and stepped back in surprise when it swung open. "Curious." The door had been forced, she noticed, with the rim lock's tin keep dangling free on a single screw. *A boot against the door could have done this. Easy peasy.*

She took a single cautious step indoors. The inside smelled damp despite the recent dry weather. A stack of unwashed glasses, dishes and plates were piled near the sink. "Someone's had a party," she said. "Late night drinkies? Whoever it was has left in a hurry." She rested her hand loosely on the dog's collar. "I assume they are not in. What do you think?" Bella looked up at her, tongue lolling happily, and barged past to snuffle around the kitchen table inhaling unseen crumbs.

"Bella. Heel" she hissed and stood, head tilted, listening for any sign that she or the dog had been heard. There was not a sound beyond Bella's panting. "Hello!" Bunch shouted. "Anybody at home? Hello!" Her voice echoed through an open door into the hallway, vibrating in that way only unoccupied spaces allow it. Despite that certainty that she was alone Bunch moved cautiously to the far door. "Hello!" she yelled again.

Bella scuttled ahead of her down the short passage and veered into the first of two interconnecting reception rooms that formed a large L shape. The curtains were half-drawn and shafts of sunlight fell on a solitary glass that had not made it to the kitchen. Bella, in that unerring way of her kind, dived on a plate half-hidden under a sofa. She snatched some part-eaten morsel, gulping it down more or less unchewed before Bunch could stop her.

"Oh, for heaven's sake dog, sit. Now stay." The spaniel lowered her ears, realising she was in disgrace, and parked her rear end on the Persian rug. Bunch picked up a cushion that had fallen to the floor, lobbed it onto the sofa and sneezed at the cloud of dust it set swirling in the air. "Knapp would have a fit," she said. "This place hasn't been swept in weeks." Bunch prowled the room examining every corner of the area and found nothing of interest. *Just in need of a thorough clean.* Nowhere was there any sign of violence. She looked around, trying to imagine what Wright would be thinking and doing in her place. *Think like a policeman. What am I looking for?*

She went back into the hallway and checked the front door mat for mail. "Not so much as a grocer's bill," she said to Bella. "There may be a great deal of dirty crockery and a lot of dust but this place feels sterile. No photos, no nick-nacks, nothing on the mantle except for that ugly and terribly expensive-looking clock. Good carpets, fashionable furnishings, but all of it impersonal. The Wallers obviously don't live here so I suppose it's no great surprise, but you'd think there'd be something of theirs. I have seen more welcoming hotel rooms."

The thwack of the curtain made her glance to the stairwell and reminded her why she had entered Haven Cottage in the first place, or rather, the excuse she initially gave herself. "Come on then, Bella, may as well see to that at least."

The open window was situated at the top of the flight of stairs where it terminated in a right-angle onto the landing corridor. It had a deep reveal with a rain-sodden cushion on the low sill to form a small window seat. *How long has this window been open?* The casement's stay-arm creaked in its wobbly catch as she came level with it, and she caught hold of the frame in case it could jump free of its moorings, though she need not have worried. The brass arm had become hooked in a tear in the heavy curtain fabric so that it could only move as far as the brocade would allow.

She reached out to haul the curtain back inside and pulled the window shut. As she snicked the catch she saw that several panes were broken; two of them were missing glass, with just jagged spurs clinging to the wood frame, with the muntin dividing them splintered outward. A third pane was crazed from its bottom corner closest to the broken section. Something had apparently hit the window with considerable force from inside the house. She examined the floor beneath the window but whatever detritus that might have fallen inside had been cleared away.

Bunch shook the wrinkles from the soiled cloth, letting the floor length curtain fall back against the wall. A glint of something metallic, round and coin-like, lodged between skirting and the floor, caught her attention. She picked it up and turned it over in her palm. A brass button, grubby and dulled for want of polish. The royal crest was easy to discern but the wording was obscured. She dampened her thumb and rubbed at the button, holding it closer to the window to make out the word CANADA.

"Those chaps were here? How interesting." She slipped the button in her pocket and turned to the upper floor. The landing window provided the only available light and with all the doors closed the hall was dingier than downstairs. She reached for the light switch. Nothing happened. She flicked the Bakelight toggle twice more. "No power. Okay."

She tried the first door to her right and found herself looking at a bedroom: a large double bed, dressing table and chair. A smaller door hid a closet and the other a washbasin and mirror, complete with two towels hanging beneath the basin counter. All of it neat, almost clinical with its lack of personal effects. She might have been viewing a holiday guesthouse room awaiting its new occupant. She slowly explored the room aided by Bella's enthusiastic snuffling under beds and chairs, and between them found one solitary wine glass hiding behind a curtain.

They then worked their way anticlockwise around the landing and discovered three more bedrooms furnished in the same fashion, plus a lavatory and a bathroom with green-and-white tiled walls, a vast cast iron bath and two wash basins.

Bunch stood in the final doorway looking at a boxroom with a narrow iron bedstead slotted beneath the window. There was just enough room to open the door, against the mattress. There was a washstand behind the door but nothing else. What surprised her was that, unlike the other bedrooms, the bed itself was not made up. No pillows or blankets, only a dingy brown candlewick bedspread pulled unevenly across the mattress. It smelled dank and sour in that room, like bath towels that had been left in a corner wet and unloved. *Not that Knapp would allow that at Perringham*, she thought. *Heaven forbid. But it happened in the ATS field shelters often enough.*

"This room isn't used much, I imagine," she said. "Maid's room perhaps?" Bella whined and paddled her feet, yipping quietly. "Exactly so." Bunch turned to leave but Bella utter an excited *gruff* and dived under the bed.

"Come out of there." Bunch knelt to peer under the bed and got a faint whiff of carbolic. "Bella, out, dammit." The spaniel scampered past as Bunch got to her feet, cannoning into the backs of her legs. She laid her hand on the bed to prevent herself falling and felt the damp bedspread under her hand. Not just clammy from an unaired house, but wet. She yanked the fluffy cotton cover aside and stared at a large dark stained patch in the centre of the black-and-cream striped-ticking mattress. "Did somebody pee in the bed?" she said. "The disgusting little tyke." Bella wiggled enthusiastically. "That would suit you wouldn't it, old girl. Nothing more fascinating to your breed than pee and poo."

Bunch sniffed cautiously, wafting her hand towards her like a chef testing the freshness of turbot on a fishmonger's slab. "Mould," she muttered, "and definitely carbolic. But there's something else too." She frowned at the stain, trying to place that elusive odour percolating through a failed-laundry attempt and it came to her: faint and distorted, but that scent of putrefaction, once recognised never forgotten.

"Damnation," she breathed. "Hell's bells. Judging by its size, several buckets of what? Blood…?"

Bella rose to place both front paws on the edge of the mattress, her keen nose whiffling excitedly at the smell. Bunch slipped two fingers under the dog's leather collar and pulled her back onto the landing.

"No secret why whoever was here abandoned ship," she said. "Time to call for re-enforcements."

~~~

"It's definitely blood," said Wright.

"Although probably not sufficient for an exsanguination," Letham said. "There's no sign of the spattering one would expect if someone was killed by a violent act. The moisture is mostly soapy water, now. Cleaned by experts, I would assume, which makes the state of the kitchen sink somewhat incongruous."

"Is it human blood?" Wright persisted.

Letham backed out to the room's doorway to view the exposed bed as a whole, now cut open to expose the sticky deposits that had pooled at its centre. "It might be pig's blood, of course, or from any other medium-sized animal. A sheep, perhaps. Have any farmers reported missing stock of late? It would not be the first time I've seen the like. I've examined the results of some very wild parties." He grinned at Bunch's stunned expression. "But human blood is far more likely."

"Oh. Good … I suppose." Bunch glanced down at her boots. She had not thought of herself as naïve but a fetish was not something she had considered. "Could that blood come from the same source? The same … person?" she said at last.

"If you mean, was it all spilled at the same time? Perhaps. I repeat, I shall need to run a few tests with the proper equipment before making any firm judgement."

Wright turned to Bunch and rolled his eyes. "Can you at least say how long ago it was spilled?"

"It's difficult to say because of the cleaning attempt. A while."

"More than a week?"

"Most probably," Letham conceded. "My job is identifying what it is. The how, the who, the why, and the where – it is completely down to you, Wright. Now I shall be running along. I have two corpses awaiting my attention back at the ranch, which I should have been slicing and dicing if you hadn't had me driving around the county like a lost lamb."

Wright laughed and shook his head. "I did tell you there was no corpse here. You could have sent that trainee of yours and saved yourself a long drive."

"It sounded intriguing, I admit, but I can't be away from my mortuary for too long. I shall see you later, Wright. Good afternoon, Miss Courtney."

"I'll look forward to your report, Letham," Wright muttered.

"Good day, Doctor Letham," Bunch added.

They watched the pathologist saunter down the stairs and then moved into one of the other bedrooms that overlooked the rear of the building to watch a pair of uniformed officers poking around the garden.

"Such a happy soul," Bunch observed. "I suppose you'd need a certain line in gallows humour in his job."

"I have never been entirely sure if he's trying to be funny. He has few expectations of his fellow man. An inveterate cynic."

Bunch sneaked a look at Wright. *Takes one to know one*, she thought, and aloud, "Any sign of a body out there?" She nodded towards the garden.

"It would seem not. This is a curious one. Judging by the dirty dishes, the occupants left in a hurry – and yet they bothered to deal with the murder site before they left. If it is a murder site. There's no evidence of a burial, which we'd spot quickly in a garden this lush."

"But you think Laura Jarman was killed here? She had the telephone number for this house. It's why I came here in the first place."

"Ah, so you did come to poke around." Wright grinned. "I told you we were waiting for a warrant to search these premises."

"I only intended to look around on the outside," she snapped. "When I found the back door unlocked and the upstairs window open … I thought I should do the neighbourly thing."

"And have a nose around while you were at it."

"Good thing I did. I thought your chaps had already been here. You said they had checked the address. How did they miss an unlocked door?"

Wright gazed down at the two constables prodding sticks into the flower borders. "I shall be asking about that later. PC Botting reported that the house was empty and secured when he visited."

"Someone could have thought there was something here so important it necessitated a forced entry. Or scrubbing clean a blood-stained mattress?"

"You entered without a warrant." He turned to look at her, a warning tone creeping in. "That would be an illegal entry for an officer of the Sussex Constabulary."

"The back door was wide open," Bunch fibbed and stared at the police constables as they finished their sweep of the rear garden and were returning to the house. "It's starting to rain."

"So it is." Wright stood next to her, holding the curtain back to watch the rain gathering momentum, bouncing off the porch roof directly below them. "I doubt the rain will change things. There's unlikely to be very much of anything left to discover in the garden."

"So, what now?"

"We'll secure the house and keep trying to contact the owners and discover who rented this cottage from them. Thus far the tenants are proving as elusive as their landlord." He ushered Bunch back to the landing and started down the stairs. "And we wait for Letham to confirm the blood belonged to Laura Jarman."

"I will attempt to uncover what rumours they may have left behind."

"Botting is checking with the local traders. There must have been post or milk delivered, or ration books stamped – even for a brothel."

Bunch raised an eyebrow. "Then there will be rumours in the village. This sort of thing will be meat and drink to some. Though why here, in this house, far from anywhere? Not much business to be had, I'd have thought."

"Not locals, perhaps, but there are two big army camps just a few miles away. And a Canadian Air Force base, which will be our best option given the button you found." They paused at the front door. "May I give you a lift?"

"No, I have my car. I couldn't have Perry tethered outside for hours on end, so I took him and Bella back to Perringham once Botting arrived and I returned in the MG." Bunch glanced at her watch. "Granny insists we eat by six o'clock these days. She says it's so the staff can get home, but really it's because she's getting rather frail these days and late dinners don't agree with her. You are welcome to join me."

"Tempting … if I didn't have a desk full of work waiting for me back in Brighton that I must deal with before I turn in. I shall call you later in the week. Call me if you learn anything."

"It's market day tomorrow so I shan't get much done then, but I shall do some badgering of folks on Saturday."

"We won't have Letham's report until Monday, I don't suppose."

"Then call me on Monday. Toodle-pip old chap."

~ ~ ~

Thirty minutes later Bunch pulled into the stable yard at the Dower house, swerving to avoid the saloon car parked alongside the garage. *Damn and blast. I forgot all about Dodo coming over today. Granny will go absolutely bananas.*

She grabbed a slice of pie from the pantry and slipped upstairs to change and wash hands and face. The family conference had already convened to discuss the christening of Dodo's daughter Georgianna. Or to be more precise, the female members were gathering to thrash out the minute details. Bunch had never enjoyed these functions but as one of the infant's godparents she was inextricably involved, and Beatrice would view her failing to turn up for the war council as a capital offence.

The women had retired to the drawing room. Bunch could hear the buzz of chatter as she came down the stairs. She paused at the door, gathering her thoughts before turning the handle. "Hello chaps. Terribly sorry for being so late. Had to wait for them to finish the search."

"Of course you did," Beatrice said, holding court from her chair in the centre of the group. Dodo and her sister-in law Emma sat together on the chesterfield, while Alice Kimber was sitting slightly apart from them, a part of the group and yet not. Bunch felt a sorry for her. Kimber had become Beatrice's companion since Theadora had gone to the Red House but had still not come to grips with her new role. "You *are* late," Beatrice added. "You really are the giddy limit."

"Terribly sorry, one and all. One hell of a kerfuffle over at Haven Cottage and it took a lot longer than I thought it would." Bunch mixed a G&T and plumped herself down next to Alice, taking a deep swallow of the drink and leaning her head against the back of her chair. "One must feel for the Wallers. Their house is a disaster."

"Is it … is it a murder scene?" Dodo asked.

"Possibly, but that is only the half of it."

"Worse than murder?"

"It appears the tenants were traders in the oldest profession."

"In Wyncombe? What rot."

"Actually, my department has been examining the increase in prostitution," Emma murmured. "With all these army camps scattered around the country, boys – young men – away from home, it's a real problem."

"I can see the police having extra work, but why you?"

"Some compromising events."

"Such as … blackmail?" Bunch suggested.

Emma nodded. "I can't give details, naturally."

"Could this be something of that kind?"

"I was just pointing out that Wyncombe is as likely a place as any. Anyway, murder is a bit of a step up from blackmail."

"We don't know for certain that it is a murder scene."

"Then there was no call for you to go back there." Beatrice made a show of taking a sip from her single malt and fixed her eldest grandchild with a glacial stare. "Daphne has asked you to be godmother to your niece. The whole reason for today's supper was to get it all planned before next Sunday. We can't keep putting things off or the poor child will be walking before she's even baptised."

"I know." Bunch pulled a face. Beatrice was right. Forgetting about this supper was unforgivable. "Sorry Dodo. I shall make it up to you and little Georgi, I promise." She grinned at Emma. "If you're the other godmother who's the godfather? Barty?"

"No, I decided parents and grandparents were out," Dodo said. "I thought of our American cousin Maurice. Aunt Bibi's son. He's been in England for a while now. Aunt Adelia wrote to tell Mummy, and Mummy told me he was here when I went to see her a fortnight ago. He joined the RAF and was stationed here last month. He trained as a pilot in Canada. I thought as he's in England it would be a nice idea to include that side of the family."

"We barely know him."

"Mummy does, sort of, and it would be a good way to keep in touch with them once … well, once Mummy…"

Beatrice leaned across and patted her granddaughter's knee. "It's a splendid idea, Daphne. We don't have nearly enough time for Theadora's family."

"Never have, I suppose," said Bunch. "Always so jolly hard to get across there just for a quick jaunt. It must be better after this war is over. More planes, I expect. I hope." She smiled, trying hard to be reassuring. "Maurice. He's a second cousin?"

"Third," said Beatrice, "by marriage. Bibi's stepson, though I suppose that should not matter. He's Cedric's eldest son and heir, which is all that matters. You really need to pay attention to these things, Rose, because when I am gone you will be the family archivist."

"Don't even think about it." Bunch avoided her grandmother's glare and ploughed on. "You will outlive us all. Anyway, family aside, it will be good for young Georgi. She will always have a place to stay if she wants to go skipping across the pond. And they are *terribly* rich." She was aware of the other women turning gimlet stares in her direction and she shrugged. "It can't do any harm."

"He's not here tonight," Emma said again.

"Honestly, Emma, do be sensible. He couldn't get leave for today, but he swears he'll be here for the christening – with bells on."

Emma and Dodo squared up for what was plainly a stale argument and Bunch exchanged tired glances with Beatrice. It was time to change the subject. *Or at least get back to another one.* "I say, before I forget, Wright wants to hear everything we know about the Wallers," she said. "Granny?"

"I don't really know them," Beatrice replied carefully. "I gather Haven Cottage was more of a weekend cottage for them, rather than a home. I did hear that Mrs Waller joined the WI when they bought the house but she never went to a meeting."

"When was that?"

"The WI is not really my arena. Knapp may recall. I am almost certain they have no children."

"And Mr Waller? What line is he in?"

"People saw even less of him. He did come to speak with Edward when the war started. You were away in France at the time."

"Speak about what?"

"I am not sure. Edward made it explicit that Waller's services were not required and he never came again."

"He was an accountant." Bunch turned to gaze at Alice, startled into remembering the quiet woman sitting next to her. "Lizzie Hurst told me one of her cousins was paid to keep the garden. Mrs Waller was only there at weekends. Him hardly ever."

"Yes, a weekend cottage is in keeping with what Granny has said. What else did she say?"

"Mrs Crisp at Wyncombe Stores told me the Wallers also have a house in Kingston or Ham or some such along the Thames."

"Kingston *is* in the country," Beatrice replied. "Positively arcadian. Or it was when I was a young thing."

"So, Mrs Waller may have spent occasional weekends here, not far from sleepy Wyncombe. Mostly without Mr Waller. They say absence makes the jolly old heart fonder…"

"And keeps them married," Beatrice growled. "I've seen many marriages that worked best when conducted at a distance. Divorce may be all the rage with film stars but it remains unthinkable for the rest of us."

"That explains a great deal," said Dodo.

"Indeed. Now enough of those people." Beatrice slapped her hand on the arm of her chair. "That is not why we are here. We have precisely two days to get young Georgianna's christening under our belts, and Cook informs me there is no icing to be had for the cake."

~ Six ~

It was late on Saturday morning before Bunch had the opportunity to drive the cart into Wyncombe. Cook needed items collecting from the village shops and that was the perfect cover for wheedling information about the Wallers and Haven Cottage from Jean Crisp, the owner of Wyncombe Stores.

Heavy overnight rain had freshened the air and left lying water here and there. Where the road dipped down into a gulley, the ditches that ran alongside had gathered runoff from the fields on either side. Those puddles bulged out from both verges to cover the narrow lane in dirty clay-coloured water. Magpie, the piebald Vanner used to pull their renovated pony cart, came to an abrupt halt at the edge of the muddy water, muttering irritably and nodding her head.

"Walk on." Bunch flipped the reins lightly across Maggie's rump and clicked her tongue. The horse snickered and stamped a few paces on the spot but refused to step in the puddle. "Oh, for heaven's sake. It can't even be six inches deep. Walk on, dammit."

"That horse of yours gets right hatchety, don't she? You picked a right handful there." A stocky figure emerged from woodland at the side of the lane. His tweed jacket and moleskin trousers of indeterminate colour had blended with the background as perfectly as the tiger's stripes in its jungle.

Which, Bunch thought, *is precisely their point.* "Mr Jenner," she said. "Good morning. Yes, the silly old goose has been along here a million times but because she can't see the bottom of that puddle she thinks it's bottomless. We can't blame her, I suppose."

"Ah, she bain't daft. Mornin' Miss Rose." Roly Jenner tipped the peak of his cap and glanced up at the sky. "Bit brighter after yesterday. This'll clear up quick enough with a bit of sun." He picked his way across the raised verge and dug the heel of his work boot in the blocked drain, raking a collection of weeds and sticks clear of the channel. The water eddied, swirling plumes of yellowish Sussex clay around the cut for a moment before gushing into the ditch. He grunted in satisfaction.

"That'll sort 'en," he said.

"Thank you. I shall get onto the parish council about having those ditches cleared."

"Ah," he agreed. "Good luck'n all. Them buggers won't do nuthin'. Too busy pokin' their noses in other folk's business."

Bunch nodded without comment. Emerging, as he had from the trees on Perringham land, she had no doubt the content of his bag was not something she should enquire too closely into. And she had no doubt the council had been onto him for something equally illegitimate. Roly and his twin brother Fred where a pair of old rogues, but she had a soft spot for the two of them. She had no intention of falling out with the old man now over a bunny or two. And he had deliberately made his presence known to her; he could as easily have slipped away unseen, which told her he certainly had something to say that was worth hearing. Except that he stood and watched the puddle recede without saying a word.

"I'm rather glad to run into you, as it happens," she said. "You're a man with a good nose for what goes on."

"Ah," he said and shifted the bulging canvas bag slung over his shoulder away from her, his expression at once sly and amused.

"Mr Jenner … what have you heard about Haven Cottage?"

"Haven?" He hopped back from the mud to firmer ground and came to stand by Maggie's flank, running his hand over the animal as he mulled over Bunch's question. "You know it were a farmhouse once over? Belonged to one of them Haynes's years back. They went bust and it got bought up by them Wallers and that were … oh, must be near four years back. Polite enough but never mixed, far as I heard. They weren't church, nor chapel."

The judgement in his tone made her smile. The Jenners, like many of the Sussex labourers, were not regular worshippers, but to be neither church nor chapel was something that roused suspicion in them. "I heard your Gabe does a bit of gardening for them," she said.

"Ah," he agreed. "He did. Lawns and hedges and such."

"I see it's a bit overgrown now. He stopped when they moved out?"

"Before then. He's a good lad, is our Gabe, but he bain't the sharpest knife in the box, and them buggers had him spend weeks sweating like buggery, clearing an old rockery to make space for more cars. Then they never paid him." Jenner grunted. "He weren't goin' to poke up with that nonsense from no furriners."

"Oh?" Her ears pricked. *Furriner* to Sussex folk generally meant anyone from beyond the county border, but the emphasis the old man gave was telling. "What sort of furriner?"

"He was from Londin. And when Gabe went to get 'is pay he 'ad a set-to with some Canadian fella. Back around Christmas it wuz." Roly leaned his elbow on the cart's shaft and reached for his baccy tin. "This bloke thought he could take our Gabe on fer bein' at 'ome."

"Not in a uniform, you mean?"

"S'right. Gabe's a big strappin' boy, but he's got this bad chest. You remember he had a while in the 'ospital when he were a sprog?"

"I do remember, yes. TB, wasn't it?"

Jenner nodded. "He c'n fight though. Put that chap on the floor quick's you like. Army still won't 'ave 'im though. His old mum's happy of course, but the lad's had a few run-ins since."

Bunch nodded. While there had been no white feathers handed around as there had been during the Great War there was still some judgement on men out of uniform, especially a strapping lad like Gabe Jenner. "This Canadian chap ... was this at Haven Cottage?"

"There's been a lot of 'em there on an' off. Weekends mostly. Music an' dancin' an' ... stuff."

"Girls?"

Jenner looked down at his fingers deftly rolling a cigarette. He took his time licking the paper and sticking it down, smoothing the straw-thin roll up before tucking it between his lips. "Ah," he agreed and glanced at her, shrewd eyes glittering as he bent his head to one side, flicking an ancient petrol lighter several times. It flared into life, incinerating the empty end of the rizla paper before the tobacco caught. It was a ritual, an aid to his thought processes and a stage-managed effect worthy of any film star. He plainly had something more to say and Bunch waited patiently as he snapped the lighter shut and returned it and baccy tin to his pocket. Experience told her it was never wise to hurry a Jenner and when one spoke at all it was wise to listen carefully. Not just because of his thick Sussex burr but because he often spoke in riddles, if it was something he deemed of interest to authority.

And so never allowing himself cause to be quoted, she thought.

"Things goin' on, such as a well-brung up maid like you shouldn't know," he said at last. "Cars comin' and goin' all hours. Sundays, even. My missus said it weren't none've our business 'cept it got so bad she were tempted to speak with old Botting." He drew on the cigarette, almost obscuring his knowing nod.

"Was she?" Bunch hoped her tone was suitably awed. "Gosh." The redoubtable Mrs Jenner was a good woman but too many magistrates' fines for poaching meals for their table left her as wary of authority as her roguish husband. That she would voluntarily offer information to the local bobby measured her concern. "And did she? Speak to Botting, I mean?"

He laughed, making the cigarette drooping from the right corner of his mouth shake. "Didn't have to in the end. Not been a soul there for best part've a month. Not till they police started trampin' all over the place."

"You said Gabe hadn't worked there for a while?"

Jenner shrugged. "He's bin workin' over the sawmills since." He looked both ways as if somebody might have crept up the deserted lane to listen. "Coffins," he added in a hoarse whisper. "Lot've call fer coffins these days. They bain't telling people they're making so many … 'cept we all knows about it, all the same." He smiled grimly, his right eye narrowed against the smoke drifting up from his lips. Then, apparently sure his point had been made, he glanced along the road and nodded. "Old Ma Crisp'd knows what's what. You mark my words." He gave Maggie's rump a slap and stood away. "Reck'n that water's low enough now for your lapsy old mare, Miss Rose. You take care now. And tell your Mrs Westgate I got them they things she were wantin', if you'd be so good."

"I shall. Good morning, Jenner." Bunch watched him melt away into the woodland to head in the general direction of his home. She shook her head. What Cook had asked him to provide she did not care to ask. "Maybe not black market but most probably a delicate shade of grey, hey Maggie?"

The horse snorted and nodded vigorously at her name, setting the harness jingling and creaking.

"Right then. Water's all gone." She flipped the reins along the animal's back and clicked her tongue. "Giddup now, Maggie."

~~~

Bunch timed her visit to coincide with the lull when most ration card keepers were trundling home to cook dinners and lunches and the afternoon shoppers had yet to appear. She pulled the cart into the space outside the store and yanked the brake in place, checking it a second time before she jumped down to fix a nosebag over the horse's head. She didn't like leaving Maggie in harness; although the animal had been trained to stand, given enough temptation she would wander off along the high street for some distance. A fistful of hay was usually enough to keep her occupied for a while.

"Good morning." Jean Crisp looked up from her ledgers and beamed a smile. She was neat and trim, her grey hair carefully pinned into a near chignon; her modish yet practical floral dress protected, as always, by a dazzling white linen apron. She seemed to Bunch to be timeless, regardless of changing fashions and advancing years. "Don't see much of you these days, Miss Courtney. Keeping well, I hope?"

"Very well thank you. Cook said you had an order made up for her, and as I had a few people to see today I said I would drop in."

"She called to say as much. Busy cooking for young Miss Tinsley's christening tomorrow?"

"That's right. A case of all hands on deck."

"Thought it might be. We were going to deliver it this afternoon anyway but good of you to collect it now."

"It will save you a bit of petrol. Is there much to take?"

She shrugged an apology. "Just the usual orders, I'm afraid. And not a smattering of icing sugar to be had."

"So I hear. Cook is working her magic with meringue." Bunch handed over the household's ration cards and waited for the shopkeeper to stamp them before lowering her voice to add, "And Mrs Watt over at Banyards has acquired a whole basket of smoked trout from somewhere."

"Well, fish isn't on ration yet, which is a wonder. Gets no better, does it. They're adding coats and coal this month." Mrs Crisp handed back the cards. "Coats and coal. What next, I wonder?" She half-turned to call over her shoulder. "Rodney! Put the order for the Dower House in Miss Courtney's cart, will you?" She smiled an apology at Bunch. "Since Ken was called up at Easter, I've been relying on the lad Rodney for deliveries. He'll be glad to have one call off his round. He's not old enough to drive the van and that trailer's heavy to pull up that hill behind the shop bike."

"You don't drive yourself?"

"I do," she conceded, "but there's no one except me to do the Post Office counter in shop hours, and I won't drive at night."

"I don't blame you in the slightest, Mrs Crisp. The amount of light we get through a half-inch slit on the headlamps is hardly worth the effort." She paused as a sudden thought struck her. "You have a stable at the back of the shop, don't you?"

"Yes, from when we had a horse van to deliver."

"Could the boy manage a donkey cart? We have one in our barn. It's too small for any of my horses, and it needs some repairs, but I could loan it to you."

"That's kind of you, Miss Courtney. Finding a donkey going spare could be a problem but I shall give it a try. Now, is there anything else I can get for you?"

"Yes, I need a bottle of ink."

"Certainly." Crisp went to the shelves alongside the post office counter and picked up a bottle in each hand. "Parker royal blue? Or Stephens blue-black? I may have one last bottle of Carters sunset green. I know your mother preferred that one and we may not get any more for quite a while."

"Stephens will be fine. Its only for the estate accounts."

"Very good, Miss." She reached behind to place the unwanted squat bottle back on the shelf and placed the other carefully on the counter. "Speaking of your mother – I was sorry to hear she's so unwell. Is she still away from home? If it's not rude to enquire."

"She's at the Red House," Bunch replied. "I saw her the other day and she was on good form, considering. Daddy's man Sutton is fetching her for the christening tomorrow."

The shopkeeper nodded and reached across to give Bunch's hand a brief pat. The significances of both the Red House and hurried christening did not escape her. "Please give her my regards."

"I shall." Bunch regarded the older woman with a fresh question. She had known Jean Crisp all her life, use to come in with Nanny for sweets in her young days, and a few years later to make clandestine purchases of cigarettes. Jean Crisp *was* the village store. "Do you remember Mummy terribly well from back then?"

"She used to come in here a lot. In the old days. Before her loss." She looked at the countertop, reaching across to return the stamp to rest on the inkpad. "I don't think there was a family in Wyncombe didn't lose someone. I lost both of my parents, as you know. They were taken in the first wave at the end of 1919. I was away in Paris. I'd left the Nursing Corp when I was offered a place studying art."

"I never realised you studied art." Bunch leaned back a little. "You're a dark horse. Tell me all."

"We all have dreams in our youth, and I lived it for an entire summer." She pushed the stamp a little further onto the velvet pad, looking down to avoid Bunch's raised eyebrows. "And then I was sent a telegram to come home and by the time I got here…" She grunted, a grim smile on her lips. "I was never able to return to Paris, of course. I had this place to run and two younger sisters to care for."

"It must have been hard for you. I had no idea. I lost track of things going on in the village when I was sent away to school. Too young to be affected by adult things, I suppose."

"Some people deal better than others. Your mother never recovered." She looked up, stricken. "Begging your pardon, Miss, I meant no offence. We all expect to lose people older than we are. Losing a child, two children, must have been devastating."

"Yes. Yes, it was." They stood for a moment, avoiding eye contact. Jean Crisp was a little different from her neighbours. Her mother had been postmistress and had run the shop before Jean had to return, and her father had been a local councillor and sidesman at the church. She came from people of substance and was thus less likely to tell Bunch what she wanted to learn, but

Bunch needed to ask anyway. *How do I steer this conversation around to Haven Cottage?* "My sister doesn't recall any of it, naturally," Bunch said. "If anyone here in Wyncombe could remember my mother as she was before ... then it would be you. Not much goes on that you aren't aware of, you and Mr Bryce between you."

Crisp laughed, and the fragile tension popped like a soap bubble. "Dafydd Bryce is a fussy old windbag. His heart's in the right place, but my God he can talk. Thinks he knows what goes on but he doesn't know the half of it."

That's my cue, thought Bunch. "What does he have to say about Haven Cottage?"

"Probably what everyone else says."

"Funny goings on?"

"Polite version, Miss, yes," Crisp agreed. "I don't suppose you need me to repeat it all?"

"I've heard they had some pretty steamy events at Haven."

"I'm told PC Botting paid it a visit last winter though the place was empty and locked and bolted when he arrived." She wagged a finger. "You can't be surprised, surely?"

"To be perfectly honest, I *can't* believe I've never heard any if this before now. After all, this is Wyncombe and nothing is private for long."

"Not for long," Crisp agreed. "Those private parties weren't for the local lads. It was all champagne and cigars."

Bunch nodded slowly "Do you think the Wallers knew what kind of people were renting Haven Cottage? I mean, did they use an agent or were they the sort to handle the let by themselves?"

"Possibly. He was in business."

"Yet not all that profitable, letting to people that may wreck the place."

"Odd," she agreed.

"What sort of people were they? The Wallers, I mean. I never knew them."

Mrs Crisp tapped her fingers to her bottom lip. "I can't say I knew them well. They were weekenders," she said. "They only bought the place a few years ago. She had people down there regular enough, but we hardly ever saw him. He was away on business."

"What type of business, do you know?"

"Finance. He came in the shop once as I was cashing up and he laughed and said he was in that line. Not banks, he was clear on that. Finance of some sort, which surprised me. Accountants have a reputation for being a mite…"

"Dour?" Bunch replied. "So they say. You don't know where he worked?"

"London, I assumed. Not in the City though, I don't think." Mrs Crisp gazed at her for a moment, puzzled.

"You only knew Mrs Waller then."

"Enough to know she was a faker." Crisp's eyes snapped and glittered. "Had the gall to tell me she was in haute couture."

"You didn't believe her?"

"Not after the big fuss over some cotton thread."

"Why?"

"She got riled up because I didn't have the exact colour to re-hem a gown. I asked her for more details to match the colour but it turned out this gown was shot silk." Crisp tutted when Bunch didn't react. "Cotton thread to hem silk? Not quality, for all her airs."

Bunch nodded, searching for a new angle to flesh out this mysterious Mrs Waller. "Being weekenders, I don't suppose they received a lot of mail."

"Only saw mail for Mrs Waller." Jean raised her forefinger for emphasis. "Always had her letters forwarded, even when she was still here."

"That makes sense. Did she make a lot of telephone calls?" Bunch nodded towards the closed door behind the post office counter to where the telephone switchboard lay.

Jean pursed her lips. "Now there's the funny thing. There have been a lot more calls since she moved out. What about I couldn't really say. We're always discreet about people's privacy."

"Of course," Bunch agreed. *Like hell. I doubt there's a single call she couldn't quote, chapter and verse.* "I thought it wasn't your voice the other day."

"I had to get in some help. So many more people with telephones now. My niece does the mornings and Nell West takes over from one until we close at six. I still do most nights so I'm glad most of the calls for Haven Cottage came after five."

"Why? What sort of calls were they?"

"There were a few Canadians of late." She pulled a face. "Some of them were very … familiar."

"Oh? You mean the calls were a little risqué?"

Crisp drew back, her face setting into a bland professional shopkeeper mask. "I can't divulge anything of that sort. The GPO is clear on that point."

"Like being a priest?" Bunch grinned, trying to lighten the mood, and was relieved to see the older woman relax. "Gosh, it's all a bit full on, isn't it. You've told Botting I presume?"

"If he'd asked I would've but he never has so far."

Wright is going to love that, Bunch thought. "I always believed Botting was a shrewd sort of chap."

"Don't get me wrong, Miss Rose. I've just not liked to bother him. He's been poorly on and off since the New Year. That young Reserve Constable is doing his rounds."

"What's wrong with Botting?"

"Stomach, his wife tells me. Ulcers."

"Poor chap." Bunch stopped short at the jangling of the doorbell as a young mother and two toddlers crowded in. The interrogation was over. Time to leave. "Well, I must go or Maggie will have the cart halfway to Worthing. "

"You get that order back quick or the cheese will start sweating out there in the sun. Good morning, Miss Courtney. "

"Good morning, Mrs Crisp. And thank you."

~ Seven ~

Wyncombe parish church was built almost five hundred years ago and like many of its kind had undergone many alterations and additions over the centuries. Its interior was dominated now by the dark-oak pews and Victorian screens. Bunch's attention wandered across the familiar wall plaques, many of which commemorated the Courtney family, as did the long brasses in the stone-paved aisle, though the mortal remains of the people named there mostly resided in the mausoleum at Perringham House. Like generations of Courtneys before her, she attended the church regularly and had seen weddings conducted there on several occasions.

Christenings had been a different matter; for as long as Perringham House had been standing the family used its small chapel for such a discreet family occasion. The refusal of the military to allow the family access for the hour or so that the ceremony required rankled more with her than with others in her family.

Or they are simply better at hiding it? She looked around the group gathered at the worn sandstone font, which some people claimed was Roman, though experts placed it as a nineteenth century facsimile. The family had gathered in a small arc beyond the key players: the closest member of Dodo's combined families, Barty Tinsley's sister and niece, and a couple more that Bunch could not identify. The Courtneys were well represented, with Beatrice as well as Edward and Theadora making a four-generation assembly.

Bunch's attention wandered to a small scattering of people seated in the pews. Though it was a private service, the church was a public place and the doings of the Courtney family were an abiding interest to the village matriarchs who saw it as their civic duty to provide a later commentary, like some floral-hatted Greek chorus. Bunch knew that they would vanish once the service ended. *So why do I find them such a distraction?* She pushed it from her mind and concentrated on her part in the service.

Barty stood at Dodo's side, taking the role of his deceased son, the father of the child. Emma stood next to Bunch, as the two godmothers, and at the end of the arc came the godfather, Cousin Maurice.

He was a curiosity. Bunch had not seen him for many years. She recalled him as a studious and a gawky creature. He had followed her around for a summer visit like a lovesick puppy and at the time she had reported him to Dodo as *all acne and asthma*. He had changed somewhat, on the outside at least. Only a little taller than herself, perhaps an inch under six feet, with dark-blond hair peeking from beneath his RAF cap. His uniform was obviously tailored by the best that Saville Row could offer, impeccably cut to show off his physique to best advantage. *Such as it is,* she thought. *He's still a bit of a skinny specimen, and not quite handsome for all that. I hope he's a little more interesting than he was.* He noticed her looking at him and broke into a wide smile, displaying white even teeth. His face was just beginning to lose its American tan after wintering in England. Emma caught her eye and tipped a knowing nod and Bunch felt herself begin to colour, and cursed her body for reacting to embarrassment like a beacon. *He will get completely the wrong impression.*

Bunch was not a lover of bawling infants but was never more relieved that Georgianna, the star of the show, chose that moment to let out several affronted squawks. The Reverend Day was trying to tip water onto the infant's forehead while Georgi, young as she was, pushed the silver scoop away with both hands. Bunch raised her gloved hand to her face to smother a giggle. There were no tears from Georgi, only indignation as the child squirmed in her mother's arms to escape this strange man throwing water in her face. Bunch managed to sneak another glance at the village worthies, knowing how a silent christening was viewed as a bad omen, and was relieved to see them nodding their approval when the child sounded her objection.

At almost ten months Georgi was older than most infants for a christening, and a little too large for the antique family christening robes: a waterfall of white silk and Olney lace, but an expert needle had let it out enough for the occasion.

"Five generations of christenings," Beatrice had said when the alteration had been made. "It has to be done." Now in the church, the old woman stood erect and serene, happy to see her own great-grandchild christened. Beatrice looked well for her advancing years, a contrast to her unwell daughter-in-law.

Theadora was leaning heavily on Edward, her right arm twined firmly with his, a silver topped cane clutched in her left hand while the ever-faithful Kimber lurked behind them with wheelchair at the ready. Theadora was managing to be both pale and deep yellow at the same time; and so desperately weary with dark bags beneath her eyes and her mouth slightly open to quietly gasp in air.

Dodo had arranged an abbreviated service precisely because their mother had become very frail, but Bunch seriously wondered if Theadora would manage to remain on her feet for even that brief time. Her mother had been adamant that she would not sit in the wheelchair for the service and nobody had they heart to argue with her too hard, especially since the service had been arranged in a hurry precisely because of her poor health. *This is as much Mummy's show as it is the child's*, Bunch thought.

~~~

It was only at the christening tea at Banyard Manor that Bunch finally got to speak properly with her cousin Maurice.

"Hi. Rose, right? Remember me? Maurice Badeaux?"

"Hello." She swapped her sherry glass to her left and shook his proffered hand. "How are you?"

"Good. I'm very well in fact. It's good to see you. We haven't met for a while."

"We met briefly when I visited Grandmama Eltham with my parents. My goodness, that has to be almost five years ago now."

Maurice laughed, far louder than Bunch thought necessary. "I remember you paid more attention to Grampa's horses than to anyone."

"Quite possibly. I find horses are generally better company."

"Sometimes." He nodded, his face serious for a moment and then splitting in a wide grin. "You have many horses left? I heard a lot of folk got rid of their stables."

"We had to whittle down to a handful. Just Daddy's hunter Robbo, and the two ponies, Perry and Maggie. We use them for

Perringham's local household transport. Daddy has his ministry car but fuel is all but non-existent for domestic use."

"Perringham … that's the ancestral pile I stayed at before?"

"Perringham House, yes. It's been requisitioned so we're all crammed in the Dower House with Granny at the moment. Dodo has more rooms here at Banyards than we do."

"Dodo?"

"Daphne." She shrugged. "Some of the family call her Dodo."

"I remember now. And they called you Bunch, right?"

"Some still do. Sometimes." She paused, aware that her mother was watching her, a half-smile on her face. "Are you returning to your station today?"

"Not until tomorrow morning. Your sister is putting me up here tonight."

He stared down at his shiny boot caps and back at her, an intensity in his gaze that made her heart sink. She had seen that puppy-dog expression so many times in the past – and it was seldom welcome. "How nice," she murmured and looked around for someone, anyone, she really needed to chat with and caught her father's attention.

"Pardon me, I hate to intrude." Edward Courtney came to stand next to his daughter, resting one hand on her shoulder. "Maurice, is it not?"

"It is, sir. Hello."

He put out his hand and Edwards shook it briefly, a quick firm tug. "Come and speak to Theadora," he said. "I want to have her back at the Red House shortly. This is all proving a little exhausting for her, but she insists that she won't dream of leaving until she's talked with our overseas cousin."

"Of course, sir." Maurice smiled easily at Edward. "Lead on."

They crossed to where Theadora sat at the fireside, Dodo next to her, cradling the sleeping Georgi on her lap. Bunch followed them across the room.

"Ma'am, Daphne." Maurice bowed his head to each in turn. "I want to thank you again for asking me to stand godfather to young Georgianna here. It's an honour, especially when—"

Theadora held up her forefinger. "Enough. It's our pleasure, Maurice."

"I am glad you could make it," Dodo added. "Now where are my manners? Do sit down." She waved at the chair on the other side of the hearth.

"Daphne wants the child to remember all of our family," said Theadora, "so when I heard you were going to be based nearby… Synchronicity. It must make being away from home a bit easier."

"Yes, ma'am. War makes being away a whole lot harder."

"Ah yes, you were in Europe in '39, weren't you?"

"I was. My father sent me to oversee some problems we had at our Rome office. We have a factory in Italy."

"I remember now," said Dodo. "Your grandfather, wasn't he a furrier?"

"Still is. The Italians are the world beaters in leather and fur fashions. It's gotten tricky with the Generalissimo. The Italians were happy to deal with us Yanks in '39, but since we signed the lease lending thing…" He shrugged. "I guess we'll have to wait and see how it all works out."

"It will certainly get tougher if the Americans enter the war," said Bunch.

"Indeed. This American has already…" He laughed nervously. "I'm sorry, Aunt Thea, not the time or place to talk business or war. How are you?"

"Italian fashions are never boring." Theadora waved a hand at him. "And I'm doing well, thank you. How is your mother?"

He smiled and shook his head. "I'd say same as always, but I do believe her voice has risen an entire octave with all this talk of war. The Doc has her on sleeping powders and stuff."

Theadora arched an eyebrow and snorted. "Yes, indeed. Bibi has always been a trifle on the nervous side. I imagine she was not happy when you went off to join the RAF in Canada?"

"She was okay about it. If it had been my brother Chris, however – now that would've been different." His voice hardened and Georgi wriggled in her mother's arms, sleepy and fretful yet far from sleep.

"Nanny." Dodo stood carefully and handed over the child. "Can you take Georgi upstairs?" She sat down and smiled at Maurice. "Sit a little longer with us. I'm sure Mummy wants a longer chat."

"Yes, darling," said Theadora. "Maurice, tell me all the gossip from across the water."

"I can't give you much. As I said, I left America to go to Canada for a while for basic training and then flight school, though I skipped most of that. Having a civilian pilot's licence was a tremendous help."

"I took flying lessons," said Bunch. "But Daddy simply refused to buy me a plane."

"It's an expensive pastime. I only got my licence because I often need to fly up to Canada and it's a whole lot faster than driving. Oh—" he turned back to Theadora "—I just thought of one thing. My sister Beth told me just before I left Stateside that she was getting engaged. I haven't heard anything official but I guess she's told our mother by now."

"Bibi hasn't written to tell me."

"Maybe Beth's just chickened out. The guy she's sweet on is not the kind my mother would have picked for her."

He smiled at Bunch and she felt that sinking feeling yet again. "Gosh, that sounds familiar. I've managed to elude the family snares so far," Bunch muttered. "And intend to do so for a while yet."

"Sure, I get that, but my mom was saying…"

Dodo's housekeeper appeared at Bunch's side and murmured, "A telephone call for you, Miss Courtney."

"For me? Here?"

"A Sergeant Carter calling on behalf of Chief Inspector Wright."

"Oh, I wonder what he wants. Sorry chaps, I shan't be long." Bunch was seldom more grateful for an interruption and almost ran to the vestibule to pick up the handset. "Hello? Rose Courtney speaking."

"Miss Courtney, the guvnor asked me to find you. I'll just fetch him."

"What does he want? Carter, is it? It's not con…" The sound coming back to her was a muffled quiet and she realised she was talking to thin air. *Or more likely to the palm of Carter's hand.* The baffle suddenly cleared

"Good afternoon, William? What may I do for you today?"

"Hello Rose—" Laughter welled from the open drawing room door and he paused. "Where are you?"

"It's Georgi's christening. I did tell you. The poor wee mite has been lumbered with me as a godmother."

"Oh God, yes you did mention it. I'm sorry, I forgot. We've had a bit of a flap on and I just told Carter to track you down. Look, I'll call you later if it's more convenient."

"They will manage without me for a few minutes. If I am honest, it was getting a little awkward."

"Family tensions?"

"Not exactly. I shall tell you about it one day. Now, what prompted you to send out search parties on a Sunday?"

Wright muttered something she did not catch and then: "Couple of things have come up today. Could you be available tomorrow to interview a Canadian Base Commander with me?"

"How funny, I was just chatting with a Canadian pilot. Well, not Canadian actually; he's American but trained in Canada for the RAF. Gosh, that sounds terribly complicated doesn't it." She smiled at the silence from the other end of the phone. "He's a cousin," she said. "Georgi's godfather. A pleasant sort but frightfully dull."

"You may come and charm some more of his colleagues for me tomorrow. I'll pick you up at around ten?"

"I assume this is at Chellcott – it's the nearest base."

"Yes."

She waited for Wright to say more but he said nothing. *What on earth is going on with him?* "Any progress with Laura Jarman?" she finally said.

"Not a thing. I have been checking with the constabulary based around the Jarman factory, looking into the work they were doing, and we're still searching for Laura's flat. It seems the address we have for her is wrong so we're not getting far. Maybe you can have another crack at her family. What we need to find out is, who were her friends since she left her home? This girl went to some lengths to lead a secret life and made a better fist of it than some villains I know. It's frustrating, to say the least."

The weariness in his voice was evident, along with something she couldn't quite put her finger on. "You shall find something,

I've no doubt," she said. "That she has gone to so much effort to stay hidden says a great deal, surely." Bunch glanced up as Edward appeared at the doorway and went through a mime of putting the phone down and driving a car. She nodded.

"It's possible she did have an argument at home," Wright was saying, "just as her family said, but I'm certain there's more to it. People aren't left in steamer trunks on railway stations unless they are deep into something unsavoury."

"I agree. Also, most families would want the police to discover who killed their child, even if she was a family pariah. Which makes you wonder what they know, what they are not telling us."

"My thoughts exactly. If we could just get one good lead." His breath whispered across the telephone mouthpiece, sounding like the crackling of paper, and she had the feeling there was more to come.

"Look, William, is that it?" she asked him. "I really need to go now."

"Yes, I'm sorry. Get back to the christening and apologise to your sister for my interrupting a family event. I wouldn't have called if I had remembered," Wright said. "I have a meeting with the Super soon and I'll be out late tonight with Carter on these grocery shop raids."

"Not at all, old thing. I must go though. Mummy is getting tired and Daddy wants to take her back to the Red House. I shall see you tomorrow. Toodle-pip."

"Yes, ten sharp. Goodbye."

The line went dead and Bunch was left with a lot of questions crashing around her head. Wright had not told her everything, and though he might have wanted her to accompany him, to soft-soap the military, he could have simply left a message. She replaced the receiver and stared at the handset as if she could draw answers from it, like rabbits from a conjurer's hat. She listened to the rise and fall of voices drifting into the vestibule. Barty's guffaw climbed above the rest for a moment and heard laughter rise to meet it.

A movement on the stairs took her attention and she turned to smile at her sister. "Bunch? Are you leaving right now? Wait until Daddy takes Mummy back. When your friend Wright calls you usually take off like a greyhound." Her sister's impatience was evident.

"No, I'm not leaving. Nothing important. Wright just called to confirm an appointment for tomorrow."

"So unimportant he tracked you down here?"

"Nothing I can do about that. I think Daddy is ready to go now."

"Is he?" She sat on the stair and blew out her breath. "Mummy looks awful, doesn't she."

"She's tired. We knew she would be."

"I know."

"She wouldn't have missed it for anything, though." Bunch went to sit beside her sister and wrapped both arms around her. "Treasure today, Dodo. Mummy is on great form, so treasure that."

~ Eight ~

"You know, you could have mentioned that another body has been discovered." Bunch stared out at the passing hedgerows, avoiding Wright's gaze. Her emotion went way beyond anger, and she knew it was not entirely fair of her. Wright said he had not intended to intrude on the family day, and she believed him, although the vague sense that he still saw her as a mere woman to be protected refused to be laid to rest. Worse, a niggling maggot of mistrust – not hers, but his – ate at her serenity, such as it was. It was nonsense of course, she knew. Wright apologised about forgetting the christening and said he didn't wish to spoil her day further with news that could wait until the following morning. *On the other hand, you'd think a corpse was the kind of thing a chap should mention to his partner.* "I would have come out, you know. This is my investigation as much as yours. I get paid and everything."

Wright snorted quietly. "There was nothing you could have done beyond going to look at another body in another trunk, just like the Jarman girl. We can go on to the mortuary after this visit, if you really want to."

"Yes, I would like that," she said. "Oh, that sounds a little morbid, doesn't it? I don't mean that but seeing this girl – the victim – it makes her real, if you see what I mean."

"I doubt it in this case."

"Besides, I might know who she is." She turned to stare at his profile. "You're being very skittish."

"I'm certain you won't recognise her."

"But is she somebody terribly well known?"

"Not at all.

She could see that he was uncomfortable and could not imagine why. *I don't like looking at these dead bodies, that's true, but I need to – and he can't possibly imagine, after all we've done together, that I am going to be squeamish.* "Why don't you want me to see her?"

"I'm just not sure it will help, and anyway we are fairly certain we already know who this woman is. We're only waiting on verifying identifying features."

"Features?"

"She had documents under the name of Kitty Shenton."

"Not her real name?"

Wright shrugged. "We've no reason to believe it isn't, except that she left the address given in her papers some months ago. Until she has been identified she is a Jane Doe."

"Do people often pretend to be someone else?"

"More often than you'd think these days."

"Why?" Wright snorted loudly, shaking his head emphatically, reminding Bunch of an old horse dislodging a fly. "It would take some effort I'd imagine," she snapped. "Being somebody else…"

"People get into bad situations and want to leave their old lives behind; be born again, so to speak. Some people lead two lives in parallel."

"Part time?"

"Women who have a home and family and need a bit extra to make ends meet…" Wright paused.

"Go on," said Bunch. "Out with it, now you've started."

"There are those at the upper end who—" Wright replied. "The high-class escorts who have a professional name. Though that also goes for the specialist trade…" He held up his hand to silence her. "The women who … indulge in certain fantasies. Soho is full of them."

"How does this body fit in with all that?"

"If this is Kitty Shenton then she has links to Jarman's factory and it's possible she was sharing a flat with Laura Jarman. We need a positive identification."

"Is her death definitely linked with Laura's?"

"She worked at Jarman's – and she was discovered in a similar type of trunk. The deaths are too alike to be a mere coincidence."

"I say … you don't think…?"

"That Laura was working as an escort? No, I don't. The initial pathology report was quite clear on that point. The Jarman girl was not – not a maiden, but neither was she a prostitute."

"A maiden? Oh William, that is priceless." Bunch laughed, dabbing beneath her eyes with the back of her fingers. "You can be such a prudish old thing sometimes."

"Does this mean I'm forgiven?"

"Perhaps."

"Thank you. Not telling you – it was self-defence, you know. Your grandmother may well have done away with me in some exotic and painful fashion if I had dragged you away from a family do."

Bunch swatted at his shoulder and permitted herself a tiny smile. "She probably would at that. It took military precision to get that christening organised in a week. And she bullied people into giving up every sugar ration she could lay hands on to make and ice that cake. Thank heavens we have butter and eggs to spare." She put her hand to her mouth. "I suppose I shouldn't own up to that."

Wright opened his eyes wide. "Own up to what, exactly?"

"Nothing. Nothing at all." The tension that had built between them had passed and she gave her attention to the job at hand. "I do so hate seeing these places go to ruin." Bunch peered out of the window once more, this time at the pockmarked lawns beyond a makeshift checkpoint across the access road to Chellcott House. The building itself was an unremarkable manor house built of sandstone and red brick, and constructed, for reasons known only to its creators, in two conjoined parts. It reminded her of two toy bricks abandoned by some careless giant toddler.

Its deterioration, she assumed since being handed over to the military, was a shock and she began to feel a little less angry at the occupants of Perringham House. At least her own family home was not being quite so systematically wrecked as Chellcott seemed to have become, with what looked like dozens of Nissen huts hurriedly thrown up in rows across a small park to the right and, no doubt, to the rear of the main house. A huge swathe of new concrete had been laid out to the left for a welter of army trucks, tanks, and staff cars. Yet more Nissen huts beyond the vehicles compounded the depressing desecration of the estate. Most of the place was strewn with straggling spiderwebs of camouflage netting, peppered throughout by a small forest of masts and aerials. It reminded her of the BEF field stations she had driven to and from when stationed in France in 1939, as a lowly ATC driver.

The realisation that these Canadians no doubt viewed their presence here in Sussex as a visiting force come to save the local population was a sobering thought.

"Chief Inspector Wright and the Honourable Miss Rose Courtney here to see the CO," Glossop announced from the from seat.

Wright wound down his window. "We are expected," he said. "I called yesterday."

The corporal bent to peer into the car, first at Glossop and then at the passengers and then took the ID they held out. He checked their names against his clipboard and nodded. "Yes, sir. Captain Ellis is waiting up at the house for you."

"I understood we were to see Colonel Pardoe?"

"The Colonel's not on the base today. It's Captain Ellis you'll be talkin' to."

"I had made an appointment to speak with Colonel Pardoe."

The sentry shrugged, unfazed by Wright's bark. "Colonel said you're to speak to Captain Ellis. He's CFMP for this station." The man sighed at the dark looks. "Military Police."

"Corporal, before we go." Bunch leaned past Wright and pointed at the house, and at the blackened stain stretching up a sidewall from a boarded-up window. "What happened there?"

"It was Lieutenant Macintyre's twenty-first party, ma'am." The corporal looked over his shoulder at the house. "Got a liddle bit out of hand. The boys like to celebrate." He glanced again at the police ID that Wright had proffered, and then at Bunch's card. "Consulting detective, huh?"

"Indeed." She met his smirk evenly and tried hard to ignore Wright's muffled snigger. The designation had begun as a joke at his expense but she was beginning to regret it. She had not allowed for the popularity of Rathbone's portrayals of the Conan Doyle character back in 1939, and she wasn't keen on being the butt of yet another joke. "The Youngs won't be happy, I can tell you," she said. "Chellcott may not be the prettiest house in the county, I grant you, but the Young family built this place and lived here for six generations, if I recall. Do you know—" she turned to look at Wright "—I do believe my father was at school with Colonel Young."

"I can't say much about that, ma'am," the Corporal replied. "I'm guessing it'll all get put right before we go home."

"Let's hope so. May we proceed?"

"Sure thing." He handed back the cards and signalled to the private to raise the barrier. "Captain Ellis is waiting for you. Go right up to the main entrance and walk right in."

"Thank you, Corporal," Wright snapped. "Carry on Glossop."

"Sir."

Wright's ATC Driver released the brake and let out the clutch, pulling away almost before the barrier had cleared the Wolseley's bonnet and Bunch had to fight the instinct to duck. Wright, she noted, was unmoved. *He's used to Glossop's driving*, she thought.

"Not able to talk to the Colonel today…" Bunch said. "Damned nerve. And their security is pretty shabby if you ask me. Try getting into Perringham House without a Whitehall pass written in blood and see how far you'd get."

"Perringham House has a few more secrets to guard than a bunch of homesick Cannucks. And having no camp commander to sweet talk might turn out for the best," Wright replied. "This Redcap chappie may be more useful. I've discovered that they usually have a better grip on the less appealing side of the average soldier."

"Or he could be a po-faced policeman with something to prove." Bunch grinned at him. "A little bird I know insists that policemen can be that way."

"It's all lies; we are always sweetness and light. And here we are." The car came to a stop just yards from the front steps. Wright waited until Glossop opened the door for him and stepped out, straightening his jacket and hat as he waited for Bunch.

"Captain Ellis, do you think?" Bunch nodded to a figure lurking in the shade beyond the open doors.

"I'd say so."

They mounted the steps in unison and left bright sunshine for the gloom of the hall where the stocky Canadian officer was waiting. The only thing that set him apart from the other men clad in army-brown serge was the distinctive red cover on the military cap tucked under his arm.

"Chief Inspector Wright?" He came forward to shake Wright's

hand. "Good to meet you. And you must be the Honourable Miss Courtney."

Ellis scrutinised her and she had to work hard not to flinch. He was barely five foot nine, Bunch judged, no taller than herself. What she could see of his close-cropped hair was a startling red, while his eyes appeared a dark grey. *Stocky, yes,* Bunch thought, *but not an ounce of fat. All muscle, like a teeny-weeny Percheron. And there are women who would kill for that alabaster skin. He could be anywhere between twenty-five and forty.* He had not attempted to shake her hand, only nodded to her, a sharp jerk of his head that Bunch hesitated to call a bow. It felt more of a dismissal than a greeting, she felt, conveying an undercurrent of supressed aggression that she found unsettling. "Miss Courtney is fine." She smiled without her usual certainty.

"Shall we get some tea? This way, please." He swept them through a pair of double doors to their left. The room was spacious, with large windows all the way down one side. There were few battered pictures hanging on the walls, and an odd assortment of armchairs and sofas were scattered around low tables. Along one wall were makeshift bookcases loaded with paperbacks and magazines. "Mess room. There won't be anyone about this time of day. The Colonel tries to keep them busy. Young lads away from home will always kick over the traces." He waved them to a group of chairs near an open window and waited until Bunch and Wright were both seated before settling himself, placing his hat on the tabletop. "Now then, how may I help you?"

"We are looking into the murder of a young woman that may have occurred not far from here." Wright put his own hat next to the military cap and leaned back to smile at the officer.

Any last vestige of warmth left Ellis's eyes, turning to pebbles of solid flint, as he looked from Wright to Bunch. "Why would that kind of thing be linked to this base?"

"Witnesses have placed some Canadians at the house in question on various occasions, where we believe she was murdered. And we found this." Wright pulled a small stiff card envelope from his pocket and shook out the uniform button into his palm. "It was lodged under the skirting just outside of the room where the murder probably took place."

Ellis stared as the button without attempting to touch it. "Uniform button," he said at last. "Which could have been left there at any time, by anyone. I notice that you say *believed* to be the murder scene. I guess that means you found the body somewhere else. Do you have any names? A rank even? No? That's slim pickings, if you don't mind me saying so, Chief Inspector. I can't see the Colonel allowing you access unless you have a great deal more to go on."

"Our investigations are still ongoing. We know there was some sort of weekend party, and as I mentioned, men from the Canadian forces have attended parties there over the past few months."

"And I repeat, that button could have been left there at any time. Do you have any proof whatsoever that it was dropped by someone from this unit? Let me see if I understand you. The body was not found at this location, wherever it is, and as evidence all you have is a *single* button. See it from my perspective, Chief Inspector – without more than that to go on the Colonel will not give you permission to interrogate the men. The effect it would have on morale would be too bad."

"There is evidence that ties our victim to those premises, and we have this button found less than ten feet from the murder site." Wright suppressed a growl of frustration. "Yes, all right, probable murder site. But surely you can see how that appears from our perspective, Captain. You are a policeman. Different uniform, yes, but we go through the same procedures. We are not implying that it was any of your men who killed the young woman, but we do know she was there and that's where she quite likely received her fatal injuries before she was moved to another location. We need to know by whom and eliminating men from this base would help us a great deal."

Ellis nodded slowly. "I grant you, a corpse isn't a good thing to have around at a party. Where was she moved to?"

"You've read about the body found in a trunk on Brighton station?" Bunch got out her cigarette case and proffered it to Ellis.

"Yes, I read about it." He waved the case away and took a cigarette pack from his pocket. "I'll stick to my own brand, if that's okay."

Bunch eyed the black cheroot that he shook from the box, evil smelling things she knew from experience. "Russian?"

"Turkish." He looked down at the black-papered tobacco between his fingers. "I don't suppose I'll be getting these for much longer." He took a slim gold lighter and flicked it into life, touching it to Bunch's cigarette before lighting his own. "Now, is there anything else that makes you want to question our guys?"

"In addition to Canadian personnel attending these parties, the porters at the railway station have provided statements placing Canadians on the platform when the air raid started on the night the body was left there," said Wright. "We only need to ascertain if any of your chaps were among them. It's all routine questioning. You know how it is."

"I expect a lot of our guys would be passing through Brighton, along with half the militia in the region," Ellis replied. "Why Chellcott? We're not the only Canadian base in the area. There must be at least five between here and the coast."

"True, but Chellcott is the closest to the murder scene," said Wright. "It seemed the most obvious place to start. It would be hard to imagine young men finding their way to the house from further afield, unless they had local knowledge."

"They could have been invited … or had a lift. Lot of our boys have relatives in this country of yours. Cousins, aunts, uncles, grandparents."

"I doubt many grandmothers would be inviting them to that kind of party, Captain Ellis," said Bunch. "It wasn't the sort that served cake. Unless there was a girl inside it." Bunch knew she had shocked them both. She sensed Wright tense, and Ellis tilted his chin up to stare at her down his nose; it was a gesture Bunch recognised, carefully slashed peaks on the caps of drill sergeants and military police – to improve added swagger to their posture, she had been told. In that instance it marked the man opposite her as a career Redcap.

"If they're seeking *that* kind of company they usually head to Brighton. Or London if they get the chance. Can I take it this girl was… was a…?"

"A prostitute?" She tweaked him a wry smile. "You may say it, Captain Ellis. I'm quite grown up."

Wright nudged her arm in warning. "We have no proof at the moment to suggest the victim was engaged in that sort of activity, Captain," he said. "Far from it. She was the daughter of an important businessman. We are certain she *was* at that house party, however. We simply don't know what she was doing there."

Ellis regarded him in silence, the muscles along his jawline twitching and jerking. "You don't have any real evidence that a man, or men, from these barracks was responsible for killing her," he said.

"Not at all," Wright replied. "As I've explained, we don't have any evidence for that. What we need is to learn if any of the men stationed here might have visited this place and if so, did they see anything that might help in our investigation. Haven Cottage, in Wyncombe, is the location we're talking about. If any of your men could give us some information on the people who ran the—"

"I can't say I know the place. Is it close to Brighton?"

"It's closer to here," Wright replied. "As I've already stated."

"What men get up to off duty is not my business."

"Until they break the law."

"Until… If … they break the law." Ellis leaned back, crossing his legs as he settled in his chair. "You say 'Wyncombe' like it's meant to mean something to me. Is it a prominent place?"

"It's a small village," said Bunch. "Picturesque."

"I've still never heard of it. Brighton I can see. Worthing, maybe. Storrington, because its close and has a lot of pubs. What would make this place so important?"

"It's where a young woman was murdered," said Wright, frustrated at having to repeat himself. It was quite evident that Ellis was leading him in circles.

"And then stuffed into a suitcase and dumped on a railway platform?" Ellis grunted, seemingly amused at Wright's noisy inhalation. "Sorry, I don't mean to sound callous. I've been a Redcap for a long while and I've seen just about everything there is to see. I ask again: why would you think one of our men killed her?"

"And I have repeatedly explained, we do not suspect any of your men of murder," Wright replied. "However, since Canadian military personnel were known to have both visited – and telephoned – Haven Cottage over the previous months, we're obliged to follow it up. You know how things are done."

"I know. You're following the tram tracks." Ellis inclined his head, apparently accepting Wright's olive branch. "I know how it goes. I guess I'm a little itchy. We've had a hell of lot of complaints since we got here. Our guys have been accused of anything and everything. The CO's had claims for damage because of fighting from half the pubs in the county. Someone just this week tried to claim for the loss of twenty laying hens. He probably never had that many chickens in the first place." Ellis gazed out of the window as he took a lung full of smoke from his cheroot and expelled a dark aromatic cloud. Bunch and Wright waited in silence. "I guess some of it's deserved," the RCMP said finally. "You gotta understand, these are boys a long way from home and looking to let off steam. Yeah, they do get a little rowdy at times. And yeah, we've had to pay for some busted furniture and a few scraped cars and such. But murder? I surely hope not."

"We know it's hard," said Wright. "And I do understand about your boys being far from home. I've been there myself."

"France?"

Wright nodded. "The fact remains that we have a young girl brutally murdered and someone on this base may well have that vital piece of information we need in order to catch her killer. If you could check with your duty roster and see who might have been off base on those occasions…"

Ellis shook his head. "You provide me with times and dates and I'll check it out. That's how it's gonna work."

"This *is* a murder enquiry," Wright snapped.

"I get that."

"I need to question your soldiers."

Another shake of the head. "Questioning these men, on this base, is my job. As I said, we've had a lot of people accusing these boys of all kinds of problems and the CO must draw a line." Ellis leaned his forearms on his knees, seemingly casual, but his fingers were laced so tightly, Bunch noticed, that every knuckle was blazing white. "Thing is, Chief Inspector," Ellis continued, "when your police come here, trampling all over my base making wild accusations without a scrap of proof, the boys get riled. Morale isn't that good as it is and I can tell you, the CO is pretty damn sick of it. Here's what's going to happen: I shall ask around, see if anyone has visited this place, or telephoned it. When you do have some conclusive proof that a member of the Canadian forces from this base was involved, you bring it to me and we'll do all the asking together."

"That is not how it's done here in England," Wright replied.

"Except you're sitting in this old house that stopped being British the moment we walked in, and you do not have jurisdiction. Yes, we're Canadian, and yes, we're part of your damn Empire—" Ellis leaned back, fingers resting now on the edge of the table "—but we have our own way of doing things. I just told you how that is going to be."

"I can get a warrant."

Ellis chuckled quietly. "Yeah. Good luck with that." He stood up, sweeping his cap over his cropped hair in a fluid move. "I think we've concluded our business for today, Chief Inspector. Miss Courtney." He nodded abruptly, plainly as close to a salute as he was going to give a civilian. "Corporal Harris will see you off the base."

~~~

Driving away from the base, Wright was unnaturally quiet. Bunch could see the muscles in his jaw were rigid. The vein sticking out on temple throbbed and she wondered if this was how the UXB boys felt, sitting next to a ticking bomb.

"Not your favourite type of person?" she asked eventually.

"Arrogant fool," he muttered. "He's police. Military, maybe, but still police, and he's doing all he can to stand in our way."

"He wasn't terribly helpful," Bunch agreed. "It will take a while to get any sort of headway, but it was no worse than getting to speak with that dratted Everett Ralph we have camped out at Perringham House. They all see themselves as little kings in their little citadels, repelling all comers. We shall prevail, however."

"It will take weeks. Bad enough jumping through military hoops in the War Office without having the Canadian consulate in the mix."

Officiousness was something that brought out the worst in her friend, and Wright was as angry as Bunch could remember seeing him. She had sympathy for the Redcap's situation. She knew all too well how people were ready to blame the Canadians or Poles or Free French or any of a dozen more overseas contingents, and she had no doubts as to the way they felt, somewhat besieged and perplexed by it all. *Doesn't help Wright, however.* "He's just protecting his own," she said aloud. "Do you want me to see if Daddy can grease the wheels?"

"Could he?"

"Probably not, but I can ask. He'll be down at the weekend to see Mummy."

"Ah yes. How is Lady Chiltcombe?"

"Mummy?" She eyed him cautiously. *He of all people knows the family barely use our titles, though if any of us ever does, it's Mummy. Maybe he's paying his respects?* "Not good," she replied. "We are rather waiting for that call from Mother Superior at the Red House."

"I'm sorry."

She pressed her fingertips lightly against his bicep and looked away from him to stare at the passing countryside. "It doesn't matter how much you expect it," she murmured. "When you know the end is near it's still…"

"Unexpected?" he said.

"Exactly." She turned towards him and found herself looking in his face at disturbingly close quarters.

"I lost my mother to TB."

"Oh, I'm sorry. Was it recent?"

He shook his head. "June 1916."

"It hit you hard?"

"Hit us all. I don't mean to make her sound like a plaster saint, but she was the best of us. It was hardest on my sister."

"Was she close to your mother?"

"Most girls are."

"Not always."

He glanced at her, brows drawn in a question that he didn't ask. "It was harder because she was the eldest. It left her in charge of the household. She was only twenty years old."

"Your father was away?" Bunch asked softly.

"Verdun."

"Oh…" She knew little about this man and she had never

pried. She hoped for more to come but Wright had apparently said all he intended to say and turned his attention to his notebook, slowly leafing through pages. *As if he hadn't dropped a bomb*, she thought. There were a dozen questions that came immediately to her mind, and she had no doubt a few dozen more would spring from those. She knew from the set of his lips that she was unlikely to draw anymore from him, not at that moment. *Perhaps not at all, but a girl has to try.* "So, your sister…"

"Is a very capable sort," he said. "Speaking of which, how is you sister coping?"

Not exactly a neat deflection, she thought, *but message received. Mind my own damned business.* "She's not bad, considering," she said aloud. "Dodo and Mummy had a close bond. Being the baby of the family and all that."

"Not any more with a child of her own that's— How old now?"

"Oh … err … nine months? Ten?" She grinned at him. "Had to think about it for a moment. That must sound unspeakably callous." She leaned closer to Wright and dropped her tone. "It may sound odd to any man, but babies don't fascinate me in the way that people seem to assume they should."

"You don't like children?"

"I never said that. Georgi's a sweet child and I adore her, but I'm perfectly happy to be Aunt Rose for the time being, thank you very much. And do you know what: we never got that cup of tea from Captain Ellis."

Glossop pulled the Wolseley into a cut along the singletrack road's verge to allow a column drab green trucks squeeze past. "Empty trucks," she said. "Wonder what they are up to. Everything is up in the air." She felt her cheeks warming and wondered what had possessed her to confess fears about motherhood that she barely admitted in her own head. Blurting them out to Wright of all people made her feel even more vulnerable. *Confession might be all well and good for the soul but it does little for the public face. Change the subject, idiot. Now.* "Would you like to stop at the Dower for lunch?" She switched on her society smile. "I am sure Cook can manage an extra one at table."

"No thank you. I need to head back. Routine stuff. Going over statements from Wyncombe and Brighton, and I'm waiting for some details to come down from London about the Jarman family business. Besides, I need to get back for the PM on the second victim's remains."

"I assume it will be Letham doing it."

"He is. This afternoon."

"Is it in the same condition as Laura's?"

"Not exactly. I'm not sure you want to know. I can telephone you with the results." He glanced at her and sighed. "You really want to be present?"

"Perhaps not in the room, but it would be useful to get a grip on the woman herself and how she died, if that's all right?" She frowned. "May we stop off at the Dower first? I left the dog with Granny and she can get a bit of a handful after a while."

"Your grandmother or the dog?"

She shaped her lips into a sly moue. "Both, now that you mention it. You don't mind the dog in your car?"

"Rather the dog in my car than me in yours— Ow!" He winced as she flicked his arm with her fingertips. "It's not a problem. Glossop can drive you back home later. It will be light until well gone nine."

"Do you really think Laura had something to do with this Shenton girl?"

"Heaven knows. Laura Jarman seems to have been leading a shadow life since she left her parent's home. We're having trouble finding what she's been up to these past months. London is in such a mess. The bombings may have eased up and that makes things a bit easier, except that it's not only lives lost and buildings destroyed. It's the records for so many places that no longer exist that makes our job much harder."

"Anything I can do?"

Wright spread his hands. "We're at a bit of a loss, to be honest. We're getting nowhere looking into old man Jarman's business. He's working on something for Whitehall, and they can be every bit as hard a nut to crack as those Cannucks. Or worse." He jerked his thumb back the way they had come. "Sorry, Canadians. Carter's slang rubbing off on me."

"Daddy says these Whitehall types are all little emperors.

Grabbing power as fast as they can and guarding every snippet of information like bulldogs with toothache."

"Colourful turn of phrase, but he's not wrong. The Canadian line of enquiry will be bogged down for the foreseeable future. I am not going to lose any sleep over it, though, because I don't think any of them were responsible. This all feels a bit – local. Personal, even."

"You don't want me to ask Daddy, see if I can get things hurried along?"

"Far from it. Please do. I still need to talk with the Canadians because they may have vital information. Meanwhile, chatting with the Jarman family again might be more useful."

"I shall drop by to see them. I can fit it in with a trip to see Mummy as I did the last time."

~ Nine ~

Bunch dabbed a little cologne under her nose, a trick that Letham had passed on, to mask the odours of a post-mortem – for which she was eternally grateful – before she followed Wright into the mortuary. She caught him rolling his eyes at her and she waggled the silver-topped phial. "Would you like any? Letham said I could use TCP but I'm not sure that smells any better than the bodies."

"I am not sure that Schiaparelli is suitable for the likes of me."

"Too *Shocking*?" She giggled at her own joke and Wright rolled his eyes once again, adding a *tsk* for good measure.

"Too expensive," he replied, "and somewhat exotic."

"Really?" She sniffed at the spicy fumes coming off the bottle cap and shrugged. "What's your preference?"

"I have no objection to Letham's TCP," he replied. "It serves a purpose."

"I won't tell you what that stuff was called in the ATS."

"I can imagine but I wish I couldn't... Ah, Letham—" Wright pushed open the swing door into the PM room and strode in "—hello ... have you finished already?"

"I have as it happens," the pathologist replied. "Cause of death was exsanguination and there's not a great deal more I can add. I don't think it was due to the decapitation, which was carried out post-mortem." He began to chuckle. "Prior to *this* post-mortem, I hasten to add. The cause of the blood loss was that perennial old favourite, a long slender blade beneath the ribs."

"She was decapitated?" Bunch looked from Letham to Wright. "You failed to mention that small fact, William."

"Not just headless," Letham said. "Also handless, as were the first two victims, though in a rather less efficient manner than the earlier cases."

"There are different killers?"

Letham shrugged. "It's possible. Or maybe they had a lack of sharp implements. This victim still retained her feet, at least, unlike the first one – and another woman found a few years back. We never were able to identify her."

"Then how did you identify this poor woman?"

"Our killer was sloppy," Letham said. "Her killer – or killers – removed every other scrap of evidence that might identify her except for the girl's identity card, which was tucked inside the top of her corset, along with a single Yale key. Without that, I imagine we'd still be trying to identify her in ten years. It points to the body's disposal being carried out in a bit of a hurry."

"Assuming it is her card," Wright growled.

"I doubt many women run around with other people's ID cards tucked inside their bustier, Chief Inspector."

"Or someone could be laying a false trail. Hopefully, though, the key may help in finding Kitty Shenton's residence."

"Indeed. Given that we have discovered as much information from the remains as we are likely to get at this stage, do you still want to view the corpse, Miss Courtney?"

Bunch wanted to shake her head. Identifying an intact corpse was one thing but— *One can almost see them as sleeping,* she thought, *but I've seen enough in this war not to relish viewing random body parts.* "Perfectly macabre, I'm sure, but if Wright thinks this death is related to Laura Jarman's, then I probably should."

"Then come this way." Letham led her to the cold room, off to one side of the mortuary, where there were three covered trolleys. He stopped by the closest one.

"You're certain about this?" Wright murmured at Bunch's side.

She wasn't sure, not in the slightest, but Wright's attempt to hide the nature of the girl's death from her, as if she were some delicate B-movie starlet, had annoyed her. "Positive," she replied and moved nearer to the covered table. "I'm ready, Doctor Letham."

"If you are sure."

She nodded.

"Then brace yourself, lass."

Letham grabbed the edge of the cloth and as he pulled it back a potent mix of Lysol and putrefaction wafted up towards her, and Bunch was glad of the perfume freshly applied to her philtrum.

The body and legs were much as she would expect, youthful pale flesh, neatly groomed and still firm, despite the relaxing of muscle tension that death brought. The arms were truncated at the wrists with the severed ends wrapped in gauze. Bunch was touched by the gesture of dignity that Letham had lent the girl but wondered if it was for Kitty's benefit or his own. The Y incision on the torso had been closed with neat but workmanlike stitches, and above it, where the head should be – was nothing. As with the hands, the neck was covered so that instead of a ruddy gash of open flesh there was only a pale wad of cloth, stained pinkish where it was pressed against the body.

"It makes no sense," she whispered. "Why take the head and hands yet leave ID cards?"

"The card was probably left by accident. The killer was in a hurry, or he was simply sloppy."

"Or perhaps it was left precisely so you could identify her? If it is indeed Kitty," said Bunch. "It seems a little odd that both Lorna and Kitty had some documents left with their corpses."

"You think the killer wanted them identified?"

"Perhaps…"

"It's possible but doubtful," Wright replied. "Besides the ID card – left by accident, I'm sure – the body is the right height, etcetera, so it's quite probably Kitty Shenton. The mutilation, I think—" he gestured at the body "—was not only intended to delay identification but as a warning to others. We've come across the like before. Right now, we're discounting ideas of a *crime passionnel* – like Violet Kays back in 1934."

"More akin to the case we called Pretty Feet," said Letham. "She had slender dancer's feet, though there was a lot more effort given to hiding that poor wee girl. Pieces of her were discovered on several different railway stations."

Bunch felt her gut lurch uncomfortably. She had been confident she could manage any of the sights and smells this place could throw at her, but this conversation had taken a more macabre direction than she had expected. Wright was looking at her, concern and pity in his eyes. He turned to glare at Letham. "Not sure Miss Courtney needed to know that."

"I'm fine." Bunch was determined not to crack though she had to swallow hard to keep her stomach contents at bay. "Comparing this murder with the Pretty Feet case… Could it have spawned the recent killings, do you think? However many there have been."

"Counting Kitty, here, we are at five – including Pretty Feet and Laura Jarman."

"Laura never lost her head," said Bunch.

"As I said, that particular killing could be a warning for others who may be involved, of the 'cross us and you lose your head' variety. The killer wanted people involved to know what happens to 'traitors'."

"People, such as her family?"

"Poor Kitty had little family to be warned off. Far more likely to be any associates of hers in various criminal activities." Wright tapped the trolley close to the blood-tinged cloth at Kitty's neck. "Telling certain people what awaits them if…"

"They're butchered like a side of venison?" said Letham. "That is quite a statement."

The second lurching of her stomach made Bunch close her eyes for a moment. She remembered her days in FANY tending patients; she recalled helping their ghillie butcher a deer up at the bothy; most of all she recalled coming across poachers butchering sheep in Hascombe Woods back in the winter of 1939. The memory of knife cutting flesh and the cracking of bone on that cold afternoon came to her clearly. Along with the sound of the gunshot and the squeal of her injured dog. Her stomach made unholy noises in sympathy.

The body before her was a whole other matter. Those animal carcasses had all been freshly slaughtered. There was none of the antiseptic miasma attempting to cover the rancid stench of week-old meat that she could detect, despite the spicy scent she had dabbed liberally on herself at the door.

Perhaps that cologne was a mistake, she told herself. *It must be. I've always considered I have cast iron guts.*

Bunch sprinted back to the main room and leant over one of the deep sinks, a hand on either side of her head, her eyes closed, sweat speckling her forehead and upper lip. She swallowed several times, willing her lunch to stay put. *Because I can't be sick in front of these two. I shall never live it down.*

A cold damp cloth pressed against her neck cooled her a little. She put her hand to her nose before she slowly straightened up.

"I am most dreadfully sorry. I can't think what came over me," she muttered.

"If I had a silver sixpence for every brawny constable I've seen leaning over that sink," Letham observed, "I could have retired already." He was smiling at her, sympathy and concern writ large in his face. "Nothing a briny breeze won't cure. Wright, get this poor wee lass outside, man. I'll send my report in the morning."

"Thank you, Letham. I'll be back to see you when I've read it." Wright set the wet towel aside and took Bunch gently by the elbow and steered her out to the waiting car where Glossop and the dog Bella waited for them.

~~~

They stopped near the West Pier so that they could walk along Kingsway towards the Royal Pavilion. It was a warm day, with the sea as calm as the Channel ever is, rolling lethargically onto the stony beach so that the pebbles in its path made little noise. For Bunch, it was a welcome stroll; but it was impossible for her to ignore the changes that a threat of invasion had wrought.

"Such a shame we can't go onto the beach." She waved at the barbed wire and concrete blocks barricading them from the pebbly foreshore and the water beyond. "Can't even let Bella off for a run." Bella looked up at mention of her name, then back to the ocean, whining softly. "Sorry old girl." Bunch reached down to stroke the dog's head. "I'd let you go, honestly I would, but it's stiff with mines down there."

"It is, but not for ever," said Wright. "One day we'll be able to take a walk along that beach."

His tone sounded odd to Bunch's ears and she used the excuse of adjusting the dog's collar to give him a sideways glance. "Perhaps," she said. "I can't see how it will ever be the same as it was before— Look at the pier: damn great chunk chewed out of its middle."

"Same as every pier all along the coast," Wright replied.

"That may be true but it is rather a shame." She gestured at the squaddies lounging near the Bofors gun at the head if the beach, smoking and chatting, as though they were not just a few feet away from several boxes of explosives. "I know the logic behind it, of course. The army doesn't want them to be used as a landing stage, yet if those chaps simply pointed that cannon of theirs straight at the pier they could take the thing down anytime they liked."

"Perhaps, but nobody wanted to be seen taking such a risk. They'll repair them when this war is all over."

"I certainly hope so." Bunch looked at the Palace Pier before turning to compare it with the distant West Jetty, with its comparable missing midriff. She had seen both of the disabled landmarks so many times over the past months, but today, after viewing a deliberately mutilated human body, they stood as metaphor for the fragility of life. *Broken*, she thought. *Win or lose this war, nothing will ever be the same.*

"You look as if you could do with tea," said Wright, "and as we're standing outside the Grand, what about it?"

"With Bella?"

Wright laughed. "They won't refuse a lady."

"Some lady, vomiting on the job. Maybe the Schiaparelli was a mistake, after all."

"Too strong to mix with the mortuary smells?"

"Too bloody expensive to have it ending up reminding me of dead bodies every time I use it," she replied. "It was— Oh, I'm not sure what happened today, really. I was reminded of Johnny, or maybe it was Roger."

Wright smiled wryly. "I can understand it reminding you of Jonathan Frampton. You two had history together… But Roger? A dog? I know you were fond of the old hound but it's not the same…"

"Actually, it was partly a flashback to the carcasses those poachers were cutting up," she said. "The look of all those butchered sheep in the woods. Odd how past and present events are connected by something as simple as sliced muscle."

"I'd be more surprised if you didn't have a flashback. It's quite normal. And in the event, you didn't spew," he replied. "Which impressed Letham no end. Most people vomit when visiting Letham's lair, usually within the first minute of watching him at work. There is a rumour he keeps a notebook and scores people out of ten. But he's always had a soft spot for you and I think he'll have you walking on water from now on."

She grinned. "Top marks?"

"I doubt you are on his list. Now tea, because if you don't want a cuppa I do. Or something stronger?"

Bunch shook her head. "I don't think I could take anything like sherry or beer. Tea will be perfectly fine."

"Shall we, then? It may be the last chance we get because this place has been earmarked for the RAF."

The Victorian Terrace at the Grand Hotel overlooked the sea and it was, Bunch noted, one of those days when the sea and sky were both close to being blue, almost merging on the horizon. She could make out a ship on the edge of the world. *Friend or foe? No way of telling from here. Three years ago this would have been a perfect afternoon. Right now, it's all about the gaps in our lives...* She glanced around the room, with its stylish velvet-covered sofas, tall stools at the bistro-styled bar, white cane chairs, with laced cloths, lining the window side. *It all seems so terribly normal, without any hint of the conflict over the Channel.* It sparked another thought, something elusive tickling at the back of her brain and she could not for the life of her grasp hold of it, or have even the slightest hint of what it was. *Something William said. Or was it me?*

"Afternoon tea," she heard Wright murmur to the waitress. "For two."

"Yes, sir."

"Are you feeling all right? Rose?"

Bunch jerked herself back into the moment. "Pardon? Yes. Perfectly, thank you, William. I was just looking out at that sea and thinking how it all seems so peaceful. Hard to think that a headless woman..."

"This is the job, I'm sorry to say," he replied. "For what it's worth, I'm truly sorry for calling you into this mess."

His face, close to hers, was a study of concern and guilt. *And with just a little hint of relief? Does he want me to step away? Well, damned if I shall.* "I know it's the job, William. It's quite ghastly. Now we have two girls to work for, their murders to solve. Yes, I had a little case of the jitters back there. The smell reminded me of— I'm better now." She beamed at him as the waitress set chinaware between them. "Shall I be mother?"

~ Ten ~

Bunch winced at Kate's grinding of gears as the Fordson shunted back and forth in the confines of the barn. The tractor's front loader had made it shorter work than the wielding of pitchforks and shovels, but hand-shovelling was still a big part of the job. They had been hauling the deep litter accumulated through the winter to a waiting trailer, for spreading on the fields for most of that week. It was an essential task but one nobody much relished. The smell of well-rotted manure and dust did not bother her too much – it was nothing compared to a mortuary. Bunch had been mucking out stables for most of her years, to her mother and grandmother's chagrin, and the smell of bovine waste was not so different from horse. But when mixed with the engine fumes inside the farm building it made her a little nauseous. *Or perhaps a leftover from Letham's slab, after all?* She stabbed her fork in the muck and leaned back against the trailer's slatted end-board while she fished for her cigarettes.

The job was accomplished a great deal quicker with aid of the tractors, of that she had no doubt, and she recognised her father's – and Parsons', the now-retired steward – foresight in buying the three vehicles at considerable expense. Nevertheless, she missed the steady quiet of the heavy horses, and with the now diminishing supplies of fuel she wondered if they should not have kept at least a couple of the great beasts.

"How are we doing, Kate?" she yelled.

"Almost done, Boss." Kate brought the Fordson to a halt by the wagon and leaned forward to switch off the fuel toggle. As always it took a few seconds for the engine to judder to a halt. "It can be finished today if we work on a bit longer. Have you got to get back to the office?"

Bunch looked down at her grubby siren suit and laughed. "The estate office might have been a feed store two years ago but Father would still have a fit if I sat in there stinking like this. And all the paperwork is positively Sisyphean. I swear there is some horrid little man somewhere in Whitehall whose sole purpose in life is dreaming up new forms to torture me for a few additional hours every week. At times like this I really do miss Cecile." The image of her old school friend was clear in her mind. It was almost a year since Cecile Benoir had left to work with the current inhabitants of Perringham House, under the inscrutably genial Colonel Ralph. Bunch missed her friend more now than ever.

"Not heard from her I suppose?" said Kate, as if she had read Bunch's thoughts. The Land Girl braced her legs against the tractor's dished metal seat and leaned over to take the cigarette Bunch offered her. "It's been a while now. She must have finished whatever training Colonel Ralph dishes out over at Perringham House."

"I gather she's no longer training with Everett Ralph's unit." Bunch took time to light her smoke and then stared at her booted feet to hide her expression. *Bad enough that Whitehall had requisitioned the family pile*, she thought, *but having men like Ralph spiriting away old pals is just too much*. She was being unfair, she knew. Cecile had volunteered to serve under Colonel Ralph in whatever secretive military game he was playing. "When Henry Marsham popped in to see how Bella was doing, he said Cecile had been sent up north. Naturally, he wouldn't say where. Nobody can say anything of course. Walls have ears."

"That's the buzz."

Bunch glanced up at Kate, surprised at the wary tone in the woman's voice. The only other sounds within the barn now were the scrabbles and yips from Bella digging furiously in the exposed rat runs. She knew why Marsham had not told her anything more. Everything he did was covered by the Official Secrets Act. In the past she had always regarded him as a boring sort, but hidden depths had him leading a life of derring-do in the various agencies of the War Office. Cecile was no doubt using her language skills in a similar vein.

Bunch's father Edward Courtney spent most of his time ensconced in some Whitehall bunker with Winnie, as did Dodo's sister-in-law Emma. Barty Tinsley was playing soldiers with the Home Guard; even Granny and Dodo were up to their ears in the new County Herb Committee, growing and collecting medicinal plants to heal the country's civilian sick.

And me? Clerk, general factotum, and captain of the ordure. I've not even heard from Wright all week – and I made such a fool of myself in front of Letham. "Dammit," she said aloud.

"Problem Boss?"

"What? Oh no. Sorry Kate. Feeling a bit … useless, I suppose. Everybody has some useful skills to offer but me."

"Who do you imagine is running all this?" Kate tilted her head and scrutinised her boss with a critical eye. "You're just tired."

"Tired, and helpless. It's so hard to see an end to it all. Don't you ever feel as if we're not doing our bit. Everyone's off doing all kinds of stuff and here we are shovelling last winter's cow shit. I know it must be done, but I can't help feeling I should be doing something with more meaning." She tapped her lips with two fingers, as if what she had just said dawned on her. "Oh God, I'm sorry Kate. I didn't mean to imply what we're doing is beneath me. I mean growing food is desperately important, but everyone else seems to be doing more – and I simply meant I feel as if I am dragging my heels when I could be out there doing … I don't know. Not making much sense, am I?" She took pull on her cigarette and folded her arms.

Kate shook her head and laughed. "Is that your idea of an inspirational speech, Boss? Not quite St Crispin's Day, is it. Believe it or not, I do know what you mean. My sister had a promotion last month. She's now a WAF Lieutenant, swanking around in her tailor-made togs, taking down messages from Air Marshalls for the squadron leaders. All so much military bullshit, of course. I felt quite jealous when I first heard about it, but—" she struck a pose, one hand aloft, chin up, like an Art Deco statuette "—this shit we're shovelling is some very important shit, I'll have you know. Produced by the finest cows the county has to offer."

Bunch looked up at Kate, agog for a moment, and both began to laugh. "You know what, Kate? I do believe you know me better than I know myself. You're right, of course. This is an exceptional midden and we are its rightful queens." She took in a lungful of smoke and exhaled slowly, rubbing her left hand across her eyes. "Just feeling a little sorry for myself, I suppose."

"You're the boss. You don't have to do the muck spreading."

"Do I think I'm much too grand to do it? Not at all. Good God, Kate, I would never expect you girls to do things I won't do myself. And yes, I'm so damnably tired. I was late back from the Red House last night."

"How is Lady Chiltcombe?"

"Mummy?" Bunch shook her head. "She might be frail in body but the rest of her is mightily angry at the world. The christening really took it out of her, you know. She spent the next day on oxygen, according to the Red House nuns. It can't be long before ... you know."

"I'm sorry. It must be difficult for you all."

"It is. Daddy is beside himself and Dodo is in absolute pieces. Poor lamb has lost rather a lot of people in her life over the past two years. It's terribly hard on her. The only good thing we can do is say a proper goodbye. So many people can't."

"Like Laura Jarman, you mean?"

"You know something about that?" asked Bunch.

"Only the usual local gossip. And all of those 'Body in Suitcase: Daughter of Prominent Businessman Killed' headlines, naturally. It's quite hard to say which are the more lurid." Kate took a last drag on her cigarette and scrubbed it out on the side of the trailer, breathing a slow stream of smoke. "Speaking of gossip, Ruth and Elsie were in the Seven Stars the other night and said they had a drink with some men from the base at Chellcott. Didn't you go there with the Inspector?"

Bunch might have wondered how Kate knew where she had been and how there was a possible link to Chellcott. *But nothing goes unnoticed around here.* "How did the girls know these chaps were from that base?"

"I gather they went to some pains to mention it, which the girls thought was peculiar. Careless talk costs lives, as they say."

"It would seem a bit unusual. Do the chaps from Chellcott go often to the Stars?" she asked. "There must be a lot of pubs far better than the Seven Stars between Chellcott and Wyncombe."

"Not often. That's why they stood out rather. According to the girls, the men turned up half-an-hour before last orders and bought a measly half-a-pint each. Ruth heard them tell the landlord they were on a last pub crawl while they had the chance, but she and Elsie swear these men were stone-cold sober. Old Burse reckons they were Redcaps doing a sweep for stray squaddies out on the tiles, probably because they were shipping out by morning."

"What made him say that?"

"He said it's what he did before he was shipped out to France in the last lot. And there have been a lot of khaki trucks zipping around these parts over the past few days."

Nothing gets past her, Bunch mused, *not a damn thing*. "I suppose it makes sense. Was one of these chaps a redhead."

"No idea. I can ask her if it's important?"

"Doesn't matter." Bunch looked through the barn's open doors, to the brightness of the afternoon. *Wright is going to love that snippet of information*, she thought. *After being given the run around by the inscrutable Captain Ellis*. "This was when?"

"Saturday. Elsie only mentioned it this morning because there were a few lorries parked up in the village much earlier, and I remembered you saying you went over to Chellcott with the Inspector."

"I did? Co-incidence, I imagine, but I'll be sure to tell Wright when he calls."

"You can't call him?"

"I may. Meanwhile we have a dung heap to shift."

"Well, I do, Boss." Kate glanced at her watch and tapped the glass. "You asked me to give you a nudge at three, and it's ten past now."

"Oh God, already? Despite what I said not two minutes ago I must dash. Granny made it crystal clear that she expects me in for tea, and I shall need a bath first, or possibly two." She sniffed at her forearm and pulled a face. "Will you be all right here?"

"Perfectly. Elsie will be back with the second trailer shortly. We'll get it done."

"I have absolute faith in you. How many more runs, do you think?"

"Two, three at the most. I'll get the team in to wash down the last of the slurry tomorrow."

"Excellent. Thank you. Bella! Come!" Bunch whistled the dog

to heel and then slapped the tractor's engine cover, smiling up at her second in command. "I really do need to go. But Kate… For what it's worth, you'd make a far better bluff King Hal than I ever could."

~~~

The bath was welcome, and Bunch turned a blind eye that it was deeper than the recommended five inches. She spent longer in it than she should, soaking aching muscles and listening to the birds through the open window. The heart to heart with Kate had been calming and her snippet of information about the Canadians enlightening. *It almost feels too convenient. Ellis was sending us a message, I'm certain of that. He struck me as the sort of chap who'd gnaw off his own arms before he'd let anything damning escape the confines of his camp.*

She raised her left arm and smoothed the soapy sponge along it, watching the suds drip from her elbow. Years of horse riding had given strength to her arms but the physical labour of farm work she had undertaken over the past year had given them form: muscles and tendons glistening in the light from the windows had a hawser-like ripple. "Not terribly ladylike, my dear," she drawled in a better-than-fair imitation of Beatrice. Her voice echoed around the tiled room and she glanced at the door hoping nobody had heard. There were still times when she forgot that the Dower House owned a fraction of Perringham's spaciousness. "What the hell is wrong with you?" she muttered. "You're getting maudlin, Rose Courtney. It simply will not do."

Bunch sloshed the soap from her arms and stood to let the water run from her before stepping onto the cotton rug next to the tub. She reached for the vast white bath towel that Kimber had left for her and wrapped it around herself. She was glad that her mother's maid had not insisted on being present to help dry her as she had done for Theadora, and now did for Beatrice. "Not going there," she murmured, and meant it. Her mother and grandmother had been used to having their personal maids for so long, but it was something Bunch had eschewed, as had Dodo, though in her sister's case not entirely from choice but because of the lack of staff. The Tinsley fortunes at Banyard Manor had suffered in recent times, but Dodo seemed quite content living there with her father-in-law Barty and her baby Georgianna. It was obvious to Bunch that their money was tight, and not only because of the war.

As she rubbed herself dry and reached for the robe hanging from the rail, Bunch wondered if Laura Jarman had been forced to make that choice. Her mother came from an old household where maids and companions would have been commonplace, but she had the impression that Charles Jarman was not the sort of man to allow the household budget to extend beyond the basics required to maintain a veneer of sophistication. *Though his kind usually like to flaunt their money.* She frowned, realising she was being an utter snob. "To paraphrase Alice," she said to her steamed reflection in the mirror, "I should learn not to make personal remarks. It's rude and— Oh, hello Kimber." She opened the connecting door to her bedroom and stopped in her tracks. "I was quoting Alice," she said, "as in Wonderland, that is. Not you. The Mad Hatter's tea party?"

"Yes, Miss," Kimber replied. "It was a favourite of yours when you were small. You went on about it so often Miss Daphne was convinced it was all about me. She wasn't much more than a baby then." She chuckled, a breathless whisper of sound. "Now, I have laid out the lemon chiffon, Miss Rose. Do you need help with your hair?"

Kimber's glance at the clock was all the unspoken language Bunch required. She had ten minutes to be dressed and ready for Tea. *With a very capital T*, she thought. "No thank you, Kimber. Go and see if Granny needs any help."

"Her ladyship has already gone down," Kimber replied.

"And she sent you up to chivvy me along? Run along and tell her I shall be there in a trice."

She dressed quickly and bounded down to the drawing room just as the gong sounded for tea. "Hello Granny. Just us today? I thought you were doing herbal things with Dodo."

"Yes, it is. Daphne—" Beatrice said, placing emphasis on Dodo's given name "—had to get back to Banyards. So much to do there. She's lucky to have Barty doing the lion's share or she'd never be able to help me."

"Did you drive her over?"

"No. Not enough of our fuel ration remaining or I'd have

taken the Crossley. Burse took Daphne in the pony cart."

Beatrice glanced at her hands and then leaned forward to pour tea. Bunch could not help noticing how her grandmother's arms shook under the weight of the filled pot and felt a pang of guilt that her grandmother's frailty was increasing. They had all been so concerned about Theadora's failing health they had taken the older woman's indomitable persistence for granted. "Shall I pour?" Bunch said.

"Don't fuss, dear." Beatrice set the pot down and rubbed at her wrist. "Damned aches. Tying herb bundles is very hard on the fingers."

"It would be, Granny." Bunch doubted Beatrice's arthritic hands could do a great deal of the tying-up, but she let it pass. "You really need to let Kimber help. I'm sure I can train her up to drive the pony trap for when it's needed."

"Alice is not confident with horses. She never had to be with your mother, of course. Theadora had never ridden that much. She prefers her creature comforts. The motorcar was made for your mother."

Kimber has suddenly become Alice. Bunch noticed. *A promotion to Granny's companion on the cards? To the satisfaction of us all.* "Mummy seemed on good form last night," she said aloud. "I said I'll try to take Kimber – I mean to say Alice – next time I go."

"That would be good of you. They must miss each other's company." She sipped at her tea and frowned at the cup. "We must be near the end of our two ounces. This tea is quite disgusting."

"Kate was telling me that the Land Girls dry out their leaves to reuse them. Do you suppose Cook is doing the same?"

"I shudder to think. But whatever this is, its resemblance to tea as a beverage is fleeting."

"Sherry, instead? At least that isn't on ration." Bunch went to the sideboard and poured two schooners. "There you are, Granny. Chin-chin."

"Good health," Beatrice replied. "Now do sit down, child."

"Sorry. Feeling somewhat restless today."

"I am not at all surprised. You should be off doing things. This was the time of year we'd be up at the bothy for the salmon. Or a quick trip down the Riviera before the summer heat."

"I don't think either of those will happen again, even after this is all over. And the house in Thurloe Square will be on the skids too."

"It was only Theodora who liked it there." Beatrice agreed.

"I meant when the war is over, then Daddy will be back here more."

"If he doesn't get shunted off to some embassy or other. Too bad of Edward to expect you to shoulder all the estate on your own."

"I have you, Granny. And Daddy is here some weekends."

"Occasionally," Beatrice muttered. "He goes to see Theadora, of course."

"And to where is all this heading? Come on Granny, you are not anywhere near as inscrutable as you imagine. What are you up to?"

Beatrice sipped at her sherry, avoiding Bunch's eyes. "Nothing. Absolutely nothing. How was young Maurice?"

"I have no idea. Do not get any ideas about him and me. He's a nice enough chap but not my type."

"Any more than Henry Marsham? I heard he called in the other day."

"Granny!" When Beatrice grinned Bunch realised she was being wound up. "Henry is fine, as it happens. He was on his way up to Town from his parent's place and popped in to see how Bella's getting on."

"Excellent. And your Chief Inspector Wright? Didn't you see him recently?"

"Also fine. Granny, just where is this leading? A grand tour of every man I have spoken to in the last six months? Do stop trying to marry me off. I am not interested in marrying anyone, right now."

"I worry about you, dear. Speaking as an old lady, I can tell you that life is brief."

And even shorter for my mother. It was not hard to see what was on Beatrice's mind. The inevitability of Theadora's end weighed on them all. "I know it is," she said. "It comes to some of us sooner than it should, but I am fine. Honestly."

"If you say so. Now, you were asking me a little while ago about the Jarmans… Well, Connie was chatting at the WVS this morning and she mentioned that she knew all about Faye Waller."

"Haven Cottage is barely a mile from here so she must have known them. And now we're fairly certain that the Jarman girl was murdered there, so…"

"Did you also know that Clement Waller was once chummy with the Jarmans?"

"How does Connie know? Oh, don't tell me, Anne Bishop?"

"I would imagine so, yes. Connie was being rather secretive so I assume she doesn't know half as much as she would have us believe."

"Yet Connie couldn't resist passing it on, regardless? Sounds like her."

"She read in the papers that the inquest is on hold – so she told me. I suppose you would have been informed of that?"

"So would I," Bunch muttered.

"I assumed you would be called as a witness."

"Apparently not." Learning that there had been a hearing and not having heard so much as a squeak from Wright was more than annoying. *It is downright insulting.* She was furious at his arrogance that she almost missed her grandmother's next bombshell. She took a mouthful of sherry and reached for the cigarette box.

"They knew each other."

"That seems rather specific for someone who may in fact not know all that much."

Beatrice waved a dismissal. "Indeed, but Connie does have a few sources, remember. The subject came up when we were wrapping things in old newspapers and somebody saw the inquest notice about poor Laura. Connie mentioned there had been some kind of contretemps and that there was a falling out because of it; but that may just be her filling in the chinks. Connie also has a fertile imagination."

"Who had a falling out? Jarman and his daughter? Or Jarman and Waller? I can perfectly believe both because Jarman appears to be that sort of man. We already know there was a family row going on."

Beatrice thought for a moment. "Do you know, I am not so

sure now. It could be a simple family drama, I suspect. No house is ever complete without one."

"No, indeed. Do we still have yesterday's papers?"

"Not to hand. We used the old newspapers today."

"Of course. Now then, how about another sherry?"

"Chief Inspector Wright is here to see you, Miss Rose."

Bunch glanced up from her glass to stare at Knapp, then to Beatrice, and back again. "He's here? Is Carter with him?"

"No, Miss."

Bunch looked to her grandmother. "He really is the limit. What can he want?"

"The only way to know will be to ask him. Knapp, invite the Chief Inspector in."

"Yes, ma'am. And his driver?"

"Glossop knows Cook well enough by now," Bunch growled. "I don't doubt tea and toast will not go amiss."

Beatrice watched on in silence as a place was set and for Wright to sidle into the room.

"Good morning, ma'am. Rose."

"William. How delightful. Do sit down. Tea? We have some fish paste sandwiches. It's not at all bad," said Bunch. "Cook made it. She assures me it's made from smoked haddock, though between me and you I am not convinced. The colour rather speaks of smoked trout. Or possibly pike. It will depend on what old Jenner has been catching of late."

"Rose." Beatrice glowered and Bunch grinned.

"Just tea, thank you. I had lunch in the canteen before I left," said Wright.

"How wise. One never knows what the day will bring. Isn't that so, Rose?"

"Yes, Granny."

"To what do we owe this pleasure?"

"I need to see Rose about developments in our investigation."

He looked at Bunch and she saw how the lines at the corners of his mouth had deepened, the shadows under his eyes a little darker. "Not another death?"

"No, but we may have discovered Shenton's home."

"Where?"

"In Surrey."

"Goodness," said Bunch. "That's a little off your territory, isn't it, William?"

"It is."

"And you came to tell me about this because…?"

"We found—" He glanced at Beatrice.

"Don't mind me." The older woman busied herself pouring tea for her guest. "Here you are. Unless you would prefer something stronger? The sun is well and truly past the yardarm."

"Tea is fine, ma'am. I am on duty."

"Of course you are. Do carry on," said Bunch.

"We finally have a lead on Laura Jarman's residence, which also turns out to be Kitty Shenton's address." He turned his attention to Beatrice again. "Does the name ring any bells with you?"

"Rose mentioned it earlier and I can't say that it does," Beatrice replied. "Shenton is not one of the names I'm familiar with."

"It may look as if Kitty shared a flat with Laura Jarman," Wright said, "but officially it was Laura who was living with Kitty." They appear to have been living there together for a number of months. We had a job tracing their address because they had moved from one apartment block to the one next door and were living there under assumed names. Kitty Shenton also worked in the offices at Jarman's factory."

"Do you believe they were victims of the same killer?"

"Almost certainly."

"What may I do to help?"

"I was hoping you would come with me to go through Laura's belongings, see if you can pick up on any references to this area. You're more likely to spot them than some London copper."

"Certainly. Where is the flat?"

"Beddington. Which is in Surrey but is a part of London, for all practical intents and purposes."

"I suppose I could. You don't mind looking after Bella, do you Granny?"

"I can manage. Are you sure it's safe that close to London, dear? According to Edward the raid on the tenth was pretty horrendous. Six hours or more."

"But almost nothing in Town since," Bunch replied. "And you heard William, it's in Surrey. I don't want to take the dog, though. If there were to be a raid they're not allowed in the public shelters."

"Rose, darling. You can be terribly blasé, especially considering we spent so long telling Theadora it was not safe for her staying in London."

"Surrey," Bunch repeated. "And if needs must, we can stay at Thurloe Square overnight. The cellars are perfectly safe." She turned back to Wright. "Let me get changed and I shall be with you."

~ Eleven ~

The route that Glossop took eventually brought them to a small cul-de-sac of three five-storey apartment blocks, built some fifteen years earlier as fashionable residences for the up-and-coming hopefuls unable to afford the rent or leases in London itself. The nearby sprawling industrial premises and serried rows of Victorian back-to-backs saw to it never reaching that goal. Now, any shreds of glamour they once possessed had been peeled away by the Blitz.

"Luckily, these blocks haven't had any direct hits," Glossop told them. "This is one of the most bombed parts of London, south of the river. I've a cousin that's a watch commander in the Croydon fire service and he's seen the numbers."

"Is it because it's en-route to the city?" said Bunch.

"That, and the considerable number of engineering works round these parts. Jerry sees it as a prime target."

"I see." Bunch exchanged glances with Wright. "Just don't tell Granny that," she muttered. "She'd have a fit."

Fenning Court was the middle of the three red-brick and white-stucco buildings. It was situated at the end of the C-shaped cul-de-sac that also embraced a wide circle of grass and small trees, in imitation of the kind of smart mews that Bunch was familiar with in the more up-market areas. *It should,* she thought, *be a snazzy place to live – but it isn't.* She sniffed the air and coughed. The ever-present Blitz-odour of smoke and damp concrete, which hung over much of the capital since the previous raid, permeated the street.

She scrambled to catch up with Wright, who had already moved ahead and was talking with a handful of policemen gathered outside the apartment block. *Old colleagues, judging by the greetings.* She waited impatiently, staring up at the building, trying to identify which of the windows might belong to 5C, and sidled into the building when she realised the constables were not paying her any attention. The vestibule was poorly lit. Ahead of her was a cantilever door covering the lift with, she noted, an Out-of-

Order notice stuck across its handles. To her left, a staircase, and to her right, a bank of mailboxes where a concierge window might have been. Beside them hung a message board with a few public notices about the air raids, waste collections, and variety of dire warnings about walls having ears and the cost of careless talk. She read them all – from habit – as she waited for Wright.

"Rose."

She spun around expecting to see the Wright, surprised that the voice had come from someone descending the stairs, and found herself staring at Henry Marsham. "Good heavens. What are you doing here?"

"I would ask you the same thing but of course we all know the answer to that." He turned his head slightly and looked in the direction of the open door and the sound of voices drifting in from the outside. "I saw you trotting about after the splendid Inspector Wright."

"Chief Inspector – and it is not like that, Henry. Wright is a colleague. And nothing more."

"Not what I've heard."

"Then you have *heard* wrong. And I would thank you not to repeat barrack-room gossip. Is. That. Clear." Bunch snarled the last three words, jabbing him in the chest with her forefinger at each word.

"Ouch. Message received. Roger and out. Whomever Roger might be."

"Henry!"

"You sound like my grandmother when you say 'Henry' like that. No, like *your* grandmother, which quite chills the marrow."

"Granny would be thrilled. She's worked hard at it."

"I can imagine," Henry replied. "Do you have any information about the former residents of 5C?"

"Not a thing. Of course, it would help if I had a vague idea of what we were looking for. What about you?"

"No, nothing specific."

Like hell. You may not want to speak of it but you've got a damned good idea. "What have Kitty and Laura to do with your lot?"

"My lot?"

"Don't be abstruse. It doesn't suit you. I mean the cloak-and-dagger brigade. When you happen to turn up out of the blue you can't expect me not to ask questions. And if you dare say I can't expect answers... I swear I shall slap you. Hard."

"Until today Kitty Shenton has been of no interest to us whatsoever. Scout's honour."

"But Laura Jarman is. Or was?"

Henry's shoulders lifted in the merest hint of a shrug.

"Stop it! I saw you at the Jarman house the other week. Please don't deny it."

"Ah, I wondered if that was your little jalopy I saw zipping out of their driveway."

"It was. What was your interest in the Jarmans?"

"You are aware they are involved in research that could be of immense importance to the war effort?"

"The old man made no secret of that fact. Which defeats the secrecy claims."

"People know what his trade is so he's telling nobody anything that isn't already well known. We have reason to believe that those parts of his business that are secret may be under threat."

"By Laura Jarman? Surely not."

"Laura may have been mixing with some dubious sorts."

"She was a spy?"

"We don't know for sure. We had as much trouble tracking her down as you chaps did. Anyway, that is why I'm here: if there is anything to discover we thought it would be in her flat."

"Rose— Oh, hello Marsham." Wright halted at Bunch's side, so close she could feel his breathing.

"Wright," Marsham drawled. The tension that fizzed between the two men was puzzling to Bunch. She took a step back to avoid being the barrier between them.

"I'm surprised to see you still here," said Wright. "The Surrey boys said you'd been in earlier."

"I never left. Came here the moment we had the tip off. When they said you were expected I hung about hoping to bump into Rose." He grinned at Bunch.

"Is there something about the Jarman case you should be sharing with us?" Wright sounded angry.

"Not a thing that I am aware of," Marsham said and added:

"Rose, will you be at the house in Thurloe Square later tonight?"

"Possibly. Why?"

"Nothing really. I shall be having supper with Sir Edward and I thought it would be rather nice to see you then." He raised his hat. "Must toddle off now. Cheery bye, Rose. Evening, Wright."

Bunch waited until Marsham was out of sight before she rounded on Wright. "What was all that about?"

"All what?"

"All of that chest beating. It was like watching a Tarzan movie – though which of you was Tarzan and which the ape I would not like to hazard a guess."

"It's not him. It's his infernal birdwatchers interfering with our investigations."

"Henry helped us out with the last bun fight. And I'm sure he was intending to help us out now – before you stamped in with your police-issue size tens."

"If he knew anything substantial it's unlikely he would be here," Wright replied. "He's casting around, the same as us, which is both good and bad. At least we are onto something if these scavengers are poking around as well … but we don't have a clue what it is. I doubt they would tell us, or tell me. Perhaps you *should* have supper with your father and Marsham this evening, see if you can glean any further information."

"That is a little cold blooded, don't you think?"

"He waited around to talk with you, Rose. Believe me, he has something to discuss."

"He said Laura had been mixing with some rum customers," said Bunch.

"If she was sharing accommodation with Kitty Shenton that seems inevitable. I've spoken with the local bobbies, so we know Miss Shenton worked at the Jarman factory—"

"That explains how the two met but not about anything illicit."

"No, but Marsham is right about one thing. Kitty Shenton did have some dubious associates in her past. I shall be checking those later. For now, we should go upstairs and have a look, see what *we* can find."

They tramped up to the fifth floor and flat number 5C. A constable guarding the butcher-blue door snapped to attention as

Wright flashed his ID. Inside was a tiny vestibule with coat pegs and one small ceramic umbrella stand. The main room beyond was furnished a little sparsely, but still comfortably. A kitchenette lurked behind a half-drawn curtain at one end of the room. Three doors all stood open onto two bedrooms and a bathroom. The one thing the rooms had in common was that they were a maelstrom of slashed upholstery and scattered personal effects.

"My goodness," Bunch murmured, "this is a bit of a shambles." She glanced at Wright and cleared her throat. "I assume it was like this when your police chaps arrived?"

"It was." He grabbed a tipped-up chair and righted it. "Fingerprint boys say that the door handles and light switches had all been wiped clean. Whoever did this was no doubt professional enough to have worn gloves. There's no sign of blood so we can be certain Kitty wasn't murdered here. The assumption is she was abducted from here, most likely, and these premises were searched later – after she was killed."

"May we look around?"

"The photo chaps have done their bit so we're clear to have a good look now."

Bunch picked her way across to the bedrooms. Laura's room was easy to identify, and she reasoned it would at least be easier to search, with less chaos to contend with compared to the jumble in Kitty's. There were few clothes, certainly not as many as Bunch would have expected for a young woman such as Laura Jarman, but they were of excellent quality. She began by slotting the drawers back into the dresser, and picking up items one at a time, shaking them to make sure they were not hiding anything within their folds, before dropping them back into the empty drawers. Creams and brushes she returned to a tray on top of the dresser, books to the shelves, dresses and shirts hung up in the cupboard. It took over half-an-hour to have the rug exposed and the bed cleared of everything but sheets and blankets.

She stood in the middle of the space and turned slowly through 360 degrees. "Bed, chest of drawers, chair, and a small walk-in wardrobe-cupboard. There is nothing else to search. What was it that they were looking for?" she asked Wright when he appeared in the doorway.

"That is the leading question." He pulled a face. "We need to go to the factory and ask around." He placed a hand on her waist and guided her out of the flat.

"It's getting late."

"Jarman's is only about half a mile from here."

"But closed for the night, I'd imagine"

"Not at all," Wright replied. "They're working longer shifts now. The factory line is only shut down between eleven p.m. and six a.m. for maintenance."

"The offices are unlikely to work the same hours as the factory floor, though. What? Do you think I don't know how factories operate? I read the newspapers, you know." Since entering the block of flats the sun had dropped behind the townscape and it would not be long before a pink glow tipped the rooftops. "It *is* getting late," said Bunch. "I suggest we go to Thurloe Square and have Gilsworth dig out some supper for us, and we can visit the factory first thing in the morning."

"I will have to pass on supper. There are records I need to check on first at Scotland Yard."

"Don't you have constables to do that for you?"

"Not as such. I also want to look up a few old colleagues and call in some favours."

"May I help?"

"Better I go alone. Besides, your chum Henry Marsham will be calling tonight so you will have someone to distract you."

"I doubt I will learn anything *really* useful, knowing Henry. He and I are merely friends, despite our grandmothers' combined efforts. Come and stay at the Square when you are finished. We have plenty of room."

"It's kind of you to offer but I shall be a while at the Yard, being nice to people. Crossing into another police division creates more paperwork than you would believe."

"Isn't this why you have Carter?"

"Yes, but I have contacts that need to be sweetened."

"Not his strongpoint?"

"Precisely. Glossop can drop you at Thurloe Square and collect you at eight tomorrow."

"That would be perfect."

~~~

Bunch was pleasantly surprised to find her father at home when she arrived at the house. The hours he worked were both long and erratic and she worried for him because of it. The evening was warm and since there had been no air raid sirens as yet, he had not retreated to the cellars. He was relaxed and settled before the French windows, brandy in one hand and cigar in the other.

"Hello Daddy. Bunch signalled him to remain seated and went to land a kiss on the top of his head. "Nice to see you."

She turned at a movement behind her and nodded at Henry Marsham as he rose briefly to greet her. "And hello to you. Twice in one day," she said. "You're a real glutton for punishment."

"I did say I might pop round."

"Yes, and that's good of you." *What else?* she thought. *If there is one thing I have come to realise about you, Henry Marsham, it's that there is far more to you then I ever imagined.* "It's always lovely to see you."

"Have you eaten?" Edward Courtney sipped at his drink and rested his head against the chair back as he gazed at her.

"No, I haven't, as it happens, Daddy."

"I thought Wright might at least have stood you supper."

"He had to rush off to Scotland Yard. He'll be back in the morning." She flopped onto the sofa next to Henry. "Gilsworth will rustle something up for me."

"I have no doubt she will be doing just that. How is your mother?"

"You haven't spoken to her?"

"Naturally, I have. I telephone the Red House every day, but it's not the same as seeing her in person," Edward replied.

"Then you know she's having a rather bad spell. I really wonder if we should have gone through with the christening thing."

"Of course we should. Your mother was so proud."

"Even when it took so much out of her?"

Edward examined his glass of brandy, swirling the liquid slowly so that it crept up the sides. "She knew the risks," he replied, "and she considered it worth the effort." He swallowed half of the warmed spirit. "It's done now. I get down there as often as I can."

The tautness in his jaw told Bunch the subject was ended and she floundered for a new topic. "Is it horribly busy in the bunker?" she asked. "I imagine Herr Hess's arrival has set a few pigeons scattering."

Edward stared at her for a moment and she wondered if she had blundered into a new minefield. "The Hess thing." He nodded and Bunch relaxed. "Plus, Greece and Africa and Atlantic convoys – and a dozen other things." He waved his brandy at Marsham. "I had hoped for an evening of relative quiet but this young man came to call me back to duty so I shall have to leave you, I am afraid. Sutton is bringing the car round."

"Oh, that is a shame. I shall be all on my own."

"I can stay for a bit," said Marsham. "If you can bear the company."

"That would be splendid. Do you want supper?"

"I have eaten, but I don't mind watching the lions feed."

Edward downed the rest of his drink and got to his feet. "I shall leave you young things to it. Have a good evening and say hello to everyone at Perringham from me." He stooped to kiss Bunch on the cheek.

Marsham rose to shake his hand. "Sorry to have spoiled your evening, sir. But they did seem to be in a bit of a flap."

"They invariably are. Goodnight to you both."

Bunch sat in the chair vacated by her father to eat the cold cuts and salad that Gilsworth brought her, feeling self-conscious, while Marsham leaned back in his chair with a fresh glass of Scotch and regaled her with tales of trainees in the Highlands.

He is being very careful not to tell me what they are training for, she thought. *In the same way that Daddy is careful not to say what tonight's flap is about. I should be used to that.* She put down her tray and drank the remains of her Sancerre. "All right," she said, "what do you really want to say to me? I assume it has something to do with Kitty Shenton. Or perhaps Laura Jarman?"

"More than that I can't say," he replied. "My job today has involved trying to stop two departments from tearing each other apart. Dammed hard, I can tell you. The police and the bloody War Department are trying to kill each other at every turn for very little advantage. If these chaps put as much effort into fighting Jerry as they do each other, we'd all be better off."

"Daddy calls them little emperors, grabbing territory and never ever admitting if the other chap might possibly have the prior claim."

"That about sums them up." He leaned forward to rest his elbows on his knees and scrubbed at his face with both hands. "It's nothing to how the Admiralty and Army squabble in my world. Supposed to be joint operations but you'd never know it. It's wearing me out."

"Poor Henry." Bunch came to sit beside him and draped her arm around his shoulders.

"How did it lead you to those flats?"

"We hadn't heard from Laura Jarman for a number of days. It seemed sensible to look her up."

"So, she did work for you?"

He shrugged. "We paid her for information. When we were looking into her employer she came into our sphere."

"Because you wanted to keep an eye on Charles Jarman? What do you suspect him of?"

"Nothing, as it turns out. Or so we thought until Laura was killed."

"Followed by poor Kitty. And somebody plainly believed one or both were concealing something," said Bunch. "Did you intend to share any of this with Wright?"

"No more than we are permitted. I would deem it a favour if you didn't divulge any of it to Wright just yet. Splendid chap, but he'll go and put it in some report or other and we can't have that. Not yet. I must check first with my chief." He shrugged. "What more is there to say? We didn't know where she had moved to, and now we do. Learned this at the same time as Wright. And my boss would consider it a huge favour if you kept it quiet. He would have told you this himself just now but he had to leave."

"Daddy? He's your boss?"

"I don't generally get my orders directly from him, but given the exceptional circum—"

"Oh." Bunch let the facts sink in for a moment. She was being asked to hide things from Wright and that felt wrong. But the man Henry answered to, who wanted that secret kept, was her own father; she wondered if she could ever reconcile these allegiances being torn apart.

"Your father is a very important man," Henry murmured. "His department has deep roots."

"I knew he worked directly for the PM – but this is a little … rum."

"He's not the average bunker mole. A lot of the time he's working at … another place."

"It's all right." She held up both hands in defeat. "I know enough to know I don't need to know anymore." From childhood, Edward's diplomatic work was something she had been raised to dance around without asking questions, but it didn't stop her being a little envious of secrets that she wasn't a part of.

She got up and turned off the lights and opened both Blackout curtains and French doors. "Such a lovely night," she said. "And nice to be off duty. When I'm back at the old pile there is always something demanding my attention. You must know how it is. You grew up in farming country. A cow is in calf, or the sheep are out – again. There was a time when we had staff to deal with all of that, but no longer. I slope off on a jolly now and then but seldom overnight." She sighed, gazing out at the garden. A waning moon but a cloudless sky provided enough light to pick out the borders and a freckling of pale blossoms in the rose garden that had been her mother's pride and joy. She breathed in to catch a hint of their perfume. "I can see why Mummy loves to be here." Her voice caught a little as she realised her mother may never stand again where she now stood. "Loved."

"Steady, old girl." Marsham came to fold her into a hug and Bunch rested her head against his shoulder.

Her tears were silent, as was Marsham, as he swayed her gently, stroking her hair. It felt safe and it was such a long time since she'd had a man in her life. Henry had never been a contender, but somehow this felt right…

Somewhere off to the east of the city a siren raised its howl and like dogs in a valley it was answered, the call being taken up closer and closer.

"We should go to your shelter," Marsham whispered against her ear.

"No." She took a half step away from him. "I don't think I

could bear to be shut in. Not tonight." She took him by the hand and led him across the room, out into the hall, and put her hand on the carved newel post at the foot of the staircase. "Do not read any more into this than mutual comfort. Understood?"

"Are you certain? I won't want to be seen to be taking advantage."

"I'm sure. There's a bloody war on. And it's May so we have an excellent reason to gather a few rose buds."

"Pun intended?"

She laughed and led him up to the first landing. "No. Happenstance."

~ Twelve ~

Bunch was woken by Gilsworth drawing back the curtains long after the sun had risen. She stretched and yawned and slowly smiled at the memory of the preceding night. Bunch was not surprised that she was alone in her bed. Henry Marsham was too much the gentleman to allow even the most trusted staff to catch him in their employer's boudoir. *Boudoir? Like some Parisian femme fatale? I wish I were in Paris. Obviously not Paris as it is now – under Hitler's boot – but Paris from before the war. A walk along the West Bank in the May sunshine would have been perfect. What will it be like there now?* She stretched and yawned once again and was about to sit up when she realised she was naked beneath the covers.

"Good morning, Miss Rose. There has been a call from an Inspector Wright. He said he would call for you at nine."

"Good morning, Gilsworth," Bunch said. "What time is it?"

"Just gone seven o'clock, Miss." The housekeeper handed Bunch her robe and diplomatically turned to pick up the breakfast tray from the dresser while Bunch shrugged the silk kimono around her. "I thought you'd want your breakfast, Miss." She set the bed tray across Bunch's lap.

"Thank you." Bunch picked a piece of toast from the rack and scraped a smear of butter on it, avoiding her housekeeper's eye – there was no disguising the housekeeper was all too aware of her night-time activities despite Marsham's early departure. As if delivering breakfast herself rather than sending the maid were not proof enough.

"Will you want me to lay out anything special?"

"The blue slacks and that little forget-me-not blouse."

"Yes, Miss. Shall I run your bath?" the older woman hesitated by the door as if she had something to add.

"Mm," Bunch murmured. "Thank you…"

The sound of water running made Bunch realise she needed to pee. Breakfast in bed was never something she enjoyed, and a slice of toast and a cup of tea was all she managed before she set the tray aside. Then she noted something resting on the bedside table. She picked up the fresh white rosebud and twirled it between her fingers.

"Damn," she muttered. "Soppy old romantic. I should have known better than think he'd be able to keep things simple." She touched the rose against her chin and laughed. "I shall have to let him down gently." *As long as Gilsworth doesn't report me to Daddy. Grown woman or not, I was an idiot to take a chance under his roof.*

She slid out of bed, padded across to the shelves, and slipped the rose between the pages of a book, slotting it back among the others on the shelf. She had no intention of becoming closer to Marsham, no plans for a rematch, but she was fond of him all the same, and grateful for his company and comfort.

"But weightier matters are at hand."

She was bathed and dressed and waiting for Wright by quarter to nine.

"Morning Wright? Did you get your paperwork sorted?"

"I did. Fortunately, the records are kept in the basement so last night's raid didn't interrupt my search. Did you have a good evening with your father?"

"We had a little chat, yes."

"And Marsham?"

"I saw him as well."

"And?"

She looked out of the window to hide her smile. "There's nothing much to tell. He hinted that there may have been informants working at Jarman's, for his department, but they'd nothing to show for their efforts."

"Really? A spy?"

"He was a little vague on that, to be honest." *Dammit Henry*, she thought, *why tell me things you shouldn't. Change the subject!*

"What did you discover?"

Wright frowned at her, saying nothing for a few moments, his lips pursed thoughtfully. *Not fooled in the slightest*, she thought. "Kitty Shenton: youngest child of four," he said at last. "Her mother is a bookkeeper currently living with her eldest son in Wimbledon. Two more brothers – all in the merchant service.

"Her father?"

"Divorced. He's the second officer on a merchant ship."

"With so many children isn't he a little old to still be second officer?"

"Not everyone has the ambition to command a ship," Wright replied. "But in his case he did once captain his own a vessel. That was before he did two years for receiving. Would have been more but Excise couldn't prove it was him smuggling cigars out of Amsterdam."

"Is smuggling tobacco worth it?"

"Not in the small quantities he was allegedly shifting. Which is how he got away with it. Magistrate couldn't see how anyone would risk so much for so little. Plus, of course, Amsterdam is better known for the diamond trade."

"He was smuggling diamonds?"

"Nobody could prove it. Anyway, he lost his master's ticket, which I gather is why the wife left him."

"For getting caught? Or losing his ticket?"

"Probably both."

"What happened to his ship?"

"It was part owned by his eldest son. Not uncommon as a tax dodge. The son bought out his half for a song while he was inside."

"Nice family," said Bunch. "Kick him when he's down. Is he back at sea now?"

"If you mean, does he have an alibi? Yes. He's out with convoys. Things being what they are, experienced officers are gold dust. Even those with a police record. He's currently en route for the Barents Sea. Can't say I envy him that."

"He doesn't know about Kitty? Poor chap. Have you seen her mother yet?"

"Carter spoke with her. It was the mother who trained Kitty as a bookkeeper, in a chandler's office on Bankside."

"You say that as if it's important."

Wright pursed his lips and watched the streets passing them by. "I don't know," he admitted. "It's a real cat's cradle. Threads going all which ways and I've no idea which one to tug at next."

"We're going straight to Mitcham now?"

"By way of Elephant and Castle." He raised an eyebrow at her blank response. "Which is close to Bermondsey."

"I know where it is. It would be important because—"

"Because before she became a respectable sea captain's wife, Kitty Shenton's mother was an associate of Lilly Kendall."

He says that as if I should know who he is talking about. "Lilly Kendall? Remind me."

"The Forty Thieves gang? Female villains and remarkably successful for a good many years. It used to be run by a hard case named Alice Diamond, until she was jailed. You don't have to think too hard about how she got that name. I thought you would have heard of them. They still operate out of Elephant and Castle. It used to be just shoplifting and fencing goods but since the Great War they've been working the society circuit. They turn over wealthy houses using gang members posing as maids, or even house guests."

"And now we are off to see this Alice of the Diamonds."

"No. Alice was caught and jailed, as I said. Lilly Kendall took her place while Alice was inside and when she was released and found she was no longer top dog, she set herself up as a madam. Lilly isn't a patch on Alice Diamond but she runs a tight ship."

"Tight enough for her to risk being involved in this?"

Wright shook his head. "I don't know. I can see her roughing people up. Even junking their homes if they got out of line. But I can't see her sinking to murder. Sadly, I can't say the same for some of the men she associates with, specifically the MacDonald brothers."

"Would any of these people stoop to espionage?"

Wright thought for a moment. "I don't believe so."

"Good to know. Do I get the feeling you know Lilly?"

"I locked horns with her once or twice when I was at Scotland Yard. She's a tough lady. She'd sell her granny for sixpence but I'd lay good odds she's no traitor."

"Then we should go and speak with her. If she knew Kitty she may well have met Laura, and have some idea of what's going on."

"That's the theory but getting her to provide us with anything useful is a completely different matter. Miss Kendall is unlikely to offer up any information voluntarily – as a matter of principle."

"Yet we're going to visit her anyway."

"It will be a short interview and I want you to stay in the car with Glossop."

"Because you think it will be dangerous?" Bunch snorted. "Then why would you walk in there on your own?"

"Lilly won't want to risk uniforms crawling all over her manor because she roughed up a copper."

"Even if he's not a London copper anymore?"

"Especially if he's not a London copper. Unless of course she's covering up something important."

"But she's not. Is she?"

"There is always something to be covered even if it's only her own rear end. It's unlikely to be vital to our case, but I need to check."

"You are completely mad. You can't walk in without any sort of backup."

"My back up is in Sussex."

"No, it isn't. It's right here."

Wright stared at her, lost for words, then looked away. They travelled in silence for a time.

"This is it, sir." Glossop pulled up in front of a large pub and pointed to a small side alley. "It's a dead end. I can squeeze the Wolseley down there but might not get out again."

"You mean not in a hurry."

"Yes, sir."

"Fair enough. Keep a wary eye, and if I'm not back in fifteen minutes call for help."

"Yes, sir."

Wright pulled at the door handle and glanced at Bunch. "If I said stay here—"

"I'd follow."

"Thought as much. Keep your wits but try to act casual. They need to see confidence, trust even."

"Okay."

They walked down the old mews side by side, slowly, warily. Bunch found it hard not to stare at the yard doors and grubby windows they passed, at the stables side by side with garages and assorted workshops. A few of the upper stories seemed to be lived in, judging by the potted plants and occasional washing line. She was aware of movement behind some of those dark panes but didn't dare look to see who or how many faces. She could hear the rush of blood in her head and feel her fingers fizzing with the pressure of her raised pulse. *What the heck am I doing here?* she thought. And at the same time knew exactly why. This was the need to test herself, to feel something other than the tedium of routine. *And this is way off routine.*

The cul-de-sac ended with a large set of wooden doors almost the width of the alley, with a sign reading The Jungle Rooms. There were light bulbs set into the wood around the sign, which Bunch assumed had not been lit since 1939. Set in the right leaf was a smaller door, which opened apparently on its own accord as they came within five paces.

"Lilly's club. She is shrewd enough to have a legitimate cover for her other operations." Wright paused, looking at Bunch. "Are you sure about this? I'd be much happier if you waited in the car."

"Positive."

"All right then. Into the breach." He stepped over the door sill into a garage space and paused for Bunch to join him. A bulky male figure lurked in the shadows, silent and watchful.

"Where now?" Bunch asked.

The henchman pointed at a doorway on the far side, with a smaller Jungle Rooms sign, lit up with multi-coloured bulbs.

"Thank you." Wright grabbed Bunch's arm and ducked through the door. "Lilly Kendall also inherited Alice Diamond's penchant for the dramatic," he murmured.

"She will make a point of controlling this meeting?"

"Precisely. Here we go." A short corridor ended in staircases, one leading up and the other down to a basement level. The distant brass of "In the Mood" clambered up to meet them, getting louder as they neared the bottom of the flight. Another pair of doors were propped open to reveal a sprawling lounge that briefly reminded Bunch of some of the swankier hotels in Nice or the Riviera, and she speculated on whether Kendall was drawing inspiration from magazines or personal observations. *She has an eye for it all, whichever it is.*

Thick wool carpets and vast sofas in velvet and leather. Thick drapes closed off the daylight from the high windows. The room was bathed in soft pools light from a dozen or more lamps dotted around the space, hazy with cigarette smoke. Across one side of the room was a long bar, backlit and mirrored with glass shelves lined with bottles of all shapes and sizes. Bunch had seen similar sights in Paris cafes. It didn't sit quite right with the rest of the club décor but somehow it worked, and she found herself smiling at its sheer audacity.

There were six women in the room, two seated at the bar and the others scattered strategically around the room, looking suspiciously nonchalant to Bunch's eyes. No men, she noticed, but had no doubt they were there, somewhere, watching every move that she and Wright made. Bunch glanced sideways at him to see what he made of it, but his attention was fixed on just one person. A woman in her middle years sitting on the largest of the sofas. She was dressed in a simple blue dress set off by a neat string of pearls and earrings to match. Her hair, carefully coloured a deep brunette, was caught up in a fashionable roll. She might have been a banker's secretary or bookkeeper for the parish relief fund, or even some well-heeled lady of leisure.

Wright stopped a few feet from the woman and tipped his hat. "Lilly. It has been a little while."

"William. How nice." The radio was turned down. "I'd heard tell you retired after that incident at the Harringay track. I hope you are recovered, Inspector." Her accent was neutral. *Schooled*, Bunch thought. *Elocution lessons?*

"More or less," said Wright. "When the balloon went up I was recalled to service. They'll even take old cripples."

"We all must do our bit. My girls and me are all signed up as fire wardens for this block." Lilly Kendall grinned, exposing even white teeth. "We're up nights anyway and we can't have this place going up in flames now, can we." She looked Bunch up and down and tilted her head expectantly. "Your taste in underlings has improved, William." Her smile switched off like a torch. "Hello dear."

Roughly translating to: who the hell are you? "Rose Courtney." Bunch held out her hand and Kendall stared at it for a moment, seeming to consider dismissing it but instead reached out to shake it briefly, even as she turned her attention back to Wright.

"Nice set up." He waved at the room. "It's new?"

"We had the floor above Mac's pub, but we were spending so much time down here these days it seemed silly not to make ourselves at home." She looked around and nodded, her accent changing as she continued. "It works for us. So, Billy-boy—" Lilly rested her gaze on Wright "—what brings you to our humble abode?"

The diminutive made Bunch blink and she stared at him, waiting for a reaction. Wright's lips twitched and then: "A little information, Lilly. As always."

"As always," said Lilly. "And as always, you should know better than to ask."

"Nothing to do with your … business. Nor any of your other dubious connections, not that I'm aware of." He looked down at the floor for a moment. "Firstly, our condolences. Kitty Shenton was one of your … associates, wasn't she? Such a young thing."

Kendall inclined her head. "Thank you. We'll miss her. Are you here about Kitty's death?"

"I'm with Sussex Constabulary now and we are investigating a series of murders. You may have read about them in the newspapers. Bodies left on railway station platforms?"

"I've heard of them." Kendall frowned. "How does that connect with Kitty?"

"Because she was the last victim."

One of the women stifled a cry, and the shock that flickered across Kendall's features at Wright's words was quickly stifled, though it was unmistakable. "Poor child," she murmured.

"Not just Kitty. There have been several other deaths. One was a young woman by the name of Laura Jarman. She shared a flat with Kitty."

Kendall nodded. "I met her. Posh girl, considering."

"Considering what?"

"Her old man. Charles Jarman might have money but he's no more quality than I am." Lilly turned away from Wright to study Bunch closely. "You're the real deal though, aren't you. I've seen your picture in the society pages." She tipped her cigarette holder to drizzle ash into a steel ashtray. "I knew a girl that worked for your family a few years ago. Kensington isn't it."

Goosebumps roused on Bunch's forearms as she realised the inference that a member if this gang had, at some point, been in her family employ. She didn't reply and Kendall's lips tweaked upwards without a hint of humour.

Wright edged in front of Bunch, taking back Lilly's attention. "You know the Jarmans?"

"Not well. Kitty worked at the factory as a clerk. She was a bright girl, had a good head for figures. We shall miss her."

"Odd that Kitty was working there – Mitcham's a bit out of your usual patch."

"My patch? Kitty bagged herself a decent job. She was offered the chance and she grabbed it. Smart girl."

"She no longer worked for you?"

"No," Kendall admitted. "But she left with my blessing, so don't go thinking it was anything to do with this place. Kitty was never cut out for our line of work. Too sweet. Too brainy. Nose stuck in a book when she wasn't totting up our accounts."

"She was your bookkeeper?"

"A good one, as I said. She'd had proper schooling before her old man was put away. We could've done without our accountant if she'd stayed here. Maybe that was why Clem introduced her to Jarman."

"Clem?"

"Our accountant – he didn't want us cutting him out." She shrugged. "Not that there was any danger. She never knew enough about the way the City worked to get ahead. Money needs traders to grow, which she wasn't. Young Kitty got herself a job with prospects. She could've progressed. And then some bastard offs her. You surely do not think it was anything to do with me, William?" Kendall raised her chin to stare at him. "I run a strict family. You know that. Strict but fair and bumping off people for no cause is not a part of that."

"That hasn't always been the case."

A rustling around the room reminded Bunch of that sense of predatory intent when she entered her Uncle Roddy's falconry mews. The jingle of bracelets replaced the sound of a falconer's bells, a faint rustle of cloth in lieu of agitated feathers. There was a rise in tension among the women perched in strategic points around the room. Behind her, Bunch heard the unmistakable click of a firing mechanism, then another. She didn't dare look around to check what she was hearing.

Wright did not take his eyes from Kendall's as he slowly batted the air down with the flats of his hands. "Lilly, please." His tone was quiet and unashamedly placatory. "I am *not* investigating your affairs. I am trying to catch a killer of young women and I would appreciate your help."

"And I hope you find them – for their sake."

"They'll hang, Lilly. I promise you."

"The short drop and a quick death," she drawled. "Relatively speaking."

An expression flitted through Kendall's brown eyes that Bunch could not interpret. *I wonder if she knows how her emotions sometimes run across her face,* Bunch thought. *Or am I meant to read her that way?*

"I assume she got to know Laura while working at the factory rather than … the other way round?"

"Whatever liaisons Kitty made were none of my business. Or yours, I suspect." Kendall's face, which Bunch had briefly thought so easily deciphered, was suddenly impassive, like the celluloid masks of a shop dummy, and far more chilling. "I can't imagine Sir Edward Courtney's heir would move in the same circles as Charlie Jarman."

"I do know him," Bunch replied. "I found Charles Jarman something of a bore."

Kendall's perfect Victory Red lips pulled back in a grin. "I agree. Nasty bit of work. Hires and fires like nobody's business, according to Kitty. Or he used to. Bit harder now, with the war on." She nodded to Wright. "Is that all, Billy-boy? Only we're busy. Things to do, people to see."

A small silence simmered between Wright and Kendall. Bunch noted that she had not heard the cocked weapons being stood down. She felt her body begin to vibrate at being held so still for so long and hoped Wright was as eager to leave as she was.

"You've been very helpful, Lilly," he said. "I'm sure we won't need to come back. But if we do…?"

"A warm welcome awaits you, as always."

"Thank you, Lilly. Goodbye for now." Wright nodded to her. "Ladies." He gave the room a rapid smile as he tugged his hat in place.

"Bye-bye, Billy-boy. Miss Courtney."

"Pleasure to meet you, Miss Kendall. Goodbye."

Wright propelled Bunch towards the stairwell and briskly up the stairs and out to the mews. The door snapped shut on their heels.

"I say—" Bunch began.

"Keep walking," Wright muttered, his hand on the small of her back pushing her towards the main road beyond. "Don't speak and don't look back." They did not utter a word even when they reached the police Wolseley.

"Where to Guv?" Glossop asked a few moments after they climbed in the car. Her eyes reflected in the rear-view mirror were questioning, though she knew better than to ask for more than basic commands.

"To Jarman's Engineering next," said Wright. "Commonside, Mitcham."

"Sir."

The silence continued for a few minutes after they had left the alley behind them.

"Tough cookies," Bunch said finally.

"Dangerous," Wright growled. "I should not have taken you in with me."

"We came out unscathed," she replied. "Was it more by luck than grace? Do you think they would have really shot us?"

Wright shook his head. "I doubt it. Kendall is much more circumspect than her old boss. Alice Diamond would have been a different prospect."

"Was it worth the risk? She didn't tell us anything we didn't already know."

"Perhaps," he said. "When you have a chat with people like Lilly, they don't give up information readily. Especially in front of potential witnesses, even if they are her own lieutenants."

"Why talk to us at all, in that case?"

"Partly bravado, but also because she wanted to see if we had any idea who killed Kitty Shenton."

"To defend them?"

"Far from it. If her girls, or worse, the chaps in the Elephant and Castle mob, find him before we do, we may never clap eyes on the killer."

"More headless corpses in trunks?"

"A shallow grave in Epping Forest would be my guess. She was telling us something though, I'm sure. The trick is reading between the lines – it requires a strong light and a code book."

"We only need to learn how to decipher it?"

"Exactly."

Bunch lit a cigarette as she considered the problem. "Piece of cake," she said. "One of our five impossible things for the day."

~ ~ ~

Despite a nightly forest of barrage balloons, Croydon Aerodrome and the factories in the surrounding areas had drawn a lot of attention from the Luftwaffe bombers. "Or perhaps because of them," said Wright as they passed another blasted factory site. "It is a wonderful way to advertise something that's worth protecting from Göring's bombers."

"I would imagine Göring's flyboys know Croydon well enough even without the party balloons." Bunch eyed the ravaged streets that were every bit as desolate as the east end of London. "Slightly bonkers having an RAF field near here, one would have thought. So many civilians."

"No less mad than having a half-dozen munitions factories a stone's throw away," Wright murmured. "Here we are," he added.

They turned into a yard similar to a few dozen others in the area. A small office section stood closest to the entrance and from it ran a long single storey building of rendered brick and shuttered windows. Its tin roof was pockmarked by skylights at regular intervals, which had once made use of as much natural light as possible but were now boarded over so that production continued during the night-time shifts.

The engineering shop floor generated a lot of noise, heard even in the confines of the offices where a half-a-dozen women worked in the main room. Two smaller offices were cordoned off by partitions, solid to a height of four feet and glazed up to the ceiling. Both were occupied though only the tops of the heads of the people sitting at desks could be seen. Next to the offices a fire door declared Authorised Personnel Only. At the far end of the space was a panelled door labelled C Jarman.

"Wait here," said Wright.

"But…"

Wright was already opening the door to one of the goldfish bowl offices, leaving her to stare at the low-ceilinged room, at the small team of typists and clerks, and wondering how they were able to concentrate with the constant hum and clatter ringing through the place. It was a world away from the quiet of her Perringham estate office, where the loudest noises she had to contend with were the rattling of a Fordson tractor out in the yard, or a swoosh of fighter planes from one of the nearby airfields. She tried hard not to breathe in the all-pervasive odours of grease, hot metals and paint, smells that were as equally different to her as farmyard odours were to city girls. She grinned. "Horses for courses."

"Not too many horses here."

She jumped as Wright appeared at her side along with a grizzled balding man dressed in a worn suit.

"Find him?" she said.

"Jarman is here. He's on the shop floor."

"So, we do get to talk with him."

"He says he won't let you down there."

"Me? Why? Who?"

"Mr Jarman," the older man growled, "doesn't allow office staff on the factory floor. He says women are too distracting."

"Nonsense, man. I was mending trucks in France just eighteen months ago."

Wright laid a hand on her arm. "Their house rules," he said and dropped his voice to a murmur. "These girls who may know more about Laura and Kitty. Talk to them."

Bunch was annoyed at being excluded even though she had no real wish to speak with Charles Jarman again. He was an arrogant pig in her opinion; however, what Wright had asked of her made sense. She nodded. "Off you go then. Talk with Jarman."

She waited until Wright had vanished with his guide before sauntering across to the nearest desk where a woman of around thirty was bent over a ledger. Her light-brown hair was fashionably brushed and permed back from her brows so that it curled around her shoulders. When she looked up to meet Bunch's gaze her face was lightly powdered, her lips carefully coloured in the same newly fashionable Victory Red worn by the women Bunch and Wright had encountered in the mews basement. It was a collective thumbed nose to Hitler's infamous dislike of women sporting brightly painted lips. The woman cast a brief glance at the windowed office and smiled at Bunch. "May I help you?"

"Rose Courtney." Bunch held out her hand.

Another nervous glance at the office and a brief shake of the hand. "Linda Manning."

Bunch twisted slightly to look at the ledger Linda was filling in. "You're a bookkeeper?"

"Yes. Well … I enter the ins and outs and keep a running line. Mr Archer does the final totting up."

"Of course." Bunch nodded slowly. "I do that sort of stuff as well. Gets tedious sometimes, doesn't it." She looked around the room. "It's quiet in here – apart from the typewriters, and that. And the awful factory noise, of course." She gestured at the fire doors and the young woman grinned.

"Mr Archer doesn't encourage chatter," she said. "Especially with anyone from the shop floor."

"I bet he doesn't. But I am categorically not from the shop floor. Have you been doing this job for long?"

Linda shook her head. "I came in February. There were three men doing my job before me. They've joined up."

"You're terribly busy, one imagines."

"Heaven knows what those men did all day, but I haven't been rushed off my feet. Or I wasn't until now." She tapped her fingers on the edge of the ledger before her. "Kitty was a bit of a whizz with numbers. They going to miss her like mad."

"You knew Kitty?"

"As well as most. She was very close to Miss Jarman."

"They shared a flat, I understand."

"Yes. Poor Kitty was devastated when Miss Jarman went missing and then we heard she was dead too." Another glance at the window.

Like a nervous tic, Bunch thought.

"Is it true what the papers said? Kitty was stuffed inside a suitcase?"

"She was, the poor woman. I gather Miss Jarman hadn't been working here for long, either."

"No. She had a terrible fall out with the boss. It was awful sitting out here listening to them. Terrible things they said."

"Oh… What about?"

"Most of it was the usual father-daughter stuff. Her saying he didn't treat her like a grown-up. Him saying she was a spoiled child. Could have been me and my dad."

Bunch mirrored Linda's fear of office gossip being reported and sat on the edge of the desk to bring herself into a conspiratorial huddle. "What about the rest of their arguments?" she murmured.

"Something to do with accounts," she replied. "It had Kitty and me nervous because it was us doing the donkey work and we thought we were going to get dragged into the office too, but it was only Mr Archer that the boss spoke with afterwards. Kitty was acting very strange. I thought it was her feeling awkward about … about Miss Jarman living at her place."

"It wasn't?"

Linda looked a little confused. "No. It was a weird to-do going on in there." She jerked her head towards the door to the workshops. "And Mr Archer—"

"That would make sense if there was a problem with the figures. Your Mr Archer oversees all that, yes?"

"Mr Jarman takes them home once a quarter to go over them. I expect that's why he's here today. When it isn't him it's one of those financial advisors."

"And who would that be?"

"Mr Archer said it was a company of chartered accountants and none of anyone's business but Mr Jarman's." She paused. "That seemed to be what Miss Jarman was angry about."

"Having books audited is normal in business."

"That's what I told Kitty but she got obsessed about it after Miss Laura…" Linda looked down at her work and Bunch turned to see who had spooked the girl.

"Miss Courtney, we meet once more. How are you?"

"Mr Jarman." Bunch slid from the desk. "I was hoping to call on Mrs Jarman again. Is she receiving visitors yet?"

"That depends on who is visiting her. The Honourable Miss Courtney or Rose Courtney, private eye?"

"Consulting detective," she growled.

"Almost a policeman – sorry, woman." He was daring her to reply.

"And I'm quite happy as I am, Charles." He flinched at her use of his first name. *Condescending old dinosaur.* She turned her back on him and smiled at Linda. "I am terribly sorry about your friend. So difficult to lose people, and it's happening so horribly often now with this bloody war." She was aware of Jarman flinching once more, this time at her language, she assumed, and felt a childish pleasure in shocking him. It was a satisfying balm to her own shock at the earlier confrontation with Lilly Kendall.

"Thank you, Mr Jarman," she heard Wright say. "We shall be back as soon as we have any information. And of course, if you think of anything…"

"I shall telephone you," Jarman said, "though I can't think I will be able to help any further."

"The smallest thing may sometimes be very important," Wright said. "Good day." He grabbed Bunch by the arm and steered her outside. "What was all that about?" he asked.

"Something odd is definitely going on here." She related her conversation with Linda Manning as they returned to the car and then headed south.

"And we arrived back just as she was about to reveal something useful?"

"I don't know. Probably not. I don't think she was a close friend of Kitty or Laura, though I rather think she wanted to be part of their circle. Even then, she made a few catty comments about them being more than good friends."

"You mean that they were lovers?"

"Don't be such a prude, William. It isn't illegal, you know. For the record, I don't think they were, at least not seriously. I suspect they were more comrades in arms. Linda hinted that Kitty and Laura were worried about something to do with the accounts."

"Jarman is cooking the books? Is that a good enough reason to kill one's own child?"

"Not Jarman. No, I don't believe so. But there is the external accountant."

"Maybe it is about money being syphoned away. You'd think Laura would have had it out with her father if she suspected someone was stealing from the family coffers."

"Perhaps she did. Perhaps the money was only a part of it." Bunch leaned back and ran her fingers through her hair. "My brain is positively fried. A good night's sleep and I might start seeing the wood for the trees."

"You didn't sleep well?"

"Not used to raids." She stared out the window, certain Wright would see guilt written all over her face. *Not that it's any of his business. God ... last night was such a mistake. What was I thinking?* "I need to get home," she said. "The estate doesn't run itself and I have to see Mummy. My father especially asked me to visit her. And frankly ... frankly, I need a little sanity after today. Those women in that club were quite frightening."

"They were as on edge as you," Wright said. "They were rattled by something connected to the deaths of Laura Jarman and Kitty Shenton. I have put out some feelers with my Scotland Yard contacts, though we'll have to wait a few days for results."

"Your friend Lilly Kendall...?"

"What about her?"

"She wasn't telling us anything at all, but I'm sure she knows a great deal."

"And we will never know the half of it."

"Surely if she has information she should provide a statement."

"Would your sister's in-law – Percy Guest – have assisted the police?"

"Well no, but he's a fugitive."

"As are half the people working for Lilly."

"You already mentioned that. You said you've had many dealings with her before."

"I never said they were good."

"You think they would have shot you if I hadn't been there?"

"God, no." He looked down at his hands. "I hope not. They

would have been a lot less polite, I'm sure. In some strange way Lilly owes me. I was part of the team that arrested her old boss."

"Where does that leave us now?"

"Not much further forward, I'm sorry to say. Lilly seems to know something about the Jarmans, but that may be because of Kitty's gossip. We will check for anything that links them. You want to stop for lunch?"

"No, I should get home. Thank you."

~ Thirteen ~

The inferences to be had from the summons from the Red House hadn't escaped them, yet by tacit agreement Bunch and Dodo talked all around the topic on the drive across the county. The chances to chat with her sister were getting fewer and farther between. Dodo had a life Bunch could not begin to understand, as a young widow and now a mother, but their similar roles as farm managers was one subject they could share. Then still avoiding their mother's impending demise, Dodo asked Bunch about a different kind of death.

"I heard from Granny that you were going to go off on your case with Wright today. Something to do with those awful bodies in suitcases?"

"Granny says far too much. Strictly speaking, they are bodies in steamer trunks." She flashed Dodo a small grin. "Did you know Laura Jarman?"

"Only in passing. She was a little younger than me, and you know how one or two years can make all the difference. We were seldom at the same gatherings."

"I doubt she would have been invited. The father is a strange one."

"I met Stephen Jarman a few times when he started walking out with Mary Carmichael – such an odd match. Mary knew Laura quite well; I assume that's how she met Stephen."

"They were married recently."

"Were they? Goodness. I am so behind with all the gossip."

"I was hoping to swing by the Jarman's home while we are out today. I know it seems insensitive, but the case is becoming increasingly difficult. I shall be happy to take you to the Red House first, though, if that suits you better?"

"Is that why you hustled me out of the house so early?" Dodo glanced at her watch. "You want to visit them before seeing Mummy?"

"I don't think I shall feel able to see the Jarmans after."

"All right, let's do it. It will be like old times. Shenanigans for the Courtney girls."

"If you're sure, that's frightfully good of you, Dodo. It's not as important as seeing Mummy, of course. The poor lamb is so dreadfully frail."

"I know what you mean. I come away from Mummy completely wrung out."

Bunch reached across and clasped her sister's hand, resting in her lap. "Chin up old thing, we'll get through it."

"We shall. So tell me, what are you hoping to learn from the Jarmans?"

"Absolutely anything," Bunch replied. "Wright is trying to find a link between Laura and some desperate villainous types from along The Old Kent Road. Or should I say, between them and Charles Jarman. If it's to be believed, Mary Carmichael and Laura were originally best pals and it was Mary who set Laura off on her London sojourn. That may have been so much eyewash though, easier to blame someone else for a daughter running away rather than looking closer to home. He's the sort of man who would never admit he might be in the wrong."

"We must speak with Mary in that case. That should be easy – I knew her older sister."

"You're a peach."

"Anything else I need to go armed with?"

"I wish there were – unless you can steer the conversation towards Haven Cottage and a reason why Laura might have visited it."

"So one, why did Laura go to London—" Dodo held up one finger "—and two, why she would have been at Haven Cottage." She held up a second finger.

"On the nail," Bunch replied. "Hang on a moment while I get my bearings. The house is just along here somewhere… Here we are." She waved her ID at the guards as she drove through, and they were soon pulling up at the front of Gellideg House. Bunch glanced up at the stream of high herringbone clouds. "I hope it doesn't rain. I like driving with the top down. Plus, we have a first hay crop to cut at Perringham."

"As do we." Dodo giggled as she untied the scarf that had held her hat down on the drive. "Gosh listen to us talking about hay and rain. Just like a pair of old farmers."

"As opposed to a pair of young ones?" Bunch clicked the MG's door shut and looked up at the house. "Can you present your card? I don't think the housekeeper liked me very much last time I called."

"Absolutely." Dodo skipped up the two steps and tugged the bell pull. "Mrs Tinsley to see Mrs Mary Jarman." She passed her card to the housekeeper who inspected it as if it were poison – and glared past Dodo at Bunch.

"I called to pay respects to Mrs Jarman senior once before." Bunch smiled sweetly. "I'm told she's receiving visitors now."

"If you will wait, Miss, I shall ask if they are home,"

They stepped into the hallway and their doorkeeper vanished towards the rear of the house.

"Cheerful soul," Dodo whispered.

"Isn't she. Makes me appreciate Knapp. I would not be surprised if Charles Jarman picked her for her scintillating door-side manner."

Dodo began to giggle. "If she were a doctor, it would be terminal."

Bunch snorted. "If she were a doctor…"

Dodo nudged her. "Shh. Here she comes again."

"This way, please." The housekeeper led them through to a large and lush Edwardian conservatory. The centre was dominated by a Carrara marble fountain so large that it blocked the view of the doors at the far side. Water cascaded from a copper fleur-de-lis at its apex with sufficient force to soak the potted plants all around it. Blinds lined the conservatory roof to protect the palms and orchids cramming both sides from harsh sunlight. Despite the shade it was warm and humid. The heat acting on the lush growth released a heavy scent of flowers and damp compost.

The housekeeper paused at the door long enough to announce "Mrs Tinsley and Miss Courtney" before striding away into the depths of the house, leaving the sisters to sidle into the dim green cavern – with not a soul in sight.

"Do you think we shall need a machete?" Dodo whispered.

"Possibly. It looks as if Johnny Weissmuller might come swinging down from that fountain at any moment."

"Hello there." A light childlike voice hailed them. "I apologise for Tanner abandoning you in the jungle. Our housekeeper does a very fair impression of a bulldog with the toothache, but she runs this house like a well-balanced clock, and she's been with my mother-in-law since forever." Mary Jarman, nee Carmichael, waved at the sisters through the depths of the greenery. She was a short stocky young woman with voluminous pale hair, and equally pale but intense eyes, and the widest grin Bunch had ever seen that didn't belong to a horse. "Daphne. How lovely to see you. Do come and sit. Mother, this is Mrs Daphne Tinsley and the honourable Miss Rose Courtney." Mary waved them to a metal garden table sited just beyond the double doors, which Mary closed behind them. "I hope you don't mind being out here. Mother likes to take coffee among the flowers, though it's rather stuffy inside – and my father-in-law is very fussy about his orchids, keeping them out of drafts."

"I hadn't imagined Mr Jarman as a gardener," said Bunch.

"Some men go shooting, others play golf. It could be far worse. Charles grows orchids. But in his favour, he doesn't drink and he's not a violent man." Selina Jarman smiled and inclined her head in a regal move that reminded Bunch of her grandmother. "Do sit down." She didn't rise to greet the sisters as she waved them to a seat.

Facially at least, Selina appeared as Laura Jarman might have looked in twenty years or so. *If a touch skinnier.* Bunch could see that the woman was so reed thin her knees made points beneath the folds of her linen skirt, and she wondered if Mrs Jarman had always been that way or if it was a result of the conflict with Laura … and her murder.

"Mrs Jarman." Bunch pulled out one of the cast metal chairs around the table and sat; Dodo followed suit. "Please accept our condolences. My grandmother wanted to send her regards and to apologise for not being able to visit in person."

"That is kind of her. I haven't seen Beatrice for such a long while."

"Granny's getting a little frail these days," Dodo added. "She doesn't get out as much. She won't admit it of course."

A sudden smile lit Selina's face and took ten years off her

appearance. "Your grandmother was always a force of nature and such an inspiration to us youngsters in the women's leagues."

"She still is," Dodo replied.

"I heard your mother has not been well," said Mary. "Is she any better?"

"I'm afraid not. She's staying at the Red House – the nursing home."

"Oh." Mary leaned forward and touched Dodo's arm. "I am sorry. If there is anything we can do, you only need ask." Her hand dropped away. "Our families seem to have had more than their fair share of grief."

"Do send her my regards," Selina added.

"I shall," Bunch replied. "We are off to visit her today, in fact, but we thought we should make a little detour to deliver Granny's message. It isn't much out of our way." Bunch paused. "I called on you before but you were not up to visitors."

"I'm sorry about that, about not receiving guests, I mean. So many people called but I simply couldn't face any of them."

"I understand. The last thing you need at a time like that was a handful of visitors stamping all around the place. I did have quite a chat with Mr Jarman, though. And Stephen, of course." She smiled briefly at Mary. "They told me that Laura had been living in London for a little while…"

"Yes." Selina flushed slightly. "She was very keen to join the war effort."

"Wasn't she already doing that here in Jarman's research facilities? It's important work, after all."

"She always said it felt rather like cheating," said Mary. "As if she wasn't making any real contribution, as most people were."

"She was, but I can empathise." Bunch rolled her eyes. "Being dragged into the family business never feels like a proper job, does it, even if the jobs for us women makes something of a change from the usual—" She could almost feel the drop in temperature and wondered if she had mistimed her quip. "But Laura worked for Jarman's in Croydon?" she went on. "Not here at the house?"

"She worked at the labs for a while," Selina said. "Then she and Charles had a falling out. I never discovered about what or why."

Charles blames Selina, who blames Charles. I wonder which is closer to the truth. "Families invariably have their disagreements," Bunch said aloud.

"Robert joining up didn't help Charles' mood, and Stephen would have followed too if it wasn't for his arm. Charles gets angry easily. That's his way. He got angry with Laura once too often. Please don't misjudge him, he's a good man really, but *his* father taught him that strength was all about never backing down."

"Men can be such idiots," said Dodo. "My father-in-law is just the same. All bluster and blow, shouting orders at anyone who's not listening." She grinned at Bunch. "He's soft as butter on the inside, isn't he?"

"Exactly, but you're not Barty's daughter. Surely you and Mr Jarman get along well most of the time?" Bunch said to Mary.

"True. Laura always bumped horns with Charles, probably because they were so terribly alike in that respect." Mary smiled at Selina.

"Both as stubborn as they come," Selina said.

"Sounds familiar. Remember the rows Daddy and I used to have, Dodo?"

"The entire estate remembers them." Dodo rolled her eyes at Mary and Selina. "He couldn't get her off to finishing school fast enough."

Selina glanced at her hands clenching and unclenching in her lap. "I'd finally persuaded Charles that we should send Laura to Munich to finish," she whispered. "She was a little older than some of the girls but I had it all arranged for '39 and then – *pocccch!*" She spread her hands as if imitating a ballooning explosion. "All of Europe went to hell." Mary grasped her mother-in-law's hands. "Our darling Laura; she always seemed to have the most rotten luck. Goodbye fun on le continent, hello mucky munitions factory."

"I promise you we shall find out what happened to her, one way or another," Bunch said.

"Poor girl," added Dodo. "When did she start working at the factory?"

"It was some months ago. Then we find out she had another huge row with Charles – and that was the last we heard from her."

"She didn't want to come back to live here? Or somewhere nearby with friends perhaps? Brighton, for example?"

"Because that was where her body was discovered?" Mary shook her head. "Not that we knew."

"Charles hinted at something of the kind but…"

"He blamed me," said Mary. "I tried to visit her several times but she was never in. I don't think she was avoiding me, or anything. She simply wasn't at the flat when I called. And she never answered the telephone. A neighbour of hers said she was on fire watch or some such most nights. Then she moved and we had no idea where…"

"You never knew where she worked after she left the factory?"

"Not a clue. We assumed she was offered work by some of her friends, and so stayed in London. You know how that sort of a thing goes."

"Was the friend Kitty Shenton?"

"Indirectly it may have been, I suppose. I knew Kitty slightly from way back." Mary blushed. "I was … removed from school and attended a small place near Wimbledon for a term. Kitty was there on a scholarship." She glanced down at her hands. "And now the poor girl is also dead. I heard that from the policeman who came round again yesterday. He seemed convinced Kitty's death was linked with Laura's, which does not make any sense when she's a victim herself."

"Chief Inspector Wright said that?"

"No, not him. It was another chap. His sergeant, I think."

Carter. Typical of him, clod hopping idiot. "Kitty was trying to help Laura and she paid for it with her life." The atmosphere dropped another degree and Bunch swore to herself. *What is wrong with me today? I am losing my touch.* "Sergeant Carter is a good man but doesn't always see the larger picture. Kitty *was* attempting to help and continued trying to do so after Laura vanished. Something was going on at the factory and it took both of their lives."

"Charles has never mentioned any suspicious activities," Selina replied. "But then he wouldn't. Since the War Department became involved in his research he has been very secretive."

"He would be," said Dodo. "Our father works for … the Ministry. He's always talking about walls and ears and all that stuff." She laughed, a little girl laugh, flicking her hair and holding the backs of her fingers to her mouth, every inch the dizzy debutante. Bunch glanced at her and suppressed a grin. She envied her sister's ability to turn on the "helpless" act, seemingly at will, something she could never get away with herself.

"Do you suspect Kitty may have been involved with anything illegal, maybe indirectly?" Mary asked. "She was recommended to Charles by our accountant."

"She was?"

"Apparently Kitty had been working for another of his clients and he thought she could do better for herself at Jarman's." Mary shrugged at Bunch's raised brow. "Charles thinks I don't take an interest in the business, but I do. My mother was quite the emancipator, you know. That was how she knew your grandmama." She shook her head. "I wanted to work for my uncle. He's in publishing, you know. I had a stint at a secretarial school, to learn shorthand and that sort of thing."

"That would be useful," said Bunch. "Did this accountant chap—"

"Ladies," said Charles Jarman.

They all turned to stare at him. Bunch swore silently and wondered how long he had been listening because his interruption seemed too perfectly timed to be coincidental. *Which is interesting. What is it he doesn't want us to know?*

"Miss Courtney. I thought I recognised that odd little motor. To what do we owe this pleasure?"

"Good morning," Bunch muttered.

"I wished to pay my respects," Dodo cut in, "and as Rose and I were motoring over to see our mother in the nursing home we thought this was the right opportunity. I knew Laura, you see, and Granny also wanted to pass on her condolences. I'm Daphne Tinsley by the way." She held out her left hand to shake his, in an odd gesture, Bunch thought, until she realised her sister was flashing her wedding band. "I'm so pleased to meet you."

"Mrs Tinsley." Jarman stepped forward to shake her hand very briefly.

There was no mistaking the venom in the look he directed towards Bunch, and the awkward silence that followed his appearance told her she was not the only one to notice. She made a show of checking her watch. "Well now, I hate to appear rude but we should be on our way. The sisters at the Red House can be quite strict about visiting hours."

They left in a hurry, waiting until they were well away from Gellideg before either mentioned their visit.

"So that was Charles," said Dodo. "Rum sort of chap."

"One way of describing him. I should like to know what he's hiding. The look he gave me!"

"I noticed, but surely you can't believe he was involved with Laura's murder?"

"No. He loved his little girl. They fought tooth and nail, yes, but I doubt he was ever as angry with her as people make out, or he'd never have let her work at his factory."

"Yet the rows between them continued after she left Gellideg," said Dodo. "She wasn't a giddy girl just out of school, as I recall, so something drastic had to have happened."

"The anger came from her, I think, but there's more to it than a simple rebellious phase. We need to talk to that office girl again."

"More importantly, find out who this accountant is."

"By 'we' I mean Wright and me," said Bunch. "Jarman's is a limited company and will be listed in Companies House. They have basic bookkeepers for the day-to-day figures — wages and such — but the external accountant would do far more than that. The police should have no problems tracing both them and any auditors." She took her eyes off the road briefly to give her sister a hard look. "This is not something you should be involved with. Taking you to the Jarman's house was risky enough because… It's not just Laura and Kitty. There have been five bodies that we know of over the past months. These people, whoever they are — they *are* animals. And they will have no problem killing you if you get too close to their operation."

"Or you, Bunch. It's no more dangerous or different for me than it is for you. I'm a grown woman and you can't treat me like your baby sister."

"I know you're a capable woman, dear heart, but there is one major difference. You have Georgi to consider and she needs you more than anything else."

"I know, but—"

"But nothing. Your job right now is for me to talk to you, to talk through the case, aloud, and for you to tell me when you think I am going off at a tangent. That is of more use than you might imagine. Deal?"

"It's a deal. So, what do you think? Is Jarman a crook?"

"Jarman doesn't need to be a crook. From what I understand, he's making cartloads of legitimate money from munitions. With the WD watching his every move he'd be mad to try anything that stupid. And I repeat, I do not believe he killed his daughter."

"What evidence is there, whether he did or didn't?"

"None, beyond the fact he employed her at his factory despite their falling out. Why would he do that if there was a real problem between them? It simply doesn't add up."

"Selina made him back down?"

"Doubtful."

"I can see another 'but' moment," said Dodo.

"He probably knows who killed his daughter," Bunch replied. "Or he suspects that he knows who."

"Then why doesn't he inform the police?"

"Who can tell what goes on with a man like him? I would bet a pony he *is* on to whomever he thinks is responsible. It would explain why he is being so offhand with the enquiry. I should not care to be in their shoes right now. You've heard the old saying: don't get mad, get even? Jarman is the sort to do both."

"Oh heavens, you think he will track down the killer, himself? Would he kill him?"

"If he gets to him – or them – first. I'm sure Jarman is more than capable to do away with someone in a quite inventive fashion." She pulled into the entrance to the Red House grounds and stopped at the end of a small line of cars near the front doors. "Not missed visiting hour, which is good. Come on old girl."

Dodo didn't make any move to leave the MG. "Am I awful if I say I'm not looking forward to this?"

Bunch paused, the car door half-open. She'd never considered that her sister, who was so much closer to Theadora than she ever was, would be anything but desperate to visit their mother. The meeting with the Jarmans had been a distraction, with all the chatter about crime and murder only putting off the moment when they had to walk through the Red House doors. "Not in the slightest, old thing," she replied. "I don't hate it any less. It's not the visiting, not the place, and not mother – it's how she is."

"It's horrid. None of us want to remember her like this."

"The only alternative is not seeing her at all."

"I know, but every time I come here it gets harder to walk through those doors." Dodo swung her legs neatly round to set both feet on the gravel driveway. "But here we are."

"Here we are." Bunch scrambled out to link arms with her. "Best foot forward, as Nanny would have said."

Theadora was not basking in the sunshine as they had expected, though the doors leading to the enclosed gardens stood open. She lay propped on a swathe of pillows, eyes closed, her jaundiced skin, which had always been stretched tight across high cheekbones, now puffy and moist. Despite the scent of her mother's favourite musk and the wafts of fresh-cut grass drifting in through the open doors, the odours of disinfectant and incontinence still crept around them.

Bunch had only visited a few days earlier and the drastic change in her mother both shocked and frightened her; because of her nurse's training she knew what the changes signalled. She watched her mother's breath coming in wheezing sighs, and eyed the oxygen cylinder next to the bed, black and sinister, its brick-red rubber face mask looped over the dial. It was new to the décor since the previous visit and seemed to sum up their being called to this bedside. A young nun, Sister Agnes, was clearing away a bowl of soapy water, sponge and towel as they entered the room and she turned to greet them with a shy smile.

"Should we go?" Bunch asked, "if she's asleep?"

"No, no, she's not really asleep. I've finished now, just giving her Ladyship a little spruce up, ready for her visitors."

"She looks as if she's sleeping," Dodo said.

"She does, but…" The nun straightened the counterpane stretched over the cage that kept its weight from the patient. "Her Ladyship drifts in and out of awareness."

"She was so much better when I was here before," said Bunch.

"Things can go downhill very quickly in these cases. And then there's the morphine. For the pain, you understand. Doctor Amis gave her an injection just half-an-hour ago and it tends to make her drowsy. We weren't expecting anyone to visit for a little while yet. Your father said he wouldn't be here until late afternoon. Of course, the illness itself makes her tired." All the while she chattered, the nun tidied the damp towels and straightened the pillows. Brisk and efficient. "There. All done. Please, ladies, sit with her for a while. Her Ladyship gets confused but she will know you are here, I'm sure. Try not to let her get excited, though. I'll toddle off and leave you to it. Don't be afraid to ring the bell." She patted the call button close to Theadora's hand and then hoisted the bowl of sudsy water, balancing it against her hip. "Right, I'll just get rid of this," she said and trotted out into the corridor.

For a few moments there was quiet, other than the in/out of Theadora's bubbling lungs and distant voices from other patients chattering with their guests out on their various verandas.

"Should we wake her?" Dodo whispered.

"The sister said she wasn't asleep." Bunch pulled one of the two chairs up to the bedside and took hold of Theadora's warm and clammy fingers. "Mummy? It's Bunch. Rose-bunch. And Daphne's here too. Mother? Mummy?"

"No need to shout, Rose. You always were a noisy child. Has that chatterbox nun finally gone?"

"Hello Mummy. If you mean Sister Agnes, yes. She seemed rather sweet."

Theadora blinked her eyes half-open. "I thought nuns were supposed to glide around in silence but that one prattles on like some demented Lyons nippy."

"Mother, that's too shocking." Bunch gave her mother's hand a gentle tap and sat back with a smile. *Glad she can make jokes, at least.* "The Augustinians are not a silent order, as you well know, and I have no doubt young Sister Agnes is a charming girl."

"Too young to be sloshing sponges around willy-nilly," Theadora snapped.

So that's what it is. Embarrassed by the blanket bath. "Being an invalid is horrible, isn't it? Embarrassing to have your body not your own, but don't be churlish, Mummy — that's what you kept telling me when I was laid up after my accident. She's doing her best for you."

Dodo glared at Bunch to shut up. "How are you feeling, Mummy?" she said. "The sister said you've been given morphine. Is it dreadful?"

"It really is hard to think." Theadora struggled to sit straighter and only made a token protest when Bunch and Dodo gently hoisted her forward and inserted a spare pillow behind her head. "Thank you, dears. It's quite strange looking at the world from the horizontal. Where's Georgi?" Theadora's eyes struggled to focus as she peered around the room.

"She's at home. I would have brought her today but Bunch's car…"

"Mm." Theadora nestled her head in the pillow and closed her eyes. After a few seconds of quiet she drew a long breath that sounded very much like a snore.

"Mummy?"

"Mother?"

The sisters looked at each other and shrugged. "Should we just leave, do you think?"

"You've only just arrived."

Dodo sat forward in her chair and draped herself over the coverlet, her cheek resting on her mother's right hand. "We thought you were asleep."

"Mostly I am. Talk to me. Tell me about the real world beyond these cloisters. What have you been doing today?"

"We went to see Selina Jarman," Dodo murmured. "Granny wanted us to pass on condolences."

"Ah yes. I heard someone here saying her daughter died. I suppose you had motives of your own as well." She held her free hand out to Bunch and smiled. "Tell me all about it."

"Well… I'm not sure…"

"Oh my dear child, I'm hardly going to tell anybody anything. There's nobody here for me to tell and I shan't be around long enough to tell them, even if there were."

"Mummy!"

A quiet throaty chuckle escaped the older woman's lips, ending in a slow and careful cough. "The family isn't summoned to a bedside for nothing." Her eyes closed again. "Which neighbour is under the Rose Courtney spy glass this time?" She yawned, showing even teeth. "I suppose it's the Jarmans. How very droll."

"I needed to ask Selina a few questions," Bunch admitted. "Her daughter was murdered, after all."

"And we want to know who their accountant is," said Dodo.

"Dodo!"

"What?"

"I told you Wright would deal with that."

"No need," Theadora whispered. "I know who it is."

"You do? But you've been in town for most of the past year, before you came here…"

"I didn't follow your father around the embassies of the world without learning how to notice the tiny details. It was my job. Rose, you're not the only one who can extrapolate once one has them – the details that is. I was Edward's … what was it he called me? His intelligencer. He found that terribly amusing." Theadora clicked her tongue. "And you can stop smirking, Rose. Nobody expects the wives to hear what's said at those sorts of events, or to remember it for more than two minutes. Especially the wives who drink. And yes, I do see the irony – you can both stop looking so guilty."

"Sorry Mummy. You were saying?"

"All those years gathering gossip for your father, and I can't believe you now have me swept up in your own little spy ring. But there we are. Never too late for something new. Clement Waller." She widened her eyes watching for Bunch's reaction.

"Haven Cottage's Clement Waller? How did you know that?"

"He approached Edward when old Parsons retired. Edward didn't really want to speak with him but he kept leaving his card, so we had him along to Thurloe Square for cocktails one evening, along with that dreadful wife of his."

"What did he want with Daddy?"

"He offered his services to the Perringham estate. Edward declined of course. He was always sure you had it in you to do an excellent job, and also because I gather he had reservations about Waller himself."

"Really? Do tell."

"Now there I am a little hazy, and not just because of this damned morphine. I only recall it at all because you mentioned the Jarmans and I knew Selina a long time ago."

"Selina said she and you were acquainted at one time. I didn't know about Waller coming to see Daddy about Perringham, though. I'm surprised Granny didn't mention it."

"I know something that Beatrice doesn't? My goodness, that must be a first." Theodora laughed out loud and then began to gasp for breath.

"Mummy." Bunch reached for the mask. "Call for help, Dodo. Use the bell," she said as she looped the mask over her mother's face and felt relieved as the oxygen hissed through the valves and her mother's paroxysms began to calm.

"Let me."

Bunch stepped back at the voice's authority and watched – not the novice Sister Agnes – the calm and efficient Sister Bertha, whom she remembered from her previous visit.

"There we are milady. Just breathe slowly. In and out. Steady now. I know that nasty rubber thing doesn't have a nice smell, but breathe in nice and deep." Sister Bertha peered closely at Theodora's face and took her wrist to test her pulse as the coughing subsided. "That's it. There now. Feeling better?"

Beatrice nodded, too exhausted to speak.

The gas stopped its hissing as Bertha laid the mask on the bedside table within easy reach. "No excitement," she said. "I asked Sister Agnes to be clear on that."

"She was," said Dodo. "And she wasn't excited. Not really. Just laughing…"

"Right now, that is often sufficient to set off a coughing fit. And the morphine on someone so weary doesn't help. Perhaps your mother needs a little time to gather herself. She's always a little more alert in the late afternoons, as I told your father. If I may suggest that you go to the refectory for some tea or a light luncheon?"

Bunch looked at her mother. Theodora screwed shut her eyes and was still breathing a little raggedly. A fine sprinkle of perspiration freckled her brow and upper lip. She seemed to have already slipped into sleep. *I need to get hold of Wright but I can't leave now*, she thought. *I can't just walk out on Mummy*. Dodo was staring at her and she shrugged. *God, I hope I didn't say that aloud*. She leaned down and dropped a light kiss on her mother's cheek and motioned to Dodo to sit at the bedside. "I shall see if I can rustle up some tea," she said. "Sister Bertha?"

"Of course. This way."

In the corridor Bunch confronted the nun. "My mother is deteriorating very quickly."

"She is. Her liver has almost failed completely and her kidneys are no longer coping."

"How long does she have? Days? Hours?"

Sister Bertha glanced back at the closed door. "You were a nurse?"

"Yes."

"Then you know it's something we cannot predict. The good Lord willing, she will see a few more days." Bunch furrowed her eyebrows and Bertha spread her hands. "The doctor thinks that she may have perhaps a week, if she's very lucky."

"On the other hand, she could go at any time?"

"That is very possible. Personally, I think a day or two."

"Thank you for being frank with me. May I assume that four visitors today might be too much for her?" *Now I am making excuses. Tell me no, Bertha. Give me a good excuse to stay.*

"Your mother tires easily. We can manage the pain but she has a fever too, and her breathing has been getting more difficult, which is not uncommon in these cases, as you may know. We are making her as comfortable as we can, and I pray she will have a few days more at least."

"Do you think me a terrible daughter that I haven't come every day?"

"Not at all. Your mother knows you are a busy woman. The estate alone would keep anyone occupied. She has been telling me that you also work with the police. She is proud of that though she will not acknowledge it."

"She never, ever, gave me that impression. Quite the contrary."

The sister chuckled softly. "She knows you do it for very good reasons. Diplomats, nurses, coenobites, and even detectives. The search for justice for others comes from a caring heart."

"I'm not sure it's that simple but thank you. I should get back in there."

"I shall have Sister Agnes bring tea."

"Thank you, but first, may I use your telephone?"

~ Fourteen ~

It was past ten a.m. when Wright finally arrived at the Dower House. "You're late," Bunch grumbled as she flung herself into the police car's rear seat. The dry spell had finally broken, but the Wolseley's interior remained stuffy, with the odours of worn leather and engine oil mixing with the petrichor from the newly dampened earth in the garden. Beneath it all Bunch detected a hint of shaving soap.

"Sorry. I had some other issues that had to be dealt with first," he replied. "What have you there?"

"Something Daddy fished out for you from his papers."

Wright took the file from Bunch and scanned the half-dozen carbon copy sheets, so heavily scored with deleted lines that Bunch had wondered it hadn't shredded. "It's old information. And with all due respect a little short on substance." He closed it slowly and shook his head. "Your father isn't giving a lot away."

"Getting this much is a favour to me. He isn't in the business of handing out information," she replied, "and I seriously doubt there is much more to be had. Clement Waller is either as innocent as he appears to be – or he's exceptionally good at covering his tracks. Did he have a couple of suspect clients? As far as Daddy knows, Waller's company dealt well within the law."

"This information looks as if it's taken from the audits Waller submitted to His Majesty's Inland Revenue," Wright replied. "We probably have this much at Scotland Yard."

"Daddy went into it all in some depth and there was nothing to indicate Waller was doing anything untoward." She put her hand on the folder lying between them. "He was convinced Waller was not all he appears but when the Whitehall bods were unable to ferret out anything whiffy, well, he had no option but to assume it doesn't exist."

"Did they consider there was a duplicate set of books?"

"I'm sure they did. If you had arrived at Perringham earlier you could have asked Daddy yourself."

"I can't just drop everything at your beck and call, you know."

"Daddy couldn't wait any longer. He's gone to see Mummy this morning for a brief visit and then he has to head back to the Bunker. He has a lot more on his plate than either of us."

"I know. I will apologise to him when we meet, but my delay was unavoidable. How is your mother, by the way?"

"Sleeping most of the time." Bunch sighed. "According to Sister Bertha, her condition took a nosedive when she got back to the Red House after the christening. Possibly a minor stroke. It feels unfair for Mummy to waste away like this. She's travelled the world for decades, has been active all her life, and the worst thing for her now is the feeling that she lacks control. We had such trouble getting her to go to a spa at the beginning of her illness. The Red House was her choice; she hoped we wouldn't see her deteriorating, though we do, quite naturally. Nevertheless, she was pleased to think she had something useful to add to our case." A small expression of pain passed over her. "Which brings me to our investigation. Without proof of some major crime, Daddy's office has far more pressing things to deal with than a bent bookkeeper. I don't understand why Waller would draw attention to himself by chasing Daddy for business if he were acting unlawfully? He must have known he'd be investigated."

"Which could be reason enough: hiding in plain sight."

"That's a bold move."

"Or very arrogant." Wright waved the file and threw it down again.

Bunch watched the pages slide out into the footwell. "It does feel over the top."

"According to these papers, his approach to your father came around the same time as the first suitcase body."

"Pretty Feet?" she asked.

"No, not that far back. Pretty Feet was the model for these later murders, but Letham says there are distinct differences. He went over the reports again and now believes the first two may well have been committed by the same killer, but the more recent deaths, which include Laura and Kitty, were carried out by another hand. Or by two people. It's only a theory so far, based on the weight of the trunks. They were very heavy and would be difficult to move single-handedly without attracting attention."

"One man with a barrow could manage it— Don't look at me like that. You would be surprised at what I've moved around in the farmyard with a wheelbarrow. The invention of the wheel was a wonderful thing. None of which helps us now. If I can chat with Linda Manning again, away from the factory, she might be more forthcoming and willing to provide further information. She said she goes straight to fire watching after work so we shall have a chance to catch her on her own territory, so to speak."

"Agreed."

"She was like an unbroken yearling in that office," Bunch said. "So terrified she might be overheard saying the wrong thing."

"Such as?"

"Such as … whatever set Laura Jarman off on a path that led to her destruction. I have the impression that Laura was an incredibly determined woman. What she was aiming for I don't know but Linda Manning may."

Wright smiled. "I'm right ahead of you. Manning will be working at Jarman's until four and should be on fire-watch duty at her local church by five at the latest." He reached inside his jacket for his notebook and flipped through the pages. "All Saints Parish Church, High Street, Carshalton. Firstly, I suggest we head up to the river for another chat with Lilly."

Two hours later they were in Elephant and Castle. The Jungle Rooms club was closed and with no reply they moved round the corner to the Lion pub, which operated from the same building but fronted from the street that backed onto Lilly's more lucrative premises. The Lion was a drinker's pub with no saloon or snug, just a large public bar that in better times would have been packed with workers drinking, playing cards, darts, dominoes and shove ha'penny. The dinnertime rush on a sultry Tuesday in May was little more than a trickle. The long bar was propped up by no more than a dozen men with a scattering of other drinkers seated at tables around the room, which, Bunch noted, were bolted to the floor. *There can't be enough patrons to keep the place going,* she thought. All the customers, to a man, turned to stare at them when they entered. All conversations ceased and drinks set down. Even the domino players ceased their clacking to watch and wait.

The smoke across the room was thick enough to partially obscure the far doors and made Bunch cough as she followed Wright to the bar where he flipped his warrant card under the barman's nose for a split second and leaned forward. "Tell Lilly that Chief Inspector Wright is back and wants a quiet word. Down here will be good."

The barman nodded at two heavies lounging at the far end of the bar and one of them vanished through the farthest of two doorways. The other moved so he was shielded from the waist down by the bar, to stare directly at the interlopers. The barman made no attempt to serve Bunch and Wright. He backed along his side of the bar to busy himself with clearing the counter.

Through a glass panel Bunch noticed a private room beyond, which as far as she could tell, was quite empty. *He's not going to serve us?* Bunch thought, eyeing the dusty gin glasses hanging above the bar. *To be honest, I don't think I'd care to drink from those. I doubt they've been thoroughly cleaned for months, let alone used.*

With the messenger despatched, a low murmur rose as Bunch and Wright's audience resumed their drinking and gaming. To Bunch, it wasn't the low buzz of a beehive but the staccato zizz of a hornet's nest, and she didn't need telling that she and Wright were the focus of each and every one of them, even if they no longer blatantly stared at them.

"Not overly keen on officers of the law intruding on their patch," Wright murmured.

"I noticed," said Bunch. "Are we safe, do you think?"

"Don't spook them with any sudden movements and we should be fine."

"Like wolves?"

"More like rats," he whispered. "Most law-abiding locals wouldn't want to be caught dead in here." He grinned. "They won't do a thing without direct orders from above. Just watch out for those two with the dominos."

"Why?"

"They have pints of draft but there are empty bottles next to them."

"Which means?"

"It's a nasty weapon – when broken against the table edge."

"Uhuh." Bunch looked back at the entrance and mentally gauged the distance in strides. She had heard of bottle fights but had never encountered one and had no intention of taking an active part now.

Someone sniggered and she turned quickly to catch the culprit but all she saw were two men who turned their faces away. A muttered comment from the table to her left was short and guttural, just a pair of words, and Bunch was certain the second one was "off". They didn't have a long wait before Lilly Kendall strode through the door and headed across to them. Wright took a couple of paces towards her. Bunch followed suit. It seemed counter intuitive to stand in the open; *Closer to the exit would be better.*

"Billy-boy. Back so soon? And your posh little friend as well." Lilly walked around Bunch and brushed a fingernail against her bobbed hair. "Slumming it, Honourable Miss?"

"Lilly," said Wright. "Behave!"

"I always do, Billy my sweet." She paused in front of him, nose to nose. "I'm going to assume you're not asking about anything private. So then, what's up?"

"Kitty Shenton was one of your girls."

"She did a little bookwork and that was all," Lilly replied. "No secret there."

"How did she come to work for you?" Wright sighed when no answer came. "Lilly, I am trying to catch her killer. Help me out here. Please."

Lilly formed her red lips into a thoughtful moue and then nodded. "Her father and mine served on the same ship – before he fell foul of your lot."

"Reg Shenton was sent down for smuggling," said Wright.

"They only found a bit of baccy. This lot in here could smoke more in a week than what Reg was pinched for."

"He was still a smuggler." The two indulged in a staring match until Wright broke into a short laugh. "He ended up in the Scrubs and you gave Kitty a job. Is that how it went? Seems like you felt a sense of obligation."

Lilly jutted her chin and stared him in the eyes for another count of five. "Reg asked me to look out for her. She didn't want to work for her brother cos they didn't get on."

"Do you know why?"

"Sometimes families don't." Lilly shrugged. "Between you and me, he's a bit of a bastard. What sort of a man swindles his own parents out of the family business? How Kitty's mother can still live in the same house with him I don't know. Mother love, maybe. Or desperation."

"With her husband in prison perhaps it was the only way to keep the creditors at bay," said Bunch. "Lots of men in business do not like dealing with a woman, even now."

"Maybe," Lilly replied. "Still doesn't make it right. It's nothing short of piracy."

"Rather like sending girls to work for well-off families with the intent to steal from them." Bunch felt Wright go tense. *Maybe not the wisest of wise cracks.* She pulled a saccharin smile.

"It all depends on where you're standing," Lilly said.

"You helped Kitty out... So how did she come to work for Jarman's?" Wright asked.

"She was promised qualifications by working for a legit company. Make something of herself. She was a sweet thing – and I didn't think she belonged here." She waved a hand at the room. "No more than she belonged with that bastard brother of hers. As it turns out, it would have been better for Kitty if I'd kept her on my books."

"Is Clem Waller your accountant? Was he the person who got her the post with Charles Jarman?"

"What's Clem Waller to you?"

The heavies at the bar stepped towards them, tall and straight, and it felt as if the temperature in the bar plummeted. Bunch heard several chairs scraping softly on the bare floor and she tensed, ready to take flight. *God, I'd hate to live like this, always on a knife edge.*

Wright raised his hands, palms out. "I am not here to make waves for you, Lilly. I promise. We're investigating the murders of Kitty Shenton and Laura Jarman and I know you're as keen as I am to get answers. Let's start with an answer from you. It's not a hard question and you know I could learn the answer by other means if I have to. It's simply quicker to come straight to the font of wisdom. All I need is a straight yes or no."

Lilly pulled a face. "He used to be on our roll till I caught him skimming. He can be a bit of a one, him and his wife. You know Faye Waller worked for Diamond Alice, way back?"

"Faye?" said Bunch. "Oh, that is too funny. My grandmother will love that."

"Faye Waller was a tom? That's interesting." said Wright.

"She had her moments. And Faye—" Lilly chuckled quietly "—is not her real name. She never missed Fay Raye at the pictures; she was besotted with her. So besotted that she kept Faye as her nom de guerre when she was out on jobs. She stuck on the 'e' to make it seem she had quality. But she was never on the game, Billy-boy, not the way you mean it. With her looks she targeted the bright young things, sinking her teeth into their wallets. Collected beaus like some boys collect butterflies." She skewered her finger against Wright's chest. "You know the drill. Chases 'em down and fleeces 'em blind, and they never feel a thing until they're pinned down and helpless."

"Blackmail?" Wright replied.

"That is such a strong word, William." Lilly made a show of straightening the tie she has disturbed. "Faye was good. She could pull the Oliver on 'em like no one else. She never took more than they could easily afford. Steamers were more scared of what their mummies would say, if they found out, than losing a few quid. They paid like good boys and never thought to call your lot in."

"What's her real name?" Wright asked.

Lilly tipped her head back and laughed and dug him in the front of his shoulder with a scarlet painted forefinger before taking a few steps back. "Do you know, she's been Faye so long now I really can't recall." She shrugged. "If it really matters, you should ask Clem. It'd be on their marriage licence ... if they'd ever bothered to get one."

"I'll come back to that another time. Right now," said Wright, "what I need to know is whether Clement Waller is still Charles Jarman's accountant."

"Yes. Can't say any plainer than that. And that's not bleating. Far as I am concerned, Waller deserves anything he gets. I thought Kitty might've come back when we gave Clem the heave-ho, but by then she'd got chummy with Jarman's daughter. I pity Faye ... but there you are."

"Kitty had no other reason for working at the Jarman factory, other than a better job?" Bunch asked.

"There are people who think Laura and Kitty might have found something ... dubious ... going on at the factory," Wright added.

"Ah." Lilly looked thoughtful, the hard lines smoothing on her face, as her aggression dropped away. "And this has something to do with their deaths?"

Wright nodded. "We think so, though we have no proof as yet."

"This is not something you'll hear me say twice, Billy-boy: I'm not a grass so don't read anything into this, but I honestly wish I could help you more. We all liked Kitty. She was like a little sister to me."

"A lot of people seemed to have liked her. We are going to find her killer, I promise you." Wright tipped his hat and began to edge casually to the exit. "Thank you, Lilly. I really do appreciate your being so kind. Goodbye."

Bunch turned to follow and smiled when she passed through the door in two fewer paces than she had anticipated. The doors had not swung fully shut behind them before Wright grabbed her arm and hustled her to the car, leaving her no time to comment before Glossop rammed the Wolsey into gear and pulled away.

"Phew. That was all rather melodramatic for such a simple question," she said. "I can't see why you didn't just call her on the telephone."

"Shaking the tree," Wright replied. "If I had telephoned, I'm certain Lilly wouldn't have taken my call. We'd never have got to see her, either. A copper calling on her twice would certainly set tongues wagging. Talking to her in public, in the pub, was the only way to obtain answers from her in a way that didn't put her in danger. I hadn't counted on Bert Avory being in the bar, though."

"Who's he?"

"The old domino player? Not a head man around these parts nowadays but one of the MacDonald clan. Not a bad thing he heard every word."

"To protect Lilly?"

"And us. Waller has obviously queered his pitch with this lot, which may explain why we can't find him. No shame, no blame, in giving him up to us, in Lilly's eyes. We shan't need to keep an eye out over our shoulders."

"But we seem to be getting somewhere. Were both Jarman and Waller fiddling the books, do you think?" Bunch said. "Although maybe not Jarman. He's a hard man and it would need to be a tremendous scam, because I can't see him sacrificing his own daughter." Bunch looked back through the rear window, then asked: "Where to now? The factory? We're here in Town so we may as well."

"I'd thought about it but not just yet. The powers-that-be are very twitchy about our investigations into Jarman Engineering. There's too much at stake with whatever they are working on, for the war effort, so we should keep clear of him – for now. I do want to make a few more enquiries about this Clement Waller."

"Do you know where he lives? I heard they went to the Cotswolds or some such."

"They have an address listed in Malvern but it turned out to be a dead-letter drop. They have a house in Richmond but nobody's seen them there for a few months. There must be a place nearer; somewhere along the Thames is as close as I've got so far. Carter is onto that one. Meanwhile, I've been informed that the Yard have finally finished with Kitty's flat so maybe we should go over later, see what we can find."

"Will it be worth the time and effort? The place was searched at least twice," said Bunch. "Once by us."

"It has but we didn't know then what we were looking for. With luck there'll be a WRC still on duty and if not there may be a caretaker with a key. Let's find a decent spot to eat first and then catch up with Linda Manning."

~~~

All Saints Church in Carshalton was a sprawling structure. To Bunch, used to the neatness of Norman masonry, it was one of the oddest parish churches she had ever seen. Additions to the place had been made over the centuries, with no apparent plan or sense of proportion, ranging from medieval stone through heavy Edwardian brick to Victorian flint.

"Much as I hate to see any building suffer damage, especially a church," said Bunch as they emerged from the car to stare at it, "I am not sure a bomb or two wouldn't improve this place."

They pushed open the west doors and stood stock still as the impact of the interior of the church hit them. Inside was a revelation. Its vaulted roof rose high above them in cathedral-like proportions. The altar and carved choir stalls were sited beyond the chancel step. Above was a vast organ loft. As they walked along the central aisle Bunch peered through the arches along one side, to a gilded cavern that was plainly the lady chapel.

Like most places of worship, it had been stripped of all moveable treasures against the fear of a direct hit, but its purpose remained. Bunch took a deep breath, inhaling the medley of old stone, beeswax candles and lavender polish, and exhaled a whispered "gosh". The space both absorbed the sound and reflected it to the furthest corners, in that way only churches can. "Hello," she called. "Miss Manning? Linda?"

There was a scuffle in one of the recesses and two figures in siren suits and battle bowlers peered from behind a pillar on the east aisle. Linda stepped forward to frown at them. "Miss Courtney?"

"Yes. And Chief Inspector Wright." Bunch waved a hand at the space around them. "Quite a surprise once you get inside."

"Isn't it. My auntie calls it God's warehouse." She shrugged. "Sorry, my family's sense of humour doesn't always travel. My mother is on the flower rota, and my aunt is married to the verger, so she spends a lot of time cleaning in here." She glanced shyly at her companion. "This is John. John Ross. My fiancé."

"Good evening." Ross bounced forward with hand extended and as Bunch shook it she noticed his dog collar.

"You're the vicar here?"

"Heavens no. I'm merely a humble curate, for now at least."

Linda stood beside him and grasped his left arm. "John had his call up," she murmured.

"That's if the medical board passes me fit for the Padres' Battle School. Right ear is fine but this—" He turned his head to show Bunch a hearing aid behind his left ear. "I'm not deaf, you know, just some loss on the one side."

He was defensive, plainly reiterating an argument he had been forced into and had used often to justify himself, and Bunch had every sympathy. As a fit young man out of uniform he would be open to all kinds of snidery and even open hostility, though she supposed his clerical collar would provide some leeway. She tapped at her damaged knee. "Awful isn't it, being failed B3s and such. I was invalided out following a crash, and with working in the agricultural business I was slapped with a reserved status."

"It is hard, but we do what we can." He squared his shoulders and ushered them to the nearest pew. "Enough of all that. How may we serve you today?"

Wright flashed his warrant card as he took a seat. "Miss Courtney has already spoken with Miss Manning about her work colleagues at Jarman's. We simply want to clarify a few points." He smiled at Ross and after a pause added, "We only need a few minutes of your time. Routine questions."

"Yes, of course." Ross rose reluctantly and patted Linda's shoulder. "I shall be securing the vestry if you need me."

"He can be protective." Linda watched him wander away. "But he means well. What do you want to know? I'm not sure I can tell you a lot else."

"People never know what they can remember until they're asked the right questions," said Wright.

"I'm not hiding anything. Truly!"

"We never thought that for a moment. Now you've had a bit of time to think, we hope you might remember a little more."

"As confirmation rather than anything else," said Bunch. "Always easier when you're not being watched by the boss."

Linda relaxed visibly. "Mr Archer watches us like a fox at a rabbit warren. Ready to pounce!"

"I had a lieutenant like that in the ATS," said Bunch. "I swear she had bat's ears."

"Absolutely." Linda leaned back in the pew, not fully at ease but looking less concerned. "Ask away. What is it you think I may know?"

"We understand that Jarman's use Belchamber & Phelps Accountants for their end of year accounts."

"They do. But surely Mr Jarman could have told you that." Linda glanced from one to the other, and then back to her fiancée, suddenly suspicious. "Why are you asking me?"

"We have some reports about certain activities Waller may be involved in, when working at Jarman's. How often did he come to the factory?" Wright asked. "Or either of his partners?"

"I don't think there is a Mr Belchamber or a Mr Phelps. Not now. Just Mr Waller."

"Mr Waller owns the company?"

"Far as I know."

Wright raised his brow at Bunch and she knew they were thinking the same. "Was there ever a Belchamber or Phelps?" she said.

"I never saw them if there was." Linda frowned. "Their letterhead said something like Est. 1890, so maybe they're retired? We saw an assistant now and then. We're always glad about that. Mr Waller's a bit of a handy sort – if you get my meaning." She shuddered.

"How often does Waller visit the factory?"

"He comes in about once a month. Often spends an afternoon in Old Jaybird … sorry, Mr Jarman's office."

"Is he friendly with Jarman? Do they get on well?" Wright asked.

"S'pose so. Though its odd now you say it, cos Mr J isn't there very often. When you came the other day it was the first time we'd seen him for months. He's all wrapped up with the new—" She put a hand to her mouth. "We aren't supposed to say anything about what we're making. Walls have ears."

"Quite right," Wright agreed. "We're not interested in Mr Jarman's engineering developments. What we need to know about is Mr Waller's work at the factory."

"Well … he goes over the books. I suppose it made sense when the old man was hardly ever there."

"Did he ever ask you to go over those books with him?"

"Not on your life. He called Mr Archer in now and then. And Kitty a few times."

"When did he last speak with Kitty?"

"It must have been a week or two after Miss Jarman had her row with her father."

"Just before she vanished?"

Linda nodded and hunched further into the pew, hands tucked beneath her thighs, staring at the wool-worked hassock tucked beneath the seat in front of her. "Kitty was noticeably quiet when she came out of the office. We all assumed Mr Waller had tried it on with her."

"She never gave a hint of anything before that?" Wright asked.

"Not a thing. Except— I remember she made a comment that her old boss wanted her back and she was going to hand in her notice. Only she wouldn't right then because she had a few things to sort out first."

"Her old boss being—?"

"Someone up Bermondsey way? Or Kennington? She was always a bit vague about that. Never wanted to talk about it."

"Would it have been at Elephant and Castle?"

Linda shrugged. "Could have been. It's up the same way. I remember she said it was some sort of ships' chandlers, so you'd think it would be right on the river."

Bunch looked sideways at Wright. "Did she ever ask you to dig out any information for her? Anything out of the usual," Bunch said.

"She was asking me to get things all the time. Dockets and invoices and letters."

"Nothing out of the ordinary?"

"She was going over old stuff those last weeks. She told me old Mr Jarman wanted her to get a new forecast together and they needed figures for the past ten years."

"Was that odd?"

"Not really. Banks ask for that stuff when there's a new business plan being written. She said Jaybird – sorry, Mr Jarman – wanted her to keep an eye out for any foreign deals because they had to be left out of new forecasts. On account of the war."

"Were there any?"

"There was correspondence with a Swedish steel company, which didn't count, what with them being neutral. And a few orders from a German factory, which were all dated back before 1938. That's not unusual, is it?" A panic crept into Linda's tone. "Should we have reported it? That was all stuff from years ago and everyone was trading with the Jerries back then. Weren't they?"

"They were," Bunch agreed. "Don't worry, you've done nothing wrong. Would you say Kitty took special notice of those records?"

"She jotted them all down in a little book."

"We found a notebook with Miss Jarman, one of those little things in a metal case with a propelling pencil. Did Kitty use that type of book?"

"No, not the sort ladies have. It was one of those cheap little red cashbooks that you can buy in Woolworths. They were both using that book and that's why I remember it. I remember seeing Miss Laura writing in it and thinking she wasn't the kind to shop in Woolies. It was notes for Mr J, Kitty told me. I didn't ask what or why – she was my boss, in a way. Senior to me, anyway, even though she was younger in age. Kitty had a good head for figures. Never made a mistake, ever. Even corrected Mr Archer one time, which didn't go down well, I can tell you. She mentioned once that there were some pages missing from a ledger and that taking pages out was wrong, and if entries were incorrect they should be scored through and the whole lot re-entered."

"Which ledgers were these? Do you know?" said Wright. "Could you point them out to us if we came to the office?"

"No. They'd be in one of the inner offices." Linda shook her head sharply enough to make her unfastened tin hat tilt at a rakish angle. "Besides, Kitty never mentioned it again."

The wail of a siren made them all pause and glance upwards. Ross was trotting down the central aisle towards them, boots clattering on the stone flags.

"First time in a while. It's early so it might just be a drill, but if that's all…?"

"You have work to do," said Wright.

"Yes. We should be on roof watch now."

"I think we have enough." He shook her hand as they stood. "You have been very helpful, Miss Manning."

Ross put his arm around Linda. "Everything all right?"

"Yes, indeed. I doubt we shall need to bother Miss Manning again," Wright said.

"Splendid. Now I must steal Linda away from you. We do need to get up top. Probably a false alarm but they were still dropping the odd incendiaries a few days ago. This may not be St Paul's but we locals value it as much." He paused, rattling the fire bucket in his left hand. "There is a crypt if you need to take shelter."

"No, thank you," said Wright. "We have a few more things to do and it's still light so we can get on with it before the Blackout."

"Then Godspeed," he called over his shoulder as he and Linda clattered away to the doors on one side of the chancel and vanished.

"He'll make a far better padre than a curate," said Wright.

"Quite bossy," Bunch agreed. "It's an admirable quality for climbing ecclesiastic ladders. He would make a good sort of archdeacon. Linda will need to watch that one."

"Well … you would know. Come on we have a lot to do."

"Where to now? Surely not back to see Lilly Kendall. Would that be wise?"

"No need today. I suspect Lilly may hold a few more pieces of the puzzle but that can wait. She may not have known or cared about Laura Jarman but she certainly wants Kitty Shenton's murderer caught, as much as we do. Perhaps more. Such as, how Kitty really ended up working for Jarman's."

"That is obvious. It was Waller."

"He's the link, yes, but we have absolutely no proof that he was involved in either death."

"And how do we gather evidence?"

Wright glanced up at the sky and smiled grimly as the siren stopped for a few seconds before wailing out an all clear. "Waller had links to a mob – and we've shaken the tree." Now we need to collect the fallen fruit."

"We return to the flat?"

"Of course.

~~~

The door to flat 5C was shut when they arrived with no sign of any War Reserve Constable on guard duty.

"Where will we find a caretaker?" said Bunch. "I didn't see any concierge window on our way in."

"Perhaps these are not service flats," said Wright. "There are three blocks of flats so a caretaker, if he exists, could live in any one of the ground floor apartments." He leaned forward and gave the door to 5C a push and smiled grimly when it refused to budge.

"Locked," said Bunch.

"Is it?" Wright rummaged in his pocket for a bunch of keys and detached a small leather-covered fob. He selected a yale key from the ring and inserted it in the keyhole.

"Your key is unlikely to work," Bunch said.

"Won't it?" He grinned but stiffened suddenly, looking past her. "Who's there?"

Bunch turned towards the stair well and spun back at a couple of sharp taps in time to see Wright swinging the door open a fraction. She watched him snap the fob's dog clip back on the keyring and pocket them. "How?"

"Door was open after all," Wright said.

"Dear me, Chief Inspector. Breaking and entering?"

"Not at all. CID may have left but these premises are still a crime scene. Keys are optional. Coming?"

He pushed the door open and stepped into the vestibule, leaving Bunch to follow, metaphorically open mouthed. *Hidden depths, Chief Inspector*, she thought. *Shocking and impressive*. She was about to close the door behind them when Wright held out his left hand to grasp her shoulder, his right forefinger to his lips.

From beyond a partly open door leading further into the flat came the faint sound of music: Al Bowlly crooning "What can I say, after I've taken the blame…" Then it ended abruptly. A single expletive. A crash.

Wright pushed Bunch against the wall, half-hiding her in the coats hanging on the pegs, and shoved the inner door wide open. "Good afternoon, sir. We were not expecting to find anyone here." Bunch untangled herself and followed him.

Charles Jarman stared back at them. Shellac remains dangled from his fingers with shattered fragments scattered around his feet. "She loved Bowlly." His voice was low, cracking under a strain Bunch had not expected to hear. Nor had she expected to see the hollowness in his eyes as he stared at them without seeming to recognise what or who he was seeing. She'd seen that look before.

Bunch came around the side of Wright and attempted to ease the broken record from Jarman's grip, using her thumb and forefinger, trying to avoid the sharp edges. He pulled the record away from Bunch's fingers.

"Hello Mr Jarman. Remember me? I came to see you at Gellideg House?"

Jarman shuddered, or maybe shook himself into awareness, and scowled at her, the puckered scars on his face bunching and paling, and suddenly he was looking more like himself. "Miss Courtney. Yes, I remember you." He nodded at a mahogany gramophone box. "You wanted to know about my daughter? Well, here's something. My wife and I bought Laura this for her last birthday. It was the latest Decca model, and she was so excited." He carefully folded the stylus, closed the lid, and gently placed the remains of Al Bowlly's voice on the top. "Selina complained about the constant din of those recordings, but really she misses them. All that quiet proves our girl has gone." He gazed around as if trying to recall where he was.

"Shall I make you tea?" Bunch said. "Or maybe there's something stronger around here."

"Cabinet." Jarman pointed at the low dresser. "I saw a bottle of London Dry when I was looking around. I'm a Scotch man generally but any port in a storm…"

Bunch found the bottle and waved it at Wright who shook his head. "Tad early for me."

"Please yourself. It's been one hell of a day so far." She scooped up two glasses. "Tonic?"

"God, yes," Jarman snarled. "That stuff's lighter fuel without it, but only a slosh."

He seemed almost human now, in his shock, or this was the real man and the one she'd seen before had been a business facade. She added a tiny splash of tonic water to Jarman's glass from an opened bottle. It was a little flat, bubbles struggling to creep up from the base of the tumbler, *But this is*, she reasoned, *an emergency*. "Here," she said.

He took the glass and slugged back half of the contents, grimacing briefly, and then downed the rest. "Was it my fault?" he muttered. "We fought like cats and dogs, but I loved my little girl. Selina said we were too much alike and yes, Laura was the one who would stand her ground, always demanding answers."

"What was it that made Laura 'stand her ground' stubbornly enough to leave home?"

Jarman stared at her, the pain clear in his eyes – and also a defiance. "That is a private matter," he said. "I know Selina blames me, and Laura and I had parted on bad terms, but in the end she left of her own accord."

"And ended up brutally murdered," said Wright. "Family secrets or not, you need to provide us with all the details."

"I've told you all that I know of her murder. She left home and some bastard killed her. What else can I say?"

"Mr Jarman, you must admit, you have not been fully co-operative throughout our investigation. You must see how that appears to a simple-minded old plod such as myself."

"I know nothing about how she died."

"Or that you may have had a hand in her death?"

Jarman glared at Wright, the muscles in his jaw working overtime, his face progressing through most of the rainbow, and his damaged skin shimmering in a curiously wave-like sequence. Bunch had a notion he was going to take a swing at Wright, and even given his slight frame and greater years Jarman had that condensed wiry physique of an athlete. She was willing to bet he had a gym somewhere in his laboratory complex and that he had a good chance of comprehensively pounding the Chief Inspector.

"Here." She swapped her untouched gin for his empty glass. "Drink up, old chap."

Her action surprised him, as she had hoped, and he peered at the glass in confusion.

"Drink up," she said again. "Good for shock. Or would you prefer that cup of tea?" Jarman growled something unintelligible and drained the glass. *Which is impressive*, thought Bunch, *because I poured a good double for us both, and I didn't have the soda in mine.*

The neat gin had the desired effect of making Jarman gasp, his eyes widening. "Lighter fluid," he gasped and sat in the armchair.

"Pretty much."

"Mr Jarman, we're sure what happened to Laura was *not* your fault," Wright said, "but we can't find and arrest the person who is responsible unless you cough up the whole story. Surely you can see that?"

"I don't know what to tell you. She seemed fine working in the office at home, teaching Mary the ropes, before she married into the family. I had given the pair of them a project, collating the results of our testing system in such a way that it would be easier to analyse. The chaps at the War Office can be surprisingly simplistic when it comes to evaluating anything experimental."

"You had Laura do that? Not Stephen?"

"It would have been Robert's area before he joined up. As for Stephen? He's more interested in gadding about Town. I thought marriage would settle him but—" Jarman scowled. "Laura has – had – a good brain. She should have been an engineer."

If only she'd been a boy? Bunch got out her cigarettes and lit one, without offering her case to Jarman. It was a petty objection to make, she knew, but it calmed her from wanting to slap him. *Let him smoke his own, arrogant old dinosaur.*

"Was your disagreement with Laura connected with your work?" Wright asked him.

"I don't know. I wish I did. She was working on the project and suddenly we were screaming at each other in the middle of the office. I couldn't have that, not in front of staff, so I said she was off the job. The air cleared a little afterwards, but she decided she rather work at the London factory. I'm not there that often and it seemed like a good compromise. Let tempers cool. When Mary mentioned that she knew somebody who wanted a flatmate, not too far from the factory, it felt like the perfect answer for Laura. So off she went."

"Did things really cool down between you?"

"Hard to tell," Jarman admitted. "I barely saw her for those months. The work we've been doing for the WO is not just top secret, it's top priority. My team has been putting in ten-hour days – and six-day weeks were not unusual. Quite often I work longer than that because… When the ideas are coming you must follow them to the end or 'lose the muse', as Laura would put it. I will admit I wasn't paying her a great deal of attention – as her father. I left it to my wife to chatter on with her the way mothers and daughters do. The last time Laura came down to the house all hell let loose. I had a call from Stephen to collect him from some party and as it was late I didn't want to dig my driver out of bed."

"Doesn't a chauffeur usually live over the garage?" said Bunch. "You would have woken him anyway."

Jarman pursed his lips and avoided eye contact.

"Was there some specific reason he telephoned you and not his wife?" Wright asked. "I assume Mary drives; most young people seem to, now."

Jarman tilted his head back to stare at the hand-painted lampshade and then sank forward, his head between his hands. "He called because he had ended up at a club without a way home. There was a friend who, Stephen said, had left without him. It was *not* somewhere he wanted Mary to know about."

"A gentlemen's club?" said Wright.

"That would be one name for it," said Jarman. "Though not the kind of gents' club you see in Mayfair or Pall Mall." He glanced at Bunch and coloured, so that the scar tissue looked more scale-like. "There were plenty of women there, and I choose my words carefully, Miss Courtney. There were very few *ladies* present, I can assure you."

"Prostitutes? I am familiar with the term." She filled her lungs from her cigarette and slowly blew the smoke out in her best Rosalind Russell imitation. While Jarman stared at her she was aware that Wright was fidgeting. "I was an ATS driver and served with the BEF in '39. Nothing much will shock me."

"Indeed." Jarman nodded. "So it would seem."

Wright sat in a chair across from Jarman. "This party," he said, "where was it?"

"Some dead spot just north of Storrington."

"Was it at a place called Haven Cottage?" Wright signalled Bunch to stay quiet.

Jarman's face crumpled. "Perhaps I should have told him to stay there until he sobered up, except he was so worried about Mary knowing where he was. He gave me very precise directions. Nobody can find anything just from a house name these days. No village signs. No road names…"

"If Stephen had driven himself there why not drive back?" said Bunch.

"He said he was taken there by one of his friends. Stephen tried to tell me it was the first time he'd been to one of these parties."

"You clearly didn't believe him."

"I have exceptionally good hearing. After I sounded the car horn for Stephen when I arrived – I didn't want to wait around – I heard a young woman call out something to the effect of, 'Stevie darling, there's some odd chap out there in your car'. It seems he had driven himself there before, in my Bentley."

"He drives your car? With his disability?"

"Stephen drives well enough," Jarman replied. "His arm is weak but functioning. If I'd had any idea he was using my car to visit brothels, Mary would have been the least of his troubles. We had some pretty stiff words about it on the journey back. I will admit I was not in the best mood when we got home."

"Did Laura see you both arrive back?"

"She saw me park the car. She didn't see her brother. I'd turned Stephen out at the entrance to the drive, to walk back before he came indoors to his brand-new wife. I told him it might be midnight but he could go to the Sheds and damn well sober up and put in a few hours to earn his keep."

"Did Laura know where you'd been?"

"As I said, she saw me park the car. The next morning she shoved a card for this damned club under my nose. She asked me what it was all about but I could tell from her expression that she knew perfectly well what went on there."

"Where did Laura get hold of the card?"

"Stephen must have dropped it in the car, I suppose. Laura said she was looking for an umbrella she'd left in the Bentley, but I have a suspicion she was searching for something. Anyway, she challenged me about it."

"Didn't you tell her it was Stephen's card?"

"She and Mary were bosom pals. I said nothing at first to protect my son's marriage. Our conversation became very heated very quickly and Laura made a lot of accusations, and I lost my temper. We both did, and yes, there was another almighty row. The last words we shared were harsh. I told her if she'd only came home to cause trouble and upset her mother she could damn well stay in London." Jarman looked up again. "Next day she told her mother she was going to visit friends before returning to her flat. I never saw her again."

"It's not quite what we have from your earlier statement," said Wright.

"I did not lie."

"Except by omittance."

Jarman nodded, hesitant.

Resigned, Bunch thought. "You protected Stephen regardless."

"I was trying to protect them all, even that damned young idiot Stephen. He grew up believing he's untouchable. His mother spoiled him. I suppose we all spoiled him, and I regret that. But I didn't see how destroying his marriage was going to help with anything. I thought if I could talk to Laura when we both had time to calm down it could all be sorted out. I never imagined that the opportunity would never arise."

"We have reason to believe that the house you collected your son from was where Laura died."

There was a silence broken by a swish of traffic in the street below. Jarman sat staring at his clasped hands and neither Wright nor Bunch felt they should break into his shock. "Why did she go there?" he said at last.

"That is what we are trying to discover. The house had been leased but the renters had provided false details to the agents."

"Does the owner not know what their tenant was up to?"

"It turns out that everyone, owner, agent, tenant, were all the same person using separate false names. It was Faye Waller."

"Clement's wife?"

"You didn't know they owned the property?"

"No. They lived in Richmond. I went there once."

"The Wallers have several addresses. Thus far we haven't been able to find them at any of their addresses. Tell me, how long have Jarman's used Belchamber and Phelps Accountants?"

"Belchambers? Years. Old Anselm Belchamber was a friend of my father."

"And Waller?"

"I believe he joined as a junior partner when Phelps died. When Anselm decided to retire a few years ago Waller bought the company. It's not uncommon for a young partner to rise through the ranks to eventually own the firm and keep the old name. Makes people feel safe."

"He seems to have branched out since," said Wright. "Fingers in some fairly unsavoury pies."

"Clem? Are you serious?"

"Very." Wright leaned forward, arms resting on his knees. "We have discovered that Clement Waller's activities were reported to Laura and subsequently to Kitty. They made notes from your factory's accounts, using their own private notebook. Do you have any idea why they would do that?"

"Make notes? You mean they were copying files? Why would they do that?"

"That is what we want to ascertain," said Wright. "A witness says that Laura kept track of various transactions. Her notebook was a cheap red affair. It wasn't found with Laura's body and we didn't find anything like that during our initial search of this flat. Since you've obviously gone through her belongings, have you have come across anything which could match that description?"

Jarman didn't reply for a few moments. Bunch tried to read his thoughts from his expression but there was a stony nothingness in those fire-torn features. Seconds ticked by and she exchanged questioning looks with Wright. "Mr Jarman?" She touched his hand lightly. "Are you well?"

"What? Yes. I mean no. I've not seen this notebook you're talking about, and I object to the inference that my daughter was some kind of spy!"

"We aren't implying anything of the kind. Quite the opposite in fact. From what we've been able to piece together so far, Laura and Kitty appeared to be working on the possibility that there were discrepancies in your company's records in respect to overseas deals. Specifically, those involving Germany."

"Then why didn't she come to me?" Jarman looked away as the implications filtered through. "Are you telling me that ... that she thought it could be me?"

"We don't know that. It may well have been Waller she suspected. Perhaps she stumbled across evidence of his activity while looking for something else. We may never know. It would have been better if she had reported it straight away, of course, but there you are…"

Jarman shook his head. "Waller was a friend, or so I thought.

You've both given me something to think about. There will be some urgent business to be sorted out. The security alone will be a nightmare."

"We need to talk with Waller."

"Of course."

"And we need to find that notebook." Wright rose to wander around the room without touching anything. "We did a thorough search of Laura and Kitty's bedrooms, so where do you suppose they might have hidden anything in this flat?"

"Not drawers or cupboards," said Bunch. "They've been pretty much ransacked already."

"I'll check again in Laura's room," said Jarman, "now I know what to look for."

"Doesn't hurt to recheck. Those conducting the initial search had no idea what they were after." Bunch waited until Jarman had moved into the bedroom. "Can we trust him?" she whispered.

"My gut tells me he is genuinely at a loss. Shellshocked, which is no surprise. I don't imagine this book will be in Laura's room, in any case. Not if Kitty Shenton was also writing in it. But it won't hurt to let him look. Give him a purpose while he takes all this in."

"I hadn't thought of that."

"I'll take Kitty's room while you can look around this sitting room."

"Fine by me." Bunch moved to the sideboard and began pulling out each drawer, sorting through the contents, even feeling beneath them in case something was taped on the underside. There were not too many places to search and she soon moved to the kitchenette, rooting through the cabinets, opening boxes and cannisters. After nearly an hour of searching, largely in silence and totally without success, all three were back where they started.

"What haven't we looked at?" said Wright. "I am not sure where else to check short of slitting open the cushions, but surely this book would be stashed somewhere it can be retrieved without causing damage."

"The floorboards?" said Bunch. "I checked under the rugs and didn't notice any loose planks."

"That's a tongue and groove floor," said Jarman. "Any loose

boards would be very visible."

"Tongue and groove. Goodness, that sounds terribly efficient. Probably." She grinned at him. "But you have a point about damage. Laura wasn't the average society flower. You called her an engineer."

"That mean something?" Wright asked.

"I spotted a screwdriver in the sideboard. Odd place to keep it, don't you think?"

"Well yes. What could she have used it for?"

"Not much in here, except perhaps..." Bunch fetched the screwdriver and went to examine the gramophone. She lifted the lid. The wallet within for holding a few records was buttoned shut. She pulled it open, fished out the four discs stored there and felt inside. "Nothing out of place." She tapped one of the wide-slotted screws that secured the wallet to the inside of the lid. "Scratched. Somebody has undone these more than once." Both the screws were loose and it took moments to undo them. She allowed the folder to fall forward into her hand. "Voila."

"I'll be damned. What made you look there?" said Jarman.

"The most obvious spot for a screwdriver in such a small apartment would be the kitchen, not rattling around with the cocktail sticks and playing cards. When you commented that Laura was an engineer, the only thing in the room that really came under the mechanical label was this gramophone. Or the wireless set on the sideboard, which was going to be my second choice. Comes of my ATS days. I may not know how to unlock a front door but I did learn how to wield the contents of a toolbox."

"We are both suitably impressed. Now let's see what we have here." Wright reached over and took the slender bright-red booklet that nestled in the recess behind the folder and thumbed through it.

Bunch crowded Wright's shoulder to look at page after page of entries made in an impatient sloping script, listing invoice dates and destinations. A few had question marks pencilled beside them; most were scored through. "She clearly had a methodical mind. What do you think she was looking for?"

"In her shoes I'd be looking for a pattern. Something out of the ordinary. See these recent dates? There are a few letters in the margin. Initials perhaps?" Wright showed the pages to Jarman. "Mean anything to you?"

The older man took the book and flicked the pages back and fore. "Invoice references, no doubt about that. The first pages are linked to foreign contacts." He shrugged apologetically. "I can see by the prefixes that most are German, some Swedish here and there. All of them pre '39. The later ones where Kitty took over are far more detailed." He held the book out for the two detectives to see the place where the handwriting changed to a rounder, more childlike script. He flipped back a page or two. "It looks as if Kitty was analysing Laura's entries as well as adding some of her own. All those initials by the entries are in her hand."

"And drawing different conclusions from Laura." Bunch tapped at a few words in the margin. "What does that say?"

"'Not said' – no, 'not paid'. And here, 'unconfirmed'." He ran a finger down the entries. "These are mostly from the last few months. Then she's gone back and entered a few from earlier. I'm not certain what Laura was looking for; her notes don't have an obvious pattern to them, and they are a little fixated on foreign contracts. But Kitty clearly thought someone was cooking the books."

"Whose work was she checking?" Wright regarded Jarman without expression.

"It can only be Waller's." Jarman's voice was quiet and neutral. "I trusted that man, gave him full reign with the accounting because I had so much on my plate with the research." He closed the book and opened his jacket to tuck it away in his inside breast pocket.

Wright held out his hand. "I shall take that if I may, sir. It is going to be a valuable piece of evidence."

"I need to see what he had his fingers in. All our government contracts could be in danger, you can see that, surely."

"Yes, sir. We shall return it all in good time."

"Do as you please." Jarman slapped the book into Wright's outstretched palm. "Make the most of it."

Wright tucked the book in his own pocket and stepped around to stand between Jarman and the door. "Thank you for your time, Mr Jarman. You understand, in light of what you've told us today, we'll need to take fresh statements from you and your family?"

"Are you going to charge me with something?"

"Given your status with the various ministries, I suspect that will not be my decision. For what it's worth, I believe you are only guilty of concealing facts in a criminal investigation. On the other hand, I don't believe that you were concealing evidence for your own ends. I shall report to that effect and I hope we may keep it that way." Wright moved closer to look Jarman in the eyes from a single pace away. "You were shielding a wayward son and there are not many people who wouldn't understand that. However, if there are any further such lapses I shall arrest you. Tank research or not."

"Thank you for your understanding, Chief Inspector." Jarman paused to tug his hat in place. "Now I must go. Duty calls. I shall be ready to make a statement for you tomorrow."

"That will be very helpful." Wright stood aside and watched until the door had closed softly. "That puts a clock on all of this," he murmured. "Dammit."

"Do you think Jarman had a hand in any of this? Why let him go if you believe him guilty of concealing evidence."

"Jarman killed nobody, well, not directly. The moral judgements on the manufacturing of tanks are not for me to make. It's a pity that he was here when we arrived and worse that he saw that damned book. He's the kind of man who believes in Old Testament morality."

"An eye for an eye."

"Precisely. Come on, we've found more here than we'd hoped for today. I'll drop you off at Perringham and then head back to Brighton, see what Carter has uncovered. We need to find the Wallers before Jarman does."

~~~

"There was a call for you, from a woman. She left a number but no name. She seemed rather anxious to speak with you." Knapp handed Wright a slip from the house telephone pad. "Will the Chief Inspector be staying for dinner?" she asked Bunch.

"Not today. He must get back to Brighton."

"I do but thank you, Knapp. Rose, may I use your telephone before I go?"

"Of course." Torn between good manners and overwhelming curiosity, Bunch lurked in the doorway until her grandmother called her away.

"Where have you been all day?"

"In Town with William. Not Town exactly, but sampling the dubious delights south of the river from Kennington to Croydon."

"Oh dear, but not exactly the fleshpots."

Bunch thought back to Lilly's club and shrugged. "It had its moments. Sherry, Granny?"

"That would be lovely dear, thank you. And what were you doing in the suburbs."

"Meeting some interesting people. Odd, but very interesting." Bunch sipped at her sherry and peered at the door. "And saw a few interesting quirks to our tame policeman. Have you heard anything from the Red House?"

"Daphne visited this morning with your cousin Maurice."

"Oh, is he still around?"

"He is. I am not sure if it's a sense of duty to his goddaughter or something else entirely."

"He seemed like a nice chap but terribly dull. Let's hope it's only friendship he's after."

"I doubt he's after the cash, darling. His father has a great deal more in the bank than your sister will ever have."

"We must keep an eye on Dodo, Granny. She's only just begun to get over losing George. It's worrying that she's attracted to another flier."

"You fear a substitute?"

"I don't know. I must be growing cynical in my decrepitude, but there are dangers for both of them."

Beatrice sipped her sherry and set the glass down, slowly, deliberately. "Hardly decrepit, my dear. Life does seem to hand you more than your share but please don't let it bring you to a place where you can only see the downside of every situation. Maurice is a nice boy. He is a pilot, but he's not in any more danger than you and William, charging around the country arresting armed criminals right and left."

"I'm doing my bit, Granny."

"Perhaps." She looked past Bunch to the door. "William, dear. Come and sit down. Rose, fetch your guest a drink."

"Sherry? Or would you prefer a Scotch?"

"Scotch, thank you."

"What did this person want?"

"It was a London number."

"Don't be infuriating, William. Who was it?"

"I have no idea how she got this number. It was Lilly Kendall."

"Lilly? What could she want?"

"Faye Waller walked into her club a couple of hours after we left. Or hobbled in, if Lilly is to be believed."

"Charles Jarman caught up with her?"

"Not Jarman. Apparently, her ever-loving husband made an attempt on her life."

"Good God! Is she all right?"

"She'll live. Bruising and a few minor cuts, though what Lilly calls minor is anyone's guess. Faye is safe for the moment, being sheltered somewhere in one of Lilly's chain of hidey holes."

"I had thought Faye and Clem were a really tight team."

"They may have been at one time but apparently no longer."

"Are we going back up to London to talk with her?"

"That would be a waste of time right now. If Lilly doesn't want us to speak with her today we shan't get within a mile. The problem for Faye is her husband. He was, or is still, very friendly with the MacDonald brothers and they run with the Elephant and Castle mob." He smiled grimly. "They are not to be confused with Lilly's pack. Allies, but not the same team. If the MacDonald fraternity decide that Faye Waller is a weak link in their dubious operations then her days are very much numbered."

"What then?"

"Faye will no longer be safe in London. Lilly said she'll send Faye down to Haven Cottage with one of her girls, as soon as it's safe to do so. Once arranged I shall meet Faye there and then see how we may proceed. If we can persuade her we can provide police protection she will be priceless in obtaining a conviction against Waller."

"Can a wife testify against her husband?"

"The fact that Faye was never legally married to Clement

Waller will make things simpler."

"They weren't?"

"Waller was married to one Elizabeth Burr prior to his meeting Faye. There has never been a death recorded and no divorce has been filed. Not that either proves anything. It looks as if Waller is more than capable of seeing off his wife."

"It's easy to understand why Faye has gone into hiding, in that case. However, I can't see Haven Cottage being safe. Surely that will be the first place Waller looks."

"It will be as safe as anywhere while he believes it's stiff with police."

"Which it is?"

"It's the safest place for her to meet us, at least in the short term. We can provide a safehouse later. I gather she wishes to make a statement about Waller's involvement in the murders of Laura and Kitty, so the least we can do is listen to her terms. Meanwhile we have little choice but to wait for her to contact us."

"Let me know and I shall be there." Wright stared at Bunch and she laughed. "You don't seriously imagine I'm not going to be in on the finale?"

"I know you well enough by now. It probably will be a few days before the 'finale'. To be honest, I'm not sure it's a terribly clever idea of Lilly's, but she's adamant that she can keep Faye safer than anyone for the next couple of days and, frankly, I've no reason to disbelieve her. For now, I shall shove off back to Brighton to get Carter's report – and see if we can discover any further information on the whereabouts of Clement Waller."

"Fine. I'll see you when it's convenient."

"Lady Chiltcombe." He nodded to Beatrice and pulled on his hat. "Rose. I shall call you tomorrow."

Beatrice waited until the door closed behind him. "Now that William has left, I can tell you the news from the Red House."

"Oh?" She reached for the cigarette box, finding comfort in the distraction, in the taste and smell as she lit the cigarette, hoping to avoid the news that her grandmother was about to impart. She looked up finally to meet Beatrice's eyes. "How is Mummy?"

"Sister Celestine called about an hour ago. Have you met her?"

"Once. Isn't she's the House Mother at the Red House?"

"I believe so. She sounds like a charming woman. She suggests it would be highly appropriate for the family to visit Theadora at our earliest convenience."

"Ah…" Bunch stubbed her barely smoked tailor-made against the side of a crystal ashtray. "Then I'd better get washed and changed and head back out again. I take it Daddy and Dodo are already on their way?"

"Barty has driven Daphne over, and Edward is going straight down from Town."

"Will you accompany me?"

Beatrice tilted her head and smiled a little sadly. "No, Rose, my dear, this is a time for Theadora to be with her husband and her children."

~ Fifteen ~

Bunch drove to the Red House in a daze; guilt at being out of touch while the rest of the close family were gathering at her mother's bedside gnawed at her, heaped on top of the guilt she felt at wishing Theadora's suffering could just end – a thought she squashed almost as soon as it had risen – because there was no question that she wanted her mother to live. Still, that wish lurked there as a crouching tiger in the darker recesses of her mind.

Despite breaking all the speed limits, the daylight was fading rapidly when she pulled the MG into the drive at the Red House. She sat for several minutes contemplating the colours on the horizon and waiting for the redness and tear-puffing to fade from under her eyes. She pulled the rear-view mirror to one side to dab powder on her cheeks and adjust her hat that the wind had dishevelled, before sliding out of the car, mindful that she was wearing a poplin skirt rather than her habitual slacks. Knowing her mother would never dream of sallying forth wearing less than immaculate clothing, she smoothed a hand over the dark blue fabric, surreptitiously checking her stocking seams. Satisfied that she would pass muster she hurried in to face the inevitable.

"Rosebunch." Edward rose from beside his wife's bed to kiss his eldest child on the cheek.

"Hello Daddy. How is she?" Bunch looked down at Theadora, seemingly asleep on her throne of pillows.

"Weak," he admitted. "Sleeping a great deal of the time." He sank back in his chair and took his wife's hand once more. Theadora stirred briefly and muttered a few words but her eyes remained closed.

"Dodo." Bunch went to hug her sister, staring at her cousin Maurice who'd stood as she entered. "Granny said Barty was driving you here."

"He was," said Maurice, "but he had Home Guard duties, and I was happy to volunteer." He stood behind Dodo and waved Bunch into his place at the bedside.

"Very kind, thank you." Bunch didn't offer to hug him. She was a little affronted by his presence, perhaps because she had left Beatrice behind, or because she found his hand resting her sister's shoulder mildly offensive. *Jealousy is not a pretty thing*, she told herself. "I got here as soon as I could." She sat in the chair opposite her father.

"I'm sure you did. Don't worry yourself over it," Edward replied. "Mother said you were up in Town with Wright."

"Yes, but only south of the river. It was an interesting day, one way or another. Wright never fails to astound."

"He had quite a reputation before he was invalided out."

"You had him vetted?"

"Naturally. I wanted to know what kind of man he was. He has led you into some extremely dangerous situations."

"He doesn't lead me," Bunch snapped. "I go where the evidence takes me."

"I suspect it's neck and neck where the two of you are concerned."

"Can you two leave it for today?" said Dodo. "Please?"

"Sorry," said Bunch. "I'm a bit tired. Please, give me the latest bulletin. What have the doctors told you?"

"That her organs are failing and it's all in the lap of the gods," said Edward.

"I was here just a day ago and the sister seemed to think she had more time left." Bunch properly looked at her mother for the first time since arriving and felt the shock, a physical jolt, running through her body. The once elegantly sculpted face was more bloated than on her previous visit. Puffy lids kept her eyes closed and a thin thread of drool leaked from one corner of her mouth as Theadora struggled to pull each breath between cracked lips. Bunch leaned forward to wring out a sponge from the bowl by the bedside to dab the moisture away. Theadora turned her head peevishly, muttering a few unintelligible words before lapsing back into rasping sleep.

"Does she wake at all?"

"She's delirious most of the time," said Edward. "But she comes back to us off and on."

"More off than on." Dodo pulled her chair close and grabbed

Bunch's hand. "I'm so glad you're here, Bunch."

"So am I. Granny sends her regards."

Dodo leaned over the bed and murmured into her mother's ear, "Did you hear that Mummy? Granny sends her love."

Theadora's lips struggled to shape a word but no sounds came with it and her eyes did not open.

They all fell into an awkward silence accentuated by the sounds of Theadora's laboured lungs until Edward rose stiffly. "I need to stretch my legs. Sister Bertha said there are tea and cakes for us in the refectory. Come along Maurice, we shall play at being butlers."

Bunch waited for them to leave before she put both arms around her sister. "I am sorry, my darling. I should have been here sooner, I know, but I came the moment I got your message."

"Just so we could spend even longer not saying anything?" Dodo held a handkerchief to her mouth. "I didn't mean it like that, truly," she said. "We've rather run out of things to say."

"The only subject that comes to mind is that damnable pachyderm…"

"… in the room." Dodo attempted a laugh.

"I agree, though if we're speaking of pachyderms, what's Maurice doing here?"

"He's been a brick, Bunch. Gets on awfully well with Daddy."

"That is a blessing. And you – are you seeing a lot of him?"

Dodo avoided her sister's eyes. "Not really. He's stationed close by and we're the nearest thing he has to family over here."

She has a point. Bunch thought. *Just because I find him dull as hell there's no reason Dodo should. And he visits, which is more than I or Emma have done of late. Being stuck at Banyards with a small child and Barty Tinsley for company can't be a lot of fun for Dodo.* The idea that it was not Maurice using her sister but the other way around, that Dodo needed his companionship, even a little harmless romance, had not occurred to her.

She grinned as her recent sweaty night's companionship with Henry Marsham came to mind. *Sod companionship, that was all about the sex.* Seeing Theadora labouring to gain her breath, Bunch mulled over the thought that most people have no idea how or when their lives would end. She had evaded the reaper several times herself now and tried not to smile as she wondered if the same count of a cat's nine lives also applied to people. She looked to the side of the bed to where the oxygen cylinder stood and frowned. Had her mother, sliding painfully into oblivion, taken any time to consider death? Laura Jarman and Kitty Shenton had been snuffed out to satisfy another's greed. Dodo's husband George had crashed to earth in a fighter plane in another country altogether, fighting a war that could take the life of anyone around her, at any moment. *And some people make the choice for themselves.* "We take our comforts where we can," she murmured.

"Pardon?"

Dodo was staring at her and Bunch reached to take her hand. "Be happy," she said. "I don't mean here in this room, but tomorrow and the next day and the next."

"Not like you to be the philosopher, Rose."

"Hello Mummy. Back with us for a bit then?"

"Thirsty," Theadora whispered.

"Of course." Bunch grabbed the porcelain sipping cup that had been sitting on the bedside cabinet and supported her mother's head and shoulders while the sick woman moistened her mouth. "Better?"

Theadora gave a feeble nod in reply. "Tell Nanny … I shall see the boys … after nursery tea…"

She mumbled a few words more and Dodo leaned in to catch them. "Something about keys but I didn't catch it all," she said. "She's been like this. A few lucid words here and there that makes you wonder if she's been lying there listening to everything we've said. Otherwise it's a string of nonsense. Mostly about the boys."

"She's never got over their loss." Bunch set the sipping cup down and crossed to the French doors, moving the curtain aside, to look out into the garden, ignoring Blackout rules. When her brothers were spoken of, which was seldom, it was always "the boys", to a point where Bunch conjured a mental image of Millais's "Two Princes" whenever they came up in conversation; that one of them was also called Edward only made it more compelling. Though the boys had died in the flu pandemic twenty years before, their memory remained a cloud that hung over Theadora, enveloping her in a pain that only alcohol had seemed able to lessen. A cure that was, slowly and painfully, killing her.

"What were they like?" said Dodo.

"Edward and Benedict?" She turned to face Dodo. "I was only eleven when the flu hit us, so it's hard to recall a great deal after all this time. They liked all the usual boy's stuff. Sports and such. Teddy had started boarding at Harrow the year that the Great War broke out – I was five or six then – so my memory of him is a little hazy if I'm honest. Ben was two years younger than me; he was due to start boarding later. I remember he'd broken his arm a few months before they fell ill. He took a tumble from his pony when he tried to jump the ditch past Shaws Corner. Got one hell of a ticking-off from Daddy for putting the pony at risk." She shrugged. "They were boys like any other – just boys."

"Teddy and Ben. I don't think I've heard them remembered in that way before."

"Nursery names. Does Mummy ever call you Dodo?" Bunch sat on the edge of the bed.

"She always calls me Daphne, but then so does everyone except you. It's only Daddy now who ever calls you Rosebunch. It's Rose for everyone else."

"Just nursery names," Bunch snapped and Dodo pulled away from her, looking so shocked that Bunch felt immediate remorse. She flapped jazz hands in her sister's direction. "Sorry. Bit on edge."

They both glanced at the door, glad of the interruption when Maurice brought in a tray of tea. "We also have cake," he said. "Courtesy of the lovely sister here."

"Hello ladies." Sister Bertha came to the bedside and looked at her patient, checking Theadora's pulse and frowning at what she saw on the chart hanging at the side of the bedhead. "Has she woken at all?"

"Briefly," Dodo replied. "Just says a few words. She seems to know we're here."

"She'll drift in and out, I expect."

"She's struggling to breathe."

Sister Bertha glanced at Edward, who had reached for the oxygen mask, and shook her head. "Her ladyship was adamant that we should only ease her pain."

"She wants to die?"

"I believe that she feels her time has come," Sister Bertha replied.

"Daddy!" said Dodo. "Did you know this? Did you know?"

Edward's chin dropped to his chest in an effort to avoid his youngest child's glare. "It wasn't my choice. She knew what treatment there was, that it only offered to extend her life a short while. She is in the most horrible pain."

"But you knew…"

"I have seen people make that choice." Bunch put both arms around her sister and held her close. "It's not anybody's fault. Not even hers. She made a choice, sweetheart, and we may not agree with it, but it is her decision."

"You as well?" Dodo sobbed.

"No. *Had* I known I doubt I could have changed her mind. You know how Mummy can be. She is going out on her own terms. Her last wish, if you will."

"She can't do that. Can she?" said Dodo.

"She can, child," said Sister Bertha. "We will ease her passing now she has refused treatment, and to respect her wishes."

"Is that passing is imminent?" said Bunch.

Sister Bertha regarded her patient critically. "The fluids are building up, as are the toxins. So yes, it will be soon. Twenty-four hours at most."

A hand bell rang from across the gardens and Sister Bertha looked up, reminding Bunch of her dog hearing a bird rise. The nun straightened the covers with a practised tug and gave Bunch a side-long look, as if she knew Bunch was the only one with the nerve to commit the crime of sitting on a patient's bed. "That is the Complin bell." The nun spoke to Edward. "Not our chapel bell, of course. We're not permitted to ring steeple bells now, not even little sisters such as us. It's an unexpected reverberation of war, but the law is the law, and we shall do what we must." She waved a hand at the dark beyond the French doors. "I shall just be across the courtyard. The next morphine dose is not due for another hour or so. If Lady Chiltcombe shows signs of discomfort before then, Sister Agnes will fetch me. She is on duty at the desk." The elderly nun closed the curtains against the darkening sky and withdrew, leaving the family in awkward silence.

"That is… Only twenty-four hours?" Bunch eventually said.

"I shall stay," Edward replied. "You girls needn't."

"We can't leave," said Dodo. "Not now we know."

Bunch was certain he was not hearing them. He stroked his wife's hand, rubbing his thumb across the ring on her left hand that seemed embedded in flesh swollen with fluid retention, lost in that act with his old memories, and in need of a little time alone to remember.

Dodo took a step towards him. "It isn't—"

"Daphne." Bunch grabbed her arm. "Come on, it's a small room for this many people. Let's get a little air, shall we? Maurice?" The three of them slipped out into the evening air, leaving Edward alone with his wife, and went to sit on one of the wooden benches dotted around the courtyard walls. Bunch handed round her cigarette case and they sat smoking in silence for some while. The chapel walls were solid stone but to Bunch the faint sound of evening prayer drifting across to them felt otherworldly. *And perhaps it is.* The notion of being part of a life dictated by bells and chants and stone walls gave her the shivers. *On the other hand, is life at Perringham all that different? Duty to a different calling?* "Daddy isn't himself," she said finally. "He's not going to leave her side and there are far too many of us in there. You have Georgi to get back to, and I've no doubt Maurice needs to be on parade first thing…"

Maurice nodded. "I wangled a twenty-four-hour pass from the CO but I need to be back on the field before seven."

"Dodo, please, let Maurice take you home. Call Granny and give her the news and Barty can run you back in the morning."

"You're so bossy," said Dodo. "I want to stay."

Bunch put her arm around Dodo's shoulders. "Go. Get some rest, my darling. Give Mummy one last hug and take it home to that daughter of yours."

"And if Mummy isn't here tomorrow?"

"There is that chance," Bunch agreed. "But you'll always have that hug to share, and Georgi needs you more than our mother does right now."

"She's right," said Maurice.

Daphne stared at the walls of the chapel on the far side of the garden. "You will call me the moment anything changes?" she said finally. "Good or bad!"

"I promise."

"All right. But only for Georgi's sake." They returned to Theadora's room. Dodo hugged Edward and then leaned across the bed and gently hugged her mother for a long twenty seconds. Bunch could see Dodo mutter in Theadora's ear, and if asked later she would swear Theadora's lips moved in reply but if so, then so softly that no-one but Dodo heard. Finally, she straightened. "Goodbye. Don't forget, telephone me the moment there is any change."

"We shall," Edward replied.

"The moment there is any change," Bunch said.

Maurice, his arm around Dodo's waist, gently moved her out into the corridor and the door closed quietly behind them.

Bunch raised an eyebrow at Edward, who gave a minute shrug of the head. "Well, he's a quick worker," she growled.

"He may not be right for her, but he's just what she needs right at this moment," Edward replied. "Your sister is not a pragmatist and she may not thank you later for sending her home."

"I wanted to spare her. She doesn't need to see the end. It will haunt her even more."

"She may feel the loss far more deeply."

"Whereas I don't love Mother enough?"

"You love her, Rosebunch, and you will grieve like the rest of us, but it won't overwhelm you. And that is not a criticism." He grasped her hands firmly in his. "You see the logic in death, that it is inevitable, which makes you a fine diplomat – or a detective." He sat down by the bed and gazed at his wife. "She's so beautiful even under the cosh of this damn disease."

"I know." Bunch took up a place on the opposite side of the bed. "Dodo takes after her. She really *is* the English rose, whereas I'm just named after one."

"Roses come in all shapes and sizes," he replied. "All of them are quite lovely."

Bunch snorted.

"Henry Marsham certainly thinks so," Edward continued. "He was rather late getting back to the bunker the other night. You must have had a very long chat." Edward took out a hip flask and took a brisk swig while the implications sank in. "Do be careful, won't you?"

There wasn't a reply she could make, and she only hoped the subdued light hid her furious blush. The swift change of subject took her by surprise. More so because it was the kind of comment she might have taken in her stride from Beatrice or Daphne, or even Theadora, but fathers are different. Realising that Edward was aware of her night with Marsham, or strongly suspected it at very least, was mortifying. Her eyes were unfocussed and it took her a moment to realise Edward was offering her a slug of Scotch and she took it, handing the flask back without meeting his gaze and without a word uttered until Sister Bertha had come and gone with a needle full of oblivion. They sat either side of Theadora and they talked and reminisced about the woman they both loved, to the fractured rhythm of her breathing. And finally they slept.

It was past four a.m. when Bunch opened her eyes. Light came through the half-open door from a faint blue emergency lamp in the corridor. The Blackout curtains covering the open window bulged inwards with the through draft, and on it came the spicy cent of Evening Stocks growing just outside Theadora's room. A single blackbird was trilling a few tentative scales, sensing that dawn was an hour away.

Bunch had fallen asleep leaning on the bed, with her head pillowed on her right arm while her left stretched out towards her mother. In her dream she had felt a pressure. On waking she found that though Theadora's left hand was covering hers, the older woman was staring directly at her husband, her jaw slack, the folds of oedema bunching beneath her chin – and she was still and silent.

Bunch raised herself gently to lean on her elbow, afraid to let the moment pass. "Mummy?" she said, and louder, "Daddy."

Theadora didn't move, even when Edward stirred and sat up with the energy of a man used to snatching sleep where and when he could. "Thea?"

"She's gone Daddy. It's over."

~ Sixteen ~

All the curtains were drawn out of respect, plunging the Dower House into shadow. Bunch lay on her bed watching the heavy fabric of her bedroom drapes shiver in the breeze, which was cool after the rain, and considered getting up to close the casement. *But that would involve effort.* She shifted to stare at the ceiling, debating which black dress she should choose when she dressed for dinner. Black had never been her colour of choice and she had precisely two black frocks, which should have made it simple. *But choosing even that involves effort.*

Bella whined and rolled onto her back, leaning against Bunch's side for a belly rub. Bunch obliged, absently but still aware that she was spoiling the dog terribly. Not even her old Labrador had been allowed the privilege of sleeping on the bed, spreading hair on the counterpane to Knapp's annoyance. Her father would say working dogs belonged out in the kennels. He was right, that a good shooting dog was not a pet, but Bunch doubted Bella was ever going to come close to being a *good* working dog, and right now a companion pet was what she needed. As she rubbed the dog's silky fur she turned her gaze to the two dresses hanging on the front of her wardrobes.

Theadora's death had hit her hard, far harder than she cared to admit, even to herself. Yes, Bunch had loved her mother, as any daughter would, but they had never been truly close. Was it the intimacy of her death that made it harder to accept? She was convinced that Theadora's final act had been to squeeze her hand, though she had no real memory of that grasp; that last handhold had become lost in a vague dreamlike state. Bunch was loathe to mention it to anyone, partly because she feared they would laugh, saying she had imagined it, and partly because of a deep guilt. If it had happened as she remembered it, or imagined it, then that last touch should have been her father's. He had quietly adored his wife for the best part of four decades and the guilt of that last grasp ate at her conscience.

She told herself it had been her mother's delirium. Theadora had seen her daughter, head and shoulders sprawled on the bed, but had not noticed the sleeping Edward leaning back in his chair. Bunch knew her father had not seen that final gesture but she could not help feeling guilty all the same. And then there was Dodo, who had screamed down the telephone at Bunch for persuading her away from Theadora's side. That was a more tangible rift and would take time to repair.

Bella whined at a gentle tap on the door.

"Miss Rose? There's a telephone call for you."

"Who is it?"

"Colonel Ralph, Miss."

Ralph? Hell, what can he want? "Thank you, Knapp. I just need to dress…" She pulled on a light jumper and grabbed the slacks she had taken off before her bath. "Tell him I shall be there in a few moments."

Dressed, at least well enough to answer the telephone, she ran down to the hallway, making a mental note that Beatrice was not the only one who needed a handset in her bedroom. "Hello?" she snapped into the mouthpiece.

"Miss Courtney? What ho! It's Everett, Everett Ralph. Your friendly lodger at P-House."

"Hello." She waited. His damnable Bertie Wooster act made her cautious because she knew to her cost that it really was an act – that Colonel Everett Ralph was a genuine piece of work. "What may I do for you, Colonel?" She maintained a neutral tone. He was a friend to her father and there was no advantage in upsetting him for no good reason.

"Firstly, please let me offer my deepest condolences. Your father told me about your mother's passing. Dashed shame. A lovely woman."

"Thank you. She'd been ill for some time so it wasn't entirely unexpected."

"I know. And the funeral is to be next week?"

"At the parish church. We would have considered the family chapel but things being as they are…" She left the accusation to float.

Ralph scooped it up as she hoped he would. "I can only offer you the same grovelling apologies that I did to your father. We're all off limits right now. Absolutely no unauthorised personnel. You do understand?"

"Yes, of course..." Bunch did understand, and having Theadora interred in the parish church was not really any hardship; so many of the family were already buried there. Bunch secretly wondered if Theadora would prefer it, since she had disliked spending time at Perringham, except that her boys were interred in Perringham's chapel vault. That aside, she enjoyed putting Ralph off his stride. She waited for him to reply.

"Miss Courtney? Are you still there?"

"Yes, sorry ... No, I don't understand, not really, but I suspect there is nothing I can do about it."

"Quite. I really am sorry, old girl. And I wouldn't be bending your ear now except that a rather disturbed, or I should say disturbing, woman has been battering at our gates. Quite literally."

"How so?"

"Dinked her car into the stone stanchions. She claims somebody was chasing after her, as if we've never heard that one before. My adjutant is keen to detain her for a little ... chat. He claims his students need some practice in their questioning techniques."

"And you stopped him? Goodness, Ralph, you must be going soft in your old age."

"It seemed the wrong thing to allow since she insisted you were expecting her. I thought I should give you a bell before I let my chaps have their own little tête-à-tête. Off the radar, so to speak."

"I suppose she gave you a name?" she said.

"She says her name is Faye, and that you would know what that meant. The thing is ... she has no papers, which is never a good sign. But since she insists you're expecting her at the Dower House, and as you know, I always like to oblige Edward's family when I can—"

I bet you do, Bunch thought. The idea of anyone being questioned by Ralph's secretive cabal made Bunch shudder. She also had no doubt it was only her father's influence that had kept Faye Waller from simply vanishing. *Keeping in with the boss?* "Oh, darling Faye. Yes, I was expecting Mrs Waller." *Like hell I was, but here goes.* "She was being chased? How very odd. I don't suppose your guard chaps saw anything out of the ordinary?"

"Looking for someone in hot pursuit isn't the first thing that springs to mind when a stonking great Sunbeam Tourer ploughs into one's gates."

"Why else would she drive into the gates?"

"It may not have been entirely accidental, it's true. A car did drive by shortly afterwards, but then I suppose if it was a pursuer they wouldn't have hung around. My chaps had a good scout around the immediate area and found nothing suspicious. In Major Askey's view, it was a clumsy attempt at gaining entrance into the grounds – for whatever reason. Which is why he is keen to question her. Naturally, we've upped the perimeter guard but meanwhile, what do you want me to do with her? Since you say she really is your guest I can hardly keep her here, can I?"

She could hear the smirk in his tone, for which she didn't really blame him. His caution made perfect sense. *No better way to attract the attention of half-a-dozen burly soldiers than driving into their sentry post. He also knows Faye's not being entirely truthful, and doubtless assumes I am somehow complicit. In which case, in for a penny*— "Tell your Mr Askey he has no cause for concern. Poor Faye has a rather difficult marriage and … well, I am sure I don't need to spell it out. Do I take it you've detained her at the House?"

"Let's say we've taken her in for safe keeping," he drawled. "You can understand why, I'm sure."

"Of course. Is she hurt?"

"I had the MO take a quick dekko and he says it's all superficial cuts and bruises. Nothing drastic. She's as jittery as hell, however."

Not surprising, Bunch thought and said aloud, "Faye has always been a little flaky. Probably her imagination running riot." Wright would say to keep her under guard until he arrived, Bunch was sure of that, but the hint of expectation in Ralph's voice convinced her that Faye Waller would be best off out of Perringham House and in the Dower as soon as humanly possible. *Faye Waller may be guilty of a great many things but she isn't a spy.* "Give me five minutes and I shall skip along to meet her."

"Why not bring that natty little car of yours to the front gates to pick her up?"

It would be far quicker, she knew, but if Faye Waller was being pursued there was a good to fair chance her MG would also be under surveillance. "There's no need," she said. "I shall use the farm lane – just in case."

"In case?"

"Let's say it's tied up with a police matter."

"Ah... Then perhaps I should call your police inspector friend. Wright, isn't it? He's your man in those trunk murder cases, or so I hear."

I could have been consulting with any policeman, over any crime; why does he make that immediate assumption? Bunch closed her eyes for a moment, struggling to keep herself calm. She knew that Ralph had ears everywhere, yet it creeped her out a little to think he was aware of her every move. "Not necessary, I can— Actually, yes please, make yourself useful—" *For once,* she thought "—and contact Wright at the Brighton CID. Tell him exactly what you have just told me and say he's to get here as quick as he can." Bunch wondered if she was being too abrupt with Ralph.

"Not just for a domestic quarrel?"

"There's more to it but nothing to give your Major Askey any concern. If you could call DCI Wright... Please?"

"Right ho. In that case I shall escort this lady to you personally. See you in a few minutes."

"Yes, please do." She was a little surprised that Ralph didn't ask further questions, but he could read between lines far better than anyone she knew, which she supposed was why he had been chosen to do what he did. *Whatever that might be. And the lines I'm reading between are that the quicker I get Faye Waller out of that viper's nest the better.*

She ran up to her room and finished dressing in suitable attire for a walk through the farm, and was halfway down the stairs when she realised she had forgotten something, or rather decided there was something she may quite possibly need. Slipping back into her room she took the British Bulldog pocket pistol from its box in her bureau. After her run in with Etta Beamish in a deranged showdown in her neighbour's garage, she had liberated the weapon from her father's collection – as insurance. It was smaller than the standard issue Webley favoured by the police, but it was more easily carried, concealed in a handbag or pocket. Insurance in theory, but in reality she had seldom taken it out of its box other than to clean it. Yet today felt like a day to give it an airing.

Once loaded she slipped it in the righthand pocket of her hounds-tooth jacket and patted it to reassure herself. Despite its small size it still weighed enough to pull the fabric to one side. "But I'm only going to the House so who's going to see, hey Bella? Come on."

Slipping out through the kitchen doors, Bunch made her way across the paddocks, past the row of cottages and the dairy yard, and onto the private lane that led to the rear of Perringham House, to meet Ralph and Faye.

Fronds of overgrown hazel and hawthorn stretched alongside the lane that had been rarely used since the Christmas of '39, when the Ministry had requisitioned Perringham House. Grass and dandelions had burrowed up through the tarmac, along with the usual hedgerow flounces of cow parsley and willow herb that now grew in the cracks in the road's surface. Bunch called Bella to heel and pushed onwards to the barrier of stakes and barbed wire that sentries had used to construct a gateway.

"Miss Courtney. Rose—"

Ralph stepped through the gap with a fair-haired woman at his side, and Bunch thought how, in another time and place, they would have made a stylish couple. He was an annoyingly attractive man; and Faye Waller a very handsome woman, slender and petite and fashionable in a tea dress and jacket and a matching sun hat. A blue-and-white bag hung from her left shoulder, the kind that had become popular because it could easily accommodate a gas mask. She was twirling a pair of sunglasses between fingers and thumb of her right hand, and calmly taking in her surroundings. She might have been heading out for tea at the Ritz – but for the bruises on her cheek and jaw that lent her an air of vulnerability.

Right now she's a walking target. "Faye, darling, you made it." Bunch reached out to shake Faye's hand and tug her closer or, to be more precise, away from Ralph. "Thank you, Everett. Good of you to help Faye out. We appreciate it."

"My pleasure." He bent to scritch the top of Bella's head.

"Nice dog you've acquired."

"She belongs to a friend. I'm looking after her for him."

"Henry Marsham. Yes, I had heard... I wonder, is everything all right? Do you need an escort back to the Dower House?"

"We shall be fine," Bunch replied. "Husband trouble. Some men simply don't know what's acceptable behaviour."

Ralph mouth curled at one side in a knowing smirk. "And so another friend in need hauls up on your doorstep. You're quite the Samaritan, aren't you?"

"Hardly that." Bunch looked away, snapping her fingers for Bella to come to heel. The oblique reference to Cecile, whom Ralph had absorbed into his shadowy cabal, was a barbed hook but she chose to ignore it. "If you do see anyone snooping around Faye's car please do call me. Or call Police House and have PC Botting see them on their way."

"I telephoned your Inspector Wright chappie, as commanded. Seems he had already left on his way to see you. Rather lucky, what?"

"Thank you, Everett. I don't suppose you know what time he left Brighton?"

"'Fraid not." He lowered his chin to stare at her. "Do you always call him when your friends come to you in dire need?"

"Not at all. Got to dash now. If it's not inconvenient for you I shall send someone over to collect Mrs Waller's car later. Come along Faye, you look as if you need a stiff drink or two." Bunch set of at such a brisk walk towards the Dower House that Faye struggled to keep up with her escort, finally yanking Bunch to a halt.

"What was going on back there? Please, don't get me wrong. I am very grateful, given what has gone on, but..." Faye peered back over her shoulder. "He's one of those complicated men, isn't he? Charming and shark-like in one neat package."

"That's a very succinct assessment based on such a short acquaintance with him," said Bunch.

"I know men," Faye replied. "I grew up with his sort. Without his polish, perhaps, but he's a man, nevertheless." She hitched her bag a little higher on her shoulder and slipped her sunglasses onto her nose. "He's not a villain, at least not the kind I come across in my world. What is his line of work? It doesn't take much to realise that lot back there—" she nodded back towards Perringham House "—are not the standard military."

"You truly do not want to know. Just be grateful my father carries a lot of clout, or you and your car might well have vanished without trace."

"Hardly my fault I crashed into those gates," said Faye.

Bunch wasn't totally convinced on that point. The Wallers must have known Perringham House had been requisitioned and that Bunch wouldn't be living there. *Desperation?* she thought. She glanced behind them. The barrier was back in place and just the vague outline of a sentry could be made out through the trees. "We should keep moving." She started off along the lane once more, eager to take Faye to the Dower as quickly as she could. "Is it your husband, you think, who followed you?"

"Yes. And one of MacDonald's gorillas. Or even that bloke Jarman."

"Charles Jarman?"

"That's the one. He came to the club," said Faye. "Kicking off something alarming until Lilly's boys taught him the error of his ways."

"Was he killed?"

Faye chuckled and shook her head. "No, but he's a bit worse for wear. He was looking for Clem. Seems he'd finally tumbled that Clem had been milking him all these years, like he did to all his legit clients." She snorted. "Never tried it with Lilly, though. Knew he'd never get away with shillin' her."

"Was that it? Did Laura Jarman discover that your husband was robbing the family firm?"

"Not entirely. She had it in her head that her father was some sort of spy. It's why Clem allowed her to go on working at Jarman's for as long as he did. But he never imagined he'd be rumbled by her."

"How do you know all this?"

"Kitty told me after the Jarman girl was murdered."

"She was looking at the same records. We found her notes."

"The stupid girl. I warned Kitty to drop it. I told her, it wasn't the old man she should worry about. It was the son."

"Stephen?"

"He's run up a lot of debts."

"With whom?"

"Me, for one. Not that I'd have killed him for a few measly quid. He came along to a few of my soirees, and they don't come cheap, you know. He only stopped when his father dragged him away one night."

"Who are his other debtors?"

"He likes the gee-gees." Faye rubbed forefinger and thumbs together. "MacDonald was leaning on him."

"Did they do that to you?" Bunch gestured at Faye's bruises.

Faye raised a hand to them, half-hidden behind the dark glasses. "No. If MacDonald's lads had worked me over I'd not be talking to you today. I got these when I hit the car's doorframe when I crashed. I've always bruised easy."

"You're convinced you were being followed?"

"I know I was. We all knew someone was watching Lilly's place. Not just the Jungle Club. It would have been madness to try hiding there so I was staying over at her flat. Maccy's goons aren't the brightest, so we didn't imagine they'd find me so quickly. But as soon as we spotted them I knew I had to do a runner. I called your inspector friend, jumped in my car, and scarpered." She shrugged. "I would have called you first but I didn't have your number and there wasn't enough time to ring enquiries."

"But why did you drive to Perringham House?"

"Because I knew where the Perringham estate is but I couldn't remember exactly how to get to its Dower House. I was followed so stopping for directions in the village wasn't a sensible option. The military checkpoint seemed like a safe place to stop, and I was trying to slow down enough to drive through the gates … but unfortunately I hit them instead."

"The car chasing you, was that MacDonald's men? Or was it your husband?"

Faye offered a grim smile. "It was Clement's Humber Imperial, all right. I've been inside it often enough to recognise it. They drove past the gates a moment or two after I crashed. I saw them slow down but they didn't stop, obviously."

"They?"

"He had a passenger but I couldn't see who it was. They drove past again a minute or two later, then sped off."

"Enough time to turn around and cruise past for a second look." Bunch glanced both ways along the lane and took Faye by the elbow. "We should get a move on. I doubt anyone would know this back lane without a map, but there's no point taking chances. We'll have to keep to the lane; it's a little longer but you'll never get across the fields in those shoes." She pointed at the black heels that were already stained with mud from the recent rain. "We shall find you some better footwear later. Do you have any luggage in your Sunbeam?"

"Only an overnight bag. I left in a bit of a hurry."

"We'll have that fetched later too. Bella, come." She set as fast a pace as Faye could manage, with the dog racing in and out of the hedgerows to either side of the lane, its head down as it followed seemingly random trails for the pure joy of it.

They passed the farm buildings and cottages and started along the short, flint-strewn track leading to the rear of the Dower before Faye called her to slow down. "Hang on a minute." Faye bent to shake a stone out of her shoe. "Damn and blast. I hate the country. Did you know that? All that bloody mud – and insects." She swatted at something flying around her face. "How much further is it?"

"How could you hate the country? You lived not ten minutes from here."

Faye laughed. "I never lived there, sweetie. Strictly business – and out again."

"Your brothel…"

"No. We were careful on that point. Our gentlemen paid a membership fee to the Haven Private Members Club, where they were able to attend social events." She laughed. "Very exclusive, or it was until those Canadian blokes from Chellcott got wind of it and forced their way in. The local yokels didn't have a clue."

"Don't be so naïve, Faye. One thing you should know about the countryside is that no secret ever stays secret for very—" Bunch looked at Bella, who standing in the middle of the track staring back the way they had come. *Probably nothing – or is there something in the yard.* Half-a-dozen pigeons flapped noisily out of the oak trees towering over the hedge. She watched them circle, glanced at Bella who was still staring back, her nose twitching. Bunch swore under her breath. "Would Clement know how to find the Dower House?" she asked.

"I don't know. He wasn't at Haven Cottage often. I'm sure he knew you were asking after him, so I imagine he'd make it his business to learn all about you."

"Damn." Bunch scanned the track and the fields to either side of them but could not see anything or anyone. *But no matter how stupid pigeons are, they don't fly up en masse for nothing at all.* The sooner the two women reached the Dower House the better. There was little point in attempting a dash across the field of late barley that lay between them and the Dower's paddocks; Faye's heels would never cope. She upped the pace as much as she dared along the stony, rutted lane.

"Slow down," Faye moaned.

"We must keep moving. I'm worried that your shadow has returned." Bunch moved to put Faye to her left and placed her right hand against her pocket to check for the Bulldog's reassuring bulk. The roof of the Dower peeped over the tops of the hedges. Had they taken a route across the field they would be very nearly home, but the cart track arched around to a bridge across a tiny brook before joining the public road a hundred yards from the entrance to the stable yard at the Dower House.

She hustled Faye along until they were just ten paces from a rough bridge constructed of railway sleepers, sturdy enough to support farm vehicles. The far side was sheltered by a stand of hazel and willow, coppiced by the Jenners for wattle fencing.

"Wait a minute. I have to stop. I've got a stitch." Faye pulled Bunch to a halt and bent over, hand against her side.

Bunch gazed along the track again.

Bella was not running ahead as she usually did. The dog had stopped to stare at the hedgerow, as close as a springer came to pointing. Her head turned, whippet fast, to check on her mistress and let out a sharp bark, stumped tail alert but not wagging.

Bunch cupped Faye's elbow and urged her into a sprint across the planks. "Grin and bear it," she hissed. "Somebody is coming up behind us."

"I have to get my breath back, please." Faye grabbed at a sapling and took a deep breath. "Just for a moment."

"Not here." Bunch peered along the lane, sure that she had seen movement beyond the hedge.

"Run, Faye, run. To the end of the lane and turn right towards the stable yard gates. Go now!" Despite her laboured breathing, Faye ran.

The dog moved closer to Bunch, its tail stump blurring for a moment, and then turned back as two men stepped through the thicket and into view.

The taller of them cut a distinguished figure in a bespoke city suit and handmade brogues. His companion was shorter and swarthier, dressed in a silk suit that Bunch guessed was not made on the eastern side of the Atlantic. Both looked wholly at odds with their surroundings.

"Hello Clem," Faye said.

The tall man smiled. "Faye, darling."

"Clement Waller," Bunch said, "this is a private road, you know." She cringed inwardly at the banality of her words, but it was all she could think of saying. "You have no business being here."

Waller gestured before him. "We're here now."

"Indeed you are. My colleague Chief Inspector Wright and I have been waiting to speak with you. You've been a hard man to find." Bunch slid her hand inside her pocket and adjusted her pose, feet slightly apart. To turn her back on them and run was not an option she favoured. She tensed, ready to dive to one side or the other. "We have a few questions about the murders of Laura Jarman and Kitty Shenton, not to mention threats to your own wife."

Waller took a few paces forward and Bella yipped again, paddling her feet as she stood her ground.

"Call off the mutt," the short man growled, his hand inside his jacket now. "Before I shoot him."

"He is a she," Bunch snapped. "And she won't do anything if you stay right where you are." She stared at them, unblinking, and prayed they were still far enough away not to see her trembling. The thug's hand dropped back to his side and she smiled at him.

"Bella, come by." She waited until the dog had curled herself around to sit at heel at Bunch's side. "So … Laura," she said. "Why?"

Waller blinked. "What?"

"Why did you murder her?"

"Straight to the point," he said. "Kudos, Miss Courtney. It wasn't by choice. Had Laura Jarman stuck to her job, and been a bit more up front on any discrepancies, like yourself, then…" He shrugged. "Had she just come to me with her concerns I could have seen to it that she was diverted elsewhere and none of this would have been necessary."

"Are you saying that if she had been less efficient she might have lived?"

"Something like that."

"That is insane. Are you seriously telling me that she brought her death on herself?" Bunch shook her head. "How can you blame her for her own murder. Or blame either of those young women for seeing you for what you were?"

"You know that it wasn't my activities Laura was looking into, not at first."

"What was it? What did she uncover?"

"That was the funny thing." He glanced at his companion and chuckled quietly. "She was convinced it was her father who had something to hide."

"What did she finally learn about you that meant she had to die? It's rather excessive for a spot of fraud."

"I see my wife has been talking to you." He peered past her to the swoosh of vehicle in the road beyond the trees. "It was a little more than draining a few pounds from that lunatic Jarman's piggy bank."

"And Kitty?"

"She knew about Laura. Dominoes. One falls and more must automatically follow. Leave your weapon alone, Miss Courtney. I can see its shape in your pocket. Besides, it's two against one."

"Given your track record I'm not sure I have much to gain by surrendering." Bunch took a step to block his view of the trees behind her, where she thought Faye had fled. She used the move the get a firm hold on the Bulldog's grip. "There had to be better ways of disposing of the bodies. Crammed into trunks on railway stations smacks of showmanship." Bunch wanted to laugh. It was adrenalin, she knew, but once conjured she couldn't evict the image of a showdown. *Or a duel. We need swords. Douglas Fairbanks and Raymond Massey. I did a little fencing at school.*

She was aware that Waller was moving again and pulled her gun from her pocket. She raised it just a second after he did. But he didn't fire. They stood, pointing weapons at each other. Waller's companion watched in silence, anticipation on his face.

The need to giggle boiled up in her once more – pure fear this time. She had to keep him talking and hope that Faye had escaped to raise the alarm. The stables were only a minute away at a run. *But Faye has a stitch, doesn't she?* "What about the other bodies in trunks?" Bunch said. "Inspector Wright told me there were several before Laura and all too similar to be a coincidence."

"They were not mine, but inspirational."

"Who then?" Bunch resisted the temptation to glance behind her and wondered again if she had bought enough time for Faye to have made it to the Dower. "Lilly? She doesn't seem to be your biggest fan."

"Lilly Kendall is small fry. I am more interested in some American associates of the MacDonalds." He could not resist a glance at the man standing behind him. "The Spataros are returning to New York. Being American won't stop them from being singled out and interned by our government. Because of their Italian name. I've learned much from them, however – such as, how to issue one hell of a warning."

"You couldn't bring yourself to behead Laura – so why Kitty?"

"I am a quick learner and I was very angry with young Kitty. Laura Jarman was a nuisance to be rid of – but Kitty was my prodigy, and she betrayed me. Now, Miss Courtney, you are standing in our way." He took a step forward, one boot on the edge of the bridge. Bella began to bark once again. "Shut that animal up or I will shoot it. And then you."

Waller turned slightly to aim at the spaniel and Bunch heard the click of a gun being cocked. *No!* Images of her old Labrador, Roger, shot by poachers, crowded her mind. "Not again." She raised her revolver and shots crackled out.

Waller stood for a moment, the neat hole in the centre of his forehead like a third eye staring in disbelief, and then crumpled forward to the ground. She barely noticed when Spataro pushed past her and thudded across the bridge.

"Oh dear God." *I should be dead.* Bella darted forward to sniff at the body and Bunch clattered across to pull the dog away. Waller was not moving. The back of his skull was a bloody mess, but she turned him over to feel for a pulse, just in case. There was a second bullet hole in the arm of his jacket.

"Got him."

Bunch spun around awkwardly, realising she had dropped her gun but ready to defend herself.

"Want a hand up?" Faye used her left hand to pull Bunch to her feet. In her right hand was a Colt .45.

"You hit him?" she said. "But I fired—" Bunch realised she had only fired one single shot.

"You only winged him. Don't ever take up pistol shooting in competition, Miss Courtney. Stick to your rifles." Faye opened her bag and secreted the weapon. "God bless Gucci. Not just a stylish bag for gas masks. That wasn't bad shooting of mine while on the move. And now that the reason for my being here has been removed—"

"What about the other chap?" Bunch interrupted. "Spataro was it? We should follow him."

Faye glanced in the direction the Italian-American had run and shrugged. "Kill one of those guys? I'm not sure I want that kind of enemy." She turned to the sound of shouting coming from far side of the trees. "Spataro has scarpered – there's no profit for him hanging around – and I need to be off too. Thank you for your help, Miss Courtney. I owe you a huge favour."

"You can't leave. Wright will be here any moment."

"I know. If I head back to the farm can I get to the road?"

"Yes, but…"

"Clement is no great loss. I doubt the police will look too hard for me." Faye gripped Bunch by the shoulders and kissed her on both cheeks. "You can say I just ran that way, which will be the truth. Goodbye, Miss Courtney."

The speed with which Faye vanished into the trees made

Bunch wonder how much of her teetering along the stony lane had been an act. Had Faye been delaying, waiting for her husband to make his move? She heard boots thudding towards her and Wright burst around the corner followed by Sergeant Carter.

"Rose!"

"I'm fine."

"Yours?" He nodded at Waller's crumpled corpse. "Good shooting."

Bunch shook her head. "Not me. Never been much of a shot with a pistol. Unlike Faye Waller."

"She's here?" He looked around them.

"Was here" Bunch drew breath, wondering what she should say about Waller's death. Had it not been for Faye she would quite likely be dead. "So has the American chap." She spread both hands at Wright's sigh. "I could hardly stop them on my own. The Yank was armed too." *Which was true*, she thought.

"American? Who was he?"

"He… Oh, never mind for now. What kept you?"

"We went to the Dower House and nobody knew where you were."

"I wasn't far…" She nodded towards the sound of a large engine being gunned along the road beyond the trees. "The Yank," she said. "On his way back to the States, I imagine."

"And Faye Waller?"

She shrugged. "Anybody's guess." She gestured at Waller's body. "We have Laura Jarman's and Kitty Shenton's killer right here… Case closed. I shall send in my bill."

~ Author's Notes ~

We do hope you enjoyed reading *In Cases of Murder*. If you did then why not leave a review with your bookseller; or spread the word to friends and acquaintances via your own blog – and don't forget to send us those links!

For further information on the other Bunch Courtney Investigations books visit
https://janedwardsblog.wordpress.com/

Sign up for our newsletter to receive the latest information at
https://janedwardsblog.wordpress.com/contact/

Jan Edwards is available for interviews and events.
Contact Penkhull Press at
https://thepenkhullpress.wordpress.com/

All books available in print and Kindle editions.
Signed print copies can be obtained directly from the author via the above links.

Finally: This is a work of fiction. Wyncombe is a fictitious Sussex village that I envisage nestling in the South Downs some 18 miles north-by-northwest of Brighton. I have tried to be accurate with all other geographical landmarks, though I did play a little fast and loose with the exact location of Brighton's mortuary/pathology services in 1941. Even the officials at Brighton Council were unable to tell me where they were located! Wyncombe's residents are likewise products of my fevered imagination. Historical figures such as Winston Churchill are referenced for verisimilitude